BRUTAL SCORE

CONTENTS

The Hawkeyes Hockey Series

Check out **www.kennakingbooks.com** for more books and information.

SCAN ME

CHAPTER ONE

Kaenan

"Mr. Altman, are you still there? Did you hear what I said?" the lawyer on the other end of my cell phone says as I stop dead in my tracks on a busy sidewalk in Seattle.

It doesn't matter that it's finally a warm, dry day as I walk down the crowded downtown sidewalk.

What this woman just dropped on me has my feet frozen in place as pedestrians curse at me, trying to move around me as I stand frozen on the spot.

"You have a daughter," she repeats.

Her statement feels as physically painful as a punch to the gut. Even the second time around.

It can't be.

She has the wrong guy.

A kid?

When? And with who?

If this is one of those stupid pranks one of the team players likes to pull, I'll make sure they taste the plexiglass the next time we run drills.

"What..." A clog in my throat makes it hard to speak. I clear my throat and then try again, "What do you mean I have a daughter? That's impossible."

There's no way I heard that right.

"Berkeley... your daughter. It's in Ms. Wallace's will that if anything ever happened to her that you would get Berkeley."

As in Mia Wallace?

As in the woman I dated briefly almost three years ago, who turned me down when I asked her to move to Seattle with me?

Chills race down my spine at what she just said. *"If anything ever happened to her."*

I don't like the fucking sound of that.

What happened to Mia?

Aside from having a daughter.

My daughter?

"Wait! Hold on! Where's Mia?"

"You don't know?" she asks, her voice higher pitched like she's surprised.

I'm done playing this back-and-forth. I just want to know what the hell is happening.

"I don't know what!? What the fuck is going on," I demand, about ready to lose my cool.

Pedestrians hearing my sharp tone start giving me a wider berth as they go around me.

I begin pacing the front of my apartment building. I should be walking through the doors of the hockey arena's corporate offices right now, not pacing the sidewalks of Seattle, waiting for news on an ex I left in the past.

There's silence on the lawyer's end for a moment.

"Mr. Altman. I'm sorry to be the one to tell you this, but Ms. Wallace suffered a cardiac arrest episode a couple of weeks ago and was on life support. Her family let her go peacefully a couple of days ago."

My stomach lodges into my throat and pressure builds behind my eyes.

How could this have happened?

She was so young.

So vibrant.

So full of life.

The last time I saw her, she was twenty-five and more vivacious than anyone I've ever met.

Her energy was contagious.

Her smile was addictive.

She's the only woman I've ever seen a future with. But she turned down my offer when I asked her to move to Seattle to make a life together.

This has to be a mistake.

They have the wrong girl.

"Cardiac arrest! How?" I ask, rubbing my forehead to distract my hands from throwing something.

The only thing I have to throw is my cell phone, and I need that right now.

"She had a heart condition. As I understand it, she was born with it."

"This can't be happening," I mutter, running my hand through my thick hair.

How did I not know about her heart condition?

Why didn't she say anything?

Yes, we'd only known each other for a couple of weeks, and it fizzled out as fast as it started once I left, but still, I thought we meant something to each other during that time. After all, I cared enough to ask her to move to Washington. I'd never been that serious about a woman before... or since.

"I'm sorry to be the one to tell you. I assumed the family had already reached out to you."

Her family?

I don't know anything about her family, except that her mom is a recovering drug addict, her twin sister is a flake... and Mia loved them.

It's the reason she gave me for why she couldn't move away to give us a real chance. She wanted to be near her mom and sister. She was the glue keeping their shattered family whole, and leaving would have meant things would fall apart.

It's the reason this child can't be mine.

"No. Of course, they haven't. I haven't seen Mia in almost three years," I tell her, staring down at the concrete crack in the sidewalk above my foot. "I can't be the kid's father."

"Berkeley," She says the little girl's name again. "She's two years old, and you're her legal guardian."

"I'm her what?"

This is not how I thought today would go. I didn't see this coming.

Why didn't Mia tell me?

Did she really think that little of me that she didn't think I would want to know my child? Or did she not trust my ability to be a father?

Berkeley isn't mine... that's the only explanation.

"I need to see the birth certificate."

"Mr.— "

"I need to see it! I need to see that Mia signed my name on the birth certificate and didn't tell me," I demand.

The silence grows for a second, but she agrees.

A ping hits my phone, and I pull it away from my ear to see that I received an email from the lawyer.

I open the attachment quickly, and the minute it loads, I see the birth certificate.

Mother: Mia Olivia Wallace
Father: Kaenan Altman
Daughter: Berkeley May Altman

She gave her my last name.

It's all there... in black and white.

She put me on the birth certificate and in her will. She made sure that I got the little girl if something happened to her. So why didn't she say a single word to me about this? Especially with a health condition. She had to know this scenario was possible, right? And that I'd be blindsided.

"What the hell?" I mutter as I look over the birth certificate a second time, just in case it reveals something that no one else but Mia can tell me.

"I know this is a difficult decision, and you should take some time to think about it. However, if you choose to sign over your rights to Berkeley, Ms. Logan, Mia's mother, would petition the courts to retain custody of her."

"What do you mean to retain custody?"

"The courts only granted Ms. Logan temporary custody while Mia was in the hospital and then an extension until the funeral next week. Then permanent custody reverts back to you."

"The funeral for Mia?"

This is getting too fucking real.

"Yes, it's next week, and then you'll be allowed to take Berkeley home with you."

Take her home.

Who'd give me a kid? How fucking irresponsible could they be?

"What if she's not mine?"

"Would you like to conduct a DNA test? I can ask the courts for one. I'm sure they'd issue it."

I consider it for a second.

"Would it hurt her?" I ask.

"No, it's just a swab on the inside of her mouth. If we do it right away, we'll have the results back before the funeral."

Something about putting a two-year-old through a DNA test feels wrong.

I can already guess what my agent's reaction is going to be when I tell him about this. *"Get the damn DNA test!"*

"Let's wait. She's been through enough. I'll make arrangements to fly out to Montana for the funeral," I tell her.

"I'll be at the funeral with paperwork for you to sign. Call my office if you have any further questions or if you change your mind about the DNA test."

"Okay," I say.

"Did you see the second attachment I sent?" she asks.

"Second attachment?"

"It's also attached to the email. It's a picture of Berkeley."

I swallow hard as I back out of the first attachment and click on the second. A picture comes up immediately.

My chest feels uncomfortably tight as I focus first on the beautiful woman with her caramel hair and soft blue eyes.

My sight shifts to the little girl in the picture.

Her dark chocolate curls and honey-brown eyes tell me everything I need to know. She looks nothing like Mia.

Berkeley looks just like me... she's mine.

"I won't be needing that DNA test," I say.

CHAPTER TWO

Isla

"Just lie on your backside and let a strange man rail you into the mattress. Stop making it so complicated," my ex-step sister turned best friend says.

I shake my head with a chuckle in the dim glow of the Vegas hotel hallway lighting. Vivi isn't one to mince words.

My dad married Vivi's mom when we were in middle school, and they divorced before we both graduated from high school. Vivi and I didn't feel as though the divorce extended to us, so we remained sisters.

I'm the idiot who told her that I need a one-night stand tonight before I head back to Colorado and face my life, but now that I've said it, the logistics of picking a random stranger in a city as big as Vegas has me second-guessing my decision.

Especially since I'm not as outgoing as Vivi. All my exes are people I met from my dad's country club or the private schools my father sent me to. The only long-term boyfriend I've had was a guy I met at Princeton who I ran track with.

He graduated before me, got a high-powered CEO job through his father's connections, and married a socialite from New York. Now, they have three kids and a vacation house in Martha's Vineyard. Pretty typical for our upbringing.

It wasn't long after that my father introduced me to Collin Westfall, another Princeton alumni. He's a decade older than me, and my father's new protégé. Not to mention the son of the mayor of Denver. I didn't make a fuss about the arrangement because I liked Collin right off the bat despite our age gap.

He had that boy-next-door golden blond hair and those piercing blue eyes. Although at almost forty, Collin wouldn't be considered a "boy," he still has that youthful bright-eyed look to him. I couldn't help but love the way his eyes lit up when he talked about a new business venture he and my father worked on.

He was funny, loved running like I do, and showed genuine interest in the small social media-driven athletic wear business I ran out of my father's house in my walk-in closet.

Now, four years later, it's the same business that Collin and I run after he convinced my father to invest. Newport Athletics made it on Forbes' top list of fastest-growing athletic wear companies.

We hit a goal I'd never dreamed of before him.

I thought I was the luckiest girl on earth to be marrying a man like Collin. Someone who believed that I have more value than just looking pretty on his arm at fundraisers and galas...until four weeks ago.

"I know, I know... it's just that going back to someone's hotel room that I don't know..." I try to explain, but I don't think I need to finish that sentence.

It says enough, right?

"Then go to ours. I can find something to do in the meantime. Don't you worry about me." She winks.

We stand in a vibrant tropical forest-themed hallway of a large hotel just off the Vegas Strip. She booked it the minute I mentioned needing one last wild adventure, like a final hurrah before I return to the dumpster fire of a life I abandoned a month ago. That was when I caught Collin in his office with our warehouse manager, Tori.

What I didn't know was that Tori and Collin had been high school sweethearts over twenty years ago. They'd broken up when Collin's father shipped him off to Princeton and told him Tori wasn't "wife material" for a Westfall man.

The second I opened the door to his office to ask him what he wanted for lunch and saw Tori bobbing behind his desk, he immediately pushed her away, but it was too late. I saw more than I ever wanted to.

I ran out of that office immediately and climbed into my Range Rover hoping I had enough clothing in my gym bag to get me to Vivi's in Seattle. I couldn't be in that warehouse for another minute, and there was no way in hell I was going back to our house.

A house my father bought for us as an engagement present two years ago.

I thought Tori and I were friends.

I thought Collin and I were in love.

I guess on all accounts, I was wrong.

Isn't there a saying that goes perfectly with this?

Oh right...

No good deed goes unpunished.

And it's not as if I can run to any of my girlfriends within my circles. They live for this drama. They'd all love to see my "perfect" life go up in flames. They'd step over my charred life without a second thought, to climb up one more rung of the socialite ladder without any pity.

I can hear it now. "Oh poor little rich girl, don't you know that all made men have affairs?"

I thought Collin was different.

I thought we had something special.

"Do you think I'm being reckless for wanting a one-night stand in Vegas, of all places? It's stupid to think it will help my situation," I say.

"Are you kidding? Of course, it will help your situation. Collin is the last man you've had sex with since he screwed the ditz with the tits," she says with a straight face.

My face scrunches up at the way she worded it. Then again... Tori couldn't figure out how to properly work a shipping box tape dispenser and frequently attached the wrong shipping labels to the wrong orders, sending customers the incorrect items. And admittedly, she does have larger breasts than mine, which is salt on the wound and only adds to my long list of body image issues.

It's not easy coming out of the pageant world without a skewed self-image.

Vivi's diss may be accurate, but I wish she would use a little more tact so that it didn't hurt *me* as much as when she said them.

"Uh, thanks for that brutal CliffsNotes version of one of the worst things to have ever happened to me. You certainly have a gift for sugarcoating it," I say, shifting in the tight second-skin pink cocktail dress Vivi brought me.

I'm used to wearing dresses and heels from both my pageant days and from the countless charity functions, garden parties, and country club events I've attended over my twenty-eight years of life. However, this might be the shortest dress I've ever worn. This is not the kind of dress you wear if you want your cooch to stay hidden. Though maybe that's Vivi's plan.

After three days of being here, I haven't gone back to anyone's hotel room for the one-night stand that I told her I wanted. Now she's pulling out the big dogs for our last night. She even brought me her crystal-encrusted designer four-inch heels. They're like fishing lures for men.

Men love shiny things, and in a sea of other fish, these bad boys will do the trick. Well, either the shoes or the dress that barely covers my bum cheeks.

"Sugarcoated? The only thing sugarcoated is that dog turd dipped in chocolate that you call Collin. I knew it from the minute I met him that he was crap. But I should have known it before I even met him because Dad picked him out," she says.

She still calls him Dad even after her mom and my dad separated.

"I haven't forgotten... You keep reminding me," I say, rolling my eyes.

In all fairness, she really didn't like Collin the times she met him, and she wasn't afraid to tell me, but I always figured it was just because she felt like Dad was pushing me into an arranged marriage since Collin's father holds the political power that my father would love to control.

My dad is a big businessman in Colorado, and his companies combined own a majority of Denver's commercial real estate.

That's where a convenient marriage between the Newport and the Westfall family was supposed to come in. He knew he could never convince Vivi, his "strong-willed" daughter, into such an arrangement. And since she's not Newport blood, it wouldn't hold as strong of a connection. He went with the blindly naive one who was conditioned to do as her father asked.

Unlike Vivi, I've only rebelled against my father twice. Once, when I joined the track team in middle school, and the second time, when I went behind his back and took a fashion design class as an elective in college.

I yank down on the hem of the short glittery pink dress, hoping it comes down a little farther while Vivi fluffs her long jet-black hair done up in loose curls. Similar to the way I styled my own hair.

Vivi runs her hands down the almost identical silver mini-dress she brought for herself.

I could never wear silver. It would wash out my much paler complexion. One of the only useful things my mother ever taught me was how to dress within my color wheel, and it has served me well, both in my selection of a pageant dress that always brought me a win no matter who I was up against, and in selecting color schemes and prints for my athletic wear.

As in, lavender or lilac.

Which one has the higher likelihood of trending, and which one looks better on the most skin tones? These seemingly insignificant decisions set us apart from the giants in our industry.

Where Vivi has dark hair and beautiful Brazilian skin from her mother's side of the family, I have a paler Nordic coloring.

We both stare into the reflective surface of the elevator doors as we wait, the lit-up elevator number above us barely moving down to our floor.

There are three other elevators on this level, other than the one we're waiting on, but those are headed up and we're headed down to the club on the first floor.

The elevator starts moving closer again. It started at the top of the hotel, probably picking up people from the suites and penthouses on level twenty-two to twenty-five, and is slowly working its way down to us, letting people on and off at different levels of the hotel. It's inching closer to us now, although I'm not sure if I should be relieved or terrified.

This is our last night out before we head back to Seattle, and I get back in my Range Rover to head home.

Back to Denver.

To the business that Collin and I still run together. Vivi will stay in Seattle where she owns and runs a successful nanny service she started back in college.

I'd do almost anything not to have to return to reality. The trouble is, I've gone through all of the rainy-day savings in the only account I didn't share with Collin.

And since I've been avoiding Collin and my father's calls for the past four weeks, I can't exactly ask for funds. Not that either of them would send it since they're trying to starve me out so that I'll come back home.

Collin controls all our personal and business accounts as the Chief Financial Officer, and my father already threatened to take away the company from me in his last voicemail if I don't return home soon and make up with Collin.

"Stop acting like a spoiled child. I've secured your future with the most powerful family in Colorado, and this is how you repay me? By causing gossip around the re-election and the Newport family name?"

Vivi warned me not to let my father buy in to Newport Athletics, and I should have listened.

Now my father has full control.

My home.

My car, which is owned by Newport Athletics.

My bank accounts.

Everything.

"I'm sorry if I say it too much. I just want you to know that you were always too good for Collin. He's lucky he had you for as long as he did."

"I know you are. Thanks for whisking me off to Vegas," I tell her with a frown I can't hide.

I glance up at the elevator, willing it to move a little faster.

"Listen..." she says with a soft voice. "Forget Dad. If you're not ready, don't go back. You could Huckleberry Finn it for a few more months, and I could get you a temporary job as a nanny for one of my clients," she offers.

Vivi's nanny service caters to wealthy families in Seattle. She built it without Dad's help, and I admire her for that. She knew better than to take our father's false praise and real money when my father tried to get in as an investor to gain control of her too.

"I'll find you a live-in situation so you don't have to pay rent in Seattle, though I still think you should tell Collin to transfer funds into your account. Not asking for your own money is a little ridiculous and Seattle's real estate market is insane."

Not only that but most places require at least a year long lease, and I know I'm starting to outstay my welcome with Vivi. She has her own life to live without her ex-stepsister taking up the spare room.

"Me... a nanny?" I ask, but I'm almost ready to agree at this point because I'll do anything to delay facing Collin, Tori, and my father again.

This offer of Vivi's sounds better and better the more I consider not having to get in my car and head to Colorado tomorrow, but how will my father and Collin take it?

"You'll be great. You've always wanted to be a mom, Isla. Collin is the one who convinced you that you two shouldn't have kids for a while and focus on your careers instead," she says, leaning in toward the reflective elevator paneling, reapplying some kind of lip shimmer, and then hands the tube to me to do the same. "You're wonderful with kids. You always have been."

I take the tube from her and pull the unscrewed lip shimmer top from the bottle, applying the pink shimmer. I don't have Vivi's full, beautiful lips, but then I see the reflection in the elevator, and I'm relieved she at least picked a more nude pinkish color instead of the deep reds and purples she probably would have chosen if her closet and makeup wasn't pulling double duty because all of my things are still in Denver.

"Tell that to your client after you tell them I came to Vegas to screw a stranger. I'm sure they'll be lining up to have me care for their children," I say, handing her back her lip gloss and then watching the elevator's illuminated sign indicate that it's only a floor above us now.

"Oh, don't be a prude. You'd be shocked by the things you find out about the families once you start nannying for them. I guarantee you'll still be the tamer one out of the bunch," she says, scrunching her nose at me and digging through her sparkly clutch that probably costs a small fortune while she drops the lipstick inside. "Just grab the first good-looking guy in the club. Ideally, one with a cock twice the size of Collin's... which shouldn't be tough since I've seen the pictures you posted of him in his swimming shorts in St. Barts last Christmas."

"Vivi!" I chuckle.

Collin isn't the biggest I've ever had, but before everything went up in flames, I thought our sexual chemistry was good.

"What?!" She widens her eyes at me. "If I were him, I would at least shove a sock down there before going out in public like that."

"Oh my God." I shake my head again and cover my laughter with the back of my hand.

"It doesn't have to be a big sock. I'm not talking about a winter wool sock for an adventurer traveling to the Antarctic searching for shipwreck treasure. I'm talking more like a respectable-sized anklet rolled up would probably do the trick to give the man some volume. I mean, really, Isla, you were okay with that being the last penis you ever have?" she asks with a side-eye.

I hear a ding sound from another elevator behind us, and I welcome the distraction from this conversation.

It feels good to laugh at Collin's expense for a moment since I've spent the last four weeks crying at my own.

"You need a good wanking by some brawny dude who spends more time in the gym than you do with your nose in your sketchbook and flipping through color swatches. Just let go tonight... can you please?" Vivi asks with a pout. "No trust fund babies, though. You've had your fill."

She's right about the rich frat boy types. I need a breather, but I suppose it should concern me that Vivi has more interest in my sex life than I do.

"Sure, let me just screw the brains out of the first man I see. Would that make you happy?" I say, joking.

"It would make *me* happy." I hear a deep voice come from behind the elevator's double doors in front of us.

Oh no!

Oh my God!

I thought it was the elevator behind us that arrived on our floor.

My stomach drops, and I break out into instant embarrassment sweats. My hands turn clammy, and I can feel my armpits warm. Thank God for deodorant, but there's nothing I can do about the fact that my cheeks and chest are probably turning tomato red at this very moment.

I glance over at Vivi and she only giggles. I'm not so sure those pre-game shots back in our hotel room were such a great idea if she thinks this is funny.

When the doors open, a large man stands to the left, leaning back against the corner with his hands in his pockets. He has dark hair, which appears like it would have a curl to it if he grew it out, and stares back at me with golden-brown eyes.

His nose is just a little bit crooked, and he looks like he lifts weights for a living, which isn't usually my type. I like a leaner body build, more like Collin's. A body built not in the gym like this guy, but more like the kind of guy who's training for a half marathon or long-distance running event.

"Shut it, Brent," the guy in the corner says, his head turning toward someone I can't see yet, standing to the right and behind the elevator paneling.

As the doors open wider, I see that it's not only one person inside but two decent-looking men who both heard what I said.

I debate running to the emergency exit staircase at the end of the hall, but then Vivi steps forward and into the elevator.

"Come on," Vivi says over her shoulder at me, taking the last step inside and turning around to face me. "We have to get down and find you the perfect one-nighter."

That gets both men's attention, and they both stare at me and gawk for a second.

"Vivi!" I say, my eyes widening.

I reluctantly do as she asks but send up a small prayer to the powers that be, requesting that the elevator harness and safety harness all inconveniently snap at the same time, sending this lift car plummeting to the bottom with all of us in it, leaving no survivors. It's the only way to escape this embarrassment.

Yes, I know it was my idea to sleep with a stranger on this trip, but I didn't plan on proclaiming it to a couple of men on an elevator.

"Where are you ladies headed?" the guy tucked farther into the elevator asks, a smile still across his lips thanks to Vivi's oversharing.

I think I heard his name is Brent.

Since I don't have a name for the other one, I'll call him Brutal Bodyguard because that's what he looks like he does for a living. Maybe he's a bodyguard for someone famous in Vegas. Or maybe a bouncer for one of the clubs.

Brent angles toward the buttons on the elevator waiting for our command with a bright white smile still across his face. The elevator doors begin to shut, and I have a flash of fight or flight coaxing me to jump out before the doors seal me in, but my feet won't move.

Out of all times when being a runner could have come in handy, this would have been the moment.

I watch in the reflection of the elevator panels as Brutal Bodyguard takes a full slow scan of my backside. My body erupts with tingles as he takes in every inch of me. He doesn't realize that I can see what he's doing and that makes this so much more thrilling.

This is exactly the kind of guy I meant when I said I want something different from Collin. They couldn't be more opposite in their build or in their eye and hair color.

Collin's light blond hair, blue eyes and smaller frame are nothing like the dark chocolate hair, deep brown eyes and six-foot-plus stature of the man behind me.

"The Club. Level one," Vivi says with an equally flirtatious smile.

"You two are headed to the club?" Brent asks, pressing the button that reads *Lobby*.

Then he glances over our heads at the Brutal Bodyguard who is no longer looking at me from behind and has an expression on his face that I can't read.

"Yes, we are. What are you two up to tonight?" Vivi asks back.

"We're meeting a couple of buddies across the street for dinner. Then we might be heading to the club after," he says.

The ride down another seven floors is quick, and the elevator stops at the lobby.

"Maybe we'll see you there," Vivi tells him.

The elevator doors open, and Brent sticks out an arm to hold the doors open for us to exit before them.

Taking the first steps out, I'm anxious to escape that small, enclosed space.

"I bet you will," Brent says back to Vivi, who steps off the elevator after me.

I can't ignore the way my body lit up when the man behind me took a full scan of my backside, but his lack of interest afterwards has me embarrassed of what he heard me say, and what Vivi confirmed.

She takes a few quick steps to catch up, and I listen for the men to exit the elevator next. Their footsteps fade away.

They're not following us, thank God.

I let out a sigh of relief.

"Wait up!" she yells. "I didn't realize you could move that fast in high heels."

I'm not going to be winning any half marathons in these heels, but a life spent in country clubs, dressing like the perfect daughter to make my dad seem like the family man, prepared me for this moment.

"He was cute," she says, a little out of breath from running in heels that are taller than mine.

"Brent? No thanks," I say, without looking back at her.

"No, not him. The mysterious one checking you out in the corner."

A little shiver shoots down my spine at the memory of his eyes gliding over me from behind.

"He wasn't checking me out," I argue.

But wasn't he?

"Yes, he was," she argues. "And he liked what he saw."

My cheeks warm, but there's no point to it. He's headed out to dinner with friends. I doubt I'll see him ever again.

Maybe that's for the best. Something about my physical reaction to him for the few minutes we were in proximity felt dangerous.

Dangerous to the order of things.

Dangerous to the life I have no choice but to return to or my dad will cut me off and take the business I built. But did I really build it if my father's money and influence were what made the company viable?

Maybe my father is right.

Maybe I am just a spoiled child who can't make it without his help.

"He's not my type either," I tell her, trying to convince myself more than her.

"What's not to like? He's big enough to flip you around and upside down in the bedroom. That should be every girl's type." She snickers.

My memory flashes to those strong arms by his side that flexed as I walked into the elevator, his hand tucked in his pockets. There's no doubt he's very capable of some bedroom acrobatics.

It's an appealing thought, I'll admit, but since we're leaving tomorrow morning and my plan is to get upstairs with the first hot guy I see in the club, there's not much chance of bumping into him again.

We veer down the wide hotel hallway and toward the vibrating bass coming from the club, still a ways from us. We pass dozens of people in various states of clothing and drunkenness the closer we get.

Brutal Bodyguard is attractive in that smoldering, mysterious way like she said. I won't deny that even though he isn't the kind of guy I would usually gravitate toward, one night in bed with a man who takes charge could be fun.

An image of the hot stranger tossing me around the bedroom and into different positions while railing into me has my teeth sliding over the lip gloss of my bottom lip.

Maybe it has been too long since I've been with a man. But still, I've never had a one-night stand.

A weekend-long fling that ended up fizzling out?

Sure, I had plenty of those in college, but usually with a guy on the track team that I thought would go somewhere and didn't. I've never just met a random guy in a bar and went to his place or mine to have sex and then never spoke to them again.

It sounds good in theory, considering anything more than one night is impossible since I'm headed back home tomorrow.

We get in line at the door and are quickly ushered through after showing our IDs to the large bouncer. The man from the elevator is almost the same size.

I bet the elevator guy would be demanding in the bedroom, taking the lead and doing whatever he wants with me. Calling me a good girl as he thrusts into me, demanding I take all of him. The kind of sex I've only ever read in smut books but have never experienced with a partner.

"Let's just start with a drink," Vivi yells over the music, passing me up and walking deeper into the club, gripping my hand and pulling me with her so we don't get separated.

I follow my fearless leader into the huge two-story club with a vaulted ceiling, packed wall to wall with people. The powerful strobe lights flash, and the bass bumps so loud that my soul can probably feel it.

She glances over her shoulder as we make our way inside to ensure I'm still behind her even though she's still holding my hand.

I nod in agreement about the drink.

She smiles back at me and then gives a little eyebrow wiggle. That's her usual sign when she has a feeling things are about to get interesting.

I take a deep inhale…

Here we go.

CHAPTER THREE

Isla

It's been a few hours since the elevator incident. After a couple of drinks with Vivi at the bar, I'm starting to loosen up and have fun.

We've been dancing our hearts out on the dance floor while the mortification from telling a hot, broody man twice my size that I want the first man I see to screw me has settled... a bit. The redness in my cheeks has probably subsided for the most part, not that you could tell in this dim lit club.

A throwback song from our college days hits, and everyone in the club starts going wild. Even more people enter the already over-packed dance floor.

A guy from earlier who bought us drinks walks up with his cute friend, and we all start dancing.

Vivi's partner is completely her type, and she seems really into him. While the guy I'm dancing with is a dead ringer for Collin. But at least he's helping me take my mind off the Brutal Bodyguard from the elevator.

Vivi and her partner get lost in their bump and grind, and before I know it, she's making out with him over her shoulder.

"I'm Alex," the guy behind me yells over the music, close to my ear.

"Isla," I yell back, but then I remember I wasn't planning on telling anyone my real name.

What if they know my family?

Or what if they're from Denver?

How horrifying would it be if in a few months, I run into them at a charity event with Collin's new engagement ring on my hand?

A new engagement ring...

The thought makes me sad, but I'm not here to feel sorry for myself. I'm here for one last day that belongs to me.

Without reason, my eyes are drawn over Vivi's shoulder to something in the bar.

Or rather, someone.

Brutal Bodyguard sits on a barstool facing out to the crowd, his eyes already locked on me.

He came.

My stomach feels like the inside of a popcorn bag with excited kernels popping everywhere.

He presses a beer bottle to his lips and takes a pull of the amber liquid, keeping his attention fixed on me. His hand engulfs the entire beer bottle, making it seem so much smaller than it usually looks in someone else's hands.

Curiosity makes me wonder what those full, beer-soaked lips would feel like against my skin. How would they taste against my tongue?

I watch as a woman stops by his side to talk to him. She flips her long dark hair over her shoulders and then lays a hand somewhere low on his body, like his thigh. The crowd is too thick for me to be sure of the exact placement, but either way, I feel a little warmth of jealousy hit my cheeks.

Where is that coming from?

She seems to get annoyed after moments go by and he doesn't give her the attention she's probably used to. He doesn't take his eyes off me, not even for a second.

Eventually, she stomps off, and he doesn't seem fazed in the least.

He watches me as I continue dancing, and I'm not sure if he's even blinked since I caught him surveying me. He doesn't seem the least bit concerned that he's been caught either.

How long has he been sitting there?

Tingles of excitement run down my spine with every second that he watches me. Those dark eyebrows and lashes, along with his intense stare fixed on me, make him seem almost a little dangerous for a girl like me.

I've never been with a man like that.

A rogue thrill hits me at the idea of spending the night with a man so intense. The kind of man who could put fear in any man who came up against him. Like say, my father...

I keep my eyes glued to him.

Forgetting the man dancing against me.

I keep swaying my hips even though too many people are between us for him to see my body. I don't release eye contact for an entire breath.

This is far bolder than I usually am, but maybe that last pomegranate martini gave me some liquid courage.

"You're a great dancer," a voice from behind me says.

I didn't consider that my tease for the guy at the bar might have Alex thinking I'm interested in more than dancing.

"Oh...thanks," I say, glancing away from the bar.

He must take my response as an invitation to get closer because he squeezes my hips back tighter against his hips and bends over my shoulder.

He's cute, I'll give him that, but he's not the man from the elevator.

Not even close.

I check back over Vivi's partner's shoulder to see if he's still watching me from the bar. When my eyes settle back on him in the distance, I'm relieved to see he's still there but disappointed to find his beer suspended up by his mouth as if he was just about to take a drink but froze when something unsavory distracted him.

His eyes aren't on me anymore.

They're narrowed on Alex, bending over my shoulder.

Whispering in my ear.

What is he thinking?

Would he have come over if I hadn't already been dancing with Alex?

I glance over my shoulder to see what Brutal Bodyguard is seeing, but Alex must have thought that was an invitation because he takes the opportunity, with my head turned toward him, to lay a kiss against my lips.

My instinct is to shove Alex away. To prove to the man at the bar that I didn't want that. That I'm not with Alex.

My eyes dart back to him the second I pull my lips off Alex's.

But it's too late.

He's gone.

I panic, thinking he might have left. Now, a blonde woman sits there with a guy standing behind her, ordering drinks.

I scour the bar but don't see him.

He's not here anymore.

He left.

And took with him the only option I'm interested in.

"Do you want to go upstairs with me?" Alex asks, pulling my long hair back over my shoulder to expose my neck.

He obviously didn't get the hint with that chaste kiss that I'm not interested.

"Excuse me. I have to use the restroom," I say urgently.

Before he can object, I grab Vivi's arm, yanking her from her dance partner.

"What?" she asks instantly with concern and a little annoyance that I'm taking her from her good time.

"Bathroom break. Now," I say over the music.

She doesn't hesitate when she can see my eyes widen and my lips flatline.

She nods.

"I'll be right back. Don't go anywhere," she tells her dance partner, pointing at him to stay put.

We exit the dance floor as quickly as we can and head for the bathroom, weaving through the crowds.

"I'm calling it," I tell her the minute we burst through the bathroom doors.

"What? Why? That guy you're dancing with is cute," she says, her eyebrows stitching together.

She knows what my type is as well as I do.

Alex looks just like Collin, and that's part of the problem.

I wanted a one-night stand with someone as opposite to Collin as possible. It doesn't help that the one guy in the bar who held my interest left, taking my ideal one-night stand with him.

"I failed. I just can't do it. I'm going to head back up to our room and pack for our flight in the morning," I tell her, my shoulders slumping at the idea that I'm giving up.

She leans in and runs her hand down my arm slowly.

"You didn't fail. And you don't have to prove yourself to me or to anyone else. A one-night stand is waiting on the dance floor for you. You're making a choice not to sleep with him. That's not failing... that's deciding what you want for yourself."

"Thanks, Vivi," I say, casting my eyes down in defeat, staring at our glittery shoes pointed toward each other.

"I'm sorry that it didn't work out. Do you want me to come upstairs with you?" she asks. "We can stream a movie or order room service, my treat?"

"No, you should keep dancing. It seems like you two are having fun."

I can make it up to the seventh floor alone.

It's only an elevator ride up.

"You're sure?" she asks even though she knows the answer.

I'm not fine.

I nod and smile. "No point in neither of us having some fun tonight."

Vivi works like a dog in Seattle. Her nanny business is flourishing, and she never gets time for herself. And even when she does, her immense success has become either a deterrent for men intimidated by her success or men looking for a free ride.

She deserves tonight, especially after everything she's done for me.

"Call me if you change your mind, and I'll can the hottie." She winks.

"Love you," I tell her.

"Love you too."

We exit the bathroom, Vivi heading back to her dance partner and me heading out the exit.

She agreed to keep me informed of where she goes and with whom so I don't worry.

I take the elevator up to level seven, and the minute I walk through our hotel room door, I kick off my heels.

I shoot a quick text to Vivi.

"Got here safe. Have fun," I tell her so she doesn't worry.

Then I kneel in front of my suitcase that I left in the back corner of the room and scrounge for my pajamas that my mother sent me last week.

I need a little pick-me-up.

I failed at my mission to prove I can make my own decisions. That I can step out of my father's expectations.

What was I really trying to prove running out of Denver like I did when, deep down, I knew the inevitable would happen?

I should have known my father would never allow me to leave Collin and still keep control of my business. And maybe he's right. Maybe I can't make it on my own.

Fleeing Denver created a wave of gossip, likely making its rounds in my father's large circles. Catching quicker than a house on fire and doused in gasoline.

His PR team, no doubt, is trying to extinguish it as fast as they can.

My little business that grosses a respectable high eight figures isn't what my father cares to save. No, it's the fact that it looks bad when a man of his clout can have government officials under his thumb but can't control his own daughter.

I can only imagine that Collin's father must be up in arms about this whole thing too. Our engagement and wedding have all been strategically timed with his re-election and were designed to boost his "family man" values with the voters.

I know what people are saying and how much it must make my father furious. He hasn't ceased to remind me that my "vacation from reality" is about to come to an end.

I walk over to my luggage bag sitting in the corner, flung open from going through it earlier. I kneel to fish out the pink silk pajama button-up top and shorts set with soft white piping. The name Gloria is stitched eloquently on the breast pocket. I pull out my favorite pair of comfy nude panties. I can't sleep in the white lace thong that I wore with the dress earlier.

Gloria... my mother sent me pajamas personalized with her name on it from her villa in Italy.

They were either a gift from my stepfather who, God forbid, ordered her the wrong shade of blush, or she forgot she ordered these years ago and sent them to me to make room in her enormous closet for more things she'll never wear.

Either way, I'm not turning down the designer jammies. They feel amazing against my fingertips and I could use some comfy pajamas for my last night of freedom.

Is that a little melodramatic?

Probably, but right now, my hopes are at an all-time low. With my impending seven o'clock departure flight tomorrow morning and then a long drive back to Colorado, I need this.

I hear my phone buzz with a text coming through. I stretch out to grab the clutch Vivi lent me to go with the dress, tug out my phone and my wallet, and toss the empty clutch onto Vivi's empty bed.

I open the text and read the name.

It's from Vivi.

I'm happy to see a text from her.

If I'm being honest, separating earlier tonight made me a little nervous. I didn't love the idea of leaving her in the club alone, but she seemed fine with it.

"Headed up to his hotel room. It's in the same hotel. Twenty-fifth floor, room 2519. Love you."

Level twenty-five has the most expensive suites in this resort.

I set my phone down on my nightstand and crawl into bed, flipping on the TV and snuggling under the comforter with no intention of doing anything else...

...or anyone, tonight.

It's almost two in the morning, and I still haven't fallen asleep. I'm lying in my Italian silk pajamas when my stomach rumbles. Binge-watching the last few hours of some baking competition show has my belly begging for sustenance.

I remember passing a vending machine with trail mix, chips, and chocolates down the hall by the ice maker. The exact final meal of a girl about to face her doom tomorrow.

Junk food.

I'm well past the "warm" stage of drunkenness. Sadly, I'm stone-cold sober... and starving.

I can't take the grumbling noises any longer and slip off my queen-sized bed. I succumb to my body's demands, grabbing the clutch off Vivi's bed, and head for the door.

I walk out the door, checking right and left to see if anyone else is moving about the hotel hallway.

This is Vegas, which seems like it's up all hours of the night. I'm sure I'll pass someone by the time I make it to the vending machine and back, but I don't like surprises. I want to know who's loafing around before I make myself visible.

The hallway is empty, so I step out and pull the door back behind me.

It's at that moment that I realize I left my phone on my nightstand. But not to worry, I'll be back in a few minutes.

I walk down the long hallway and find the vending machines brightly lit and as happy to see me as I am to see them.

I look over the selection as my mouth waters. Chocolate-covered peanut butter, salty cheddar chips, and sweet and sour gummies.

I make my decision and then open Vivi's clutch. My stomach drops the minute I remember that I tossed my wallet in my luggage so I wouldn't forget it.

I have no money to pay for snacks.

Then panic sets in when I realize that my room key is in my wallet, my phone is sitting on my nightstand, and I am dressed in my mother's pajamas.

This is not how I wanted today to start out.

I'm left with only two options:

Head downstairs to the front desk and ask for a new room key while dressed in my pajamas.

That's not an ideal option since I'm sure the resort is still packed with well-dressed individuals just getting back from a show on the Strip or the club. Being raised by an image-conscious mother, she'd die if she knew I was even considering it.

There's also a possibility that my efforts will all be for naught since I don't have a driver's license with me to prove my identification.

Or option two, I go up to the room Vivi said she'd be at and barge in on their night in order to borrow her room key. This could turn out to be far more embarrassing than walking around in my jammies, depending on what progress Vivi and her club friend have made since she texted me a while ago.

What room did she say again?

Room 2529?

No.

2509?

Yeah, I think that's it.

There was definitely a nine at the end.

I make up my mind. I'm going up to find Vivi and borrow her card.

I make a dash for the elevator, wanting to get this moment over with and get back into my bed as quickly as possible.

The elevator door opens quickly, and I'm relieved when no one is inside. I'm not wearing a bra, and my silk pajamas in the air-conditioned hallways have my nipples embarrassingly hard. I smash my hand against level twenty-five, and it doesn't take long before the elevator stops on the twenty-fifth floor.

When the doors open, I take a peek to my right first, reading the room number.

2501

Even numbers are on the left and odd numbers are on the right.

Got it.

I start walking quickly as I pass the rooms. The distance between the doors is farther apart than on our floor since the rooms are probably a lot bigger.

I read each door as I go by.

2503.

2505.

2507.

Here it is, 2509. I'm almost positive.

I step up to the door. If it's not Vivi or the guy from the club who answers the door, I might die of humiliation.

Knock.

Knock.

My knuckles lightly tap on the door.

I try not to knock too loudly. It's two in the morning, and the fear of some cranky old couple opening the door to yell at me has me trying to keep my feet from running back to the elevator.

"Vivi," I whisper at the door.

Hoping that somehow, she can hear me through the thick and soundproof painted indigo wooden slab keeping me from entering the room. I haven't heard a single sound in our room from the hallways so I'm sure she can't in this room either.

Heavy footsteps echo from inside the room, and my heart kicks up in speed.

Breathe.

You're fine.

A few seconds later, I hear the sound of the person on the other side unlocking the deadbolt and gripping the door handle.

The door opens, and nothing could prepare me for the man standing on the other side, bare-chested in a pair of basketball shorts and that sexy disheveled hair look from lying in bed.

It's him.

It's the guy from the elevator.

CHAPTER FOUR

Isla

An indistinguishable noise comes out of my throat as I stand face-to-face with the man from the elevator.

"Oh... I..." I stutter.

He glances down at me, one eyebrow lifted slightly.

"Uh... hi," he says, his throat a little groggy like I woke him up.

"I'm sorry, I got the wrong room," I say quickly.

I can't read his facial expression.

He doesn't seem upset that I just woke him, but he's not smiling either. Although, does this man smile?

"How did you find my room?" he asks.

Oh my God, he thinks I'm stalking him. I'm completely mortified.

My face freezes, and I can no longer feel my toes.

I'm going into shock.

I've always thought that being struck by lightning or drowning would be the worst way to die, but now I'm pretty sure I would take either of those over dying by way of absolute humiliation.

"I... umm, was searching for the room my friend said she was headed to. I got locked out, and I don't have my phone," I say, my face regaining movement.

"Really? I'm supposed to believe that?" he says and then bends a little to look at my shirt. "...Gloria."

He gives a smirk and then leans against the doorframe, a little twinkle in his eye.

"Gloria?" I ask, my eyebrows stitching together.

How does he know my mother's name?

He's not from Denver, is he?

"Your shirt," he says, pointing at my silk jammies.

When I glance down, I see my mother's name stitched on the pocket. I forgot about that, but then my eyes narrow on my hard nipples.

I forgot about those too.

I cross my arms over my breasts quickly, but I know he's already seen them.

"I went out to buy a snack and forgot my wallet," I say, trying to distract myself from my torpedo nipples and give an explanation for how we're bumping into one another again by coincidence. "My friend said she came up to this floor, and I thought she said room 2509."

I flash a peek at the door number again. Maybe it'll have changed since I've been standing here. I'm not sure how that would help at this moment but at least I'd know where to look for Vivi next.

"That's my room number. And I can assure you, she's not in here," he says, giving my Pepto-Bismol-colored outfit a once-over.

I felt so cute in my room alone.

Now I feel like a birthday cake pop from the coffee shop.

"Yeah well, I thought that's what she said in her text, but I don't have my phone to double-check the number. And now I have no way of getting back into my room," I tell him.

He nods slightly as he mulls it over.

Does he really think I'm lying and that I would march up here in this ensemble to seduce him?

"Do you want to come in and call her on my phone?" he asks.

It still doesn't seem like he's buying my story, but he pushes his shoulder off the doorframe anyway and pulls the door open a little more as an offer.

He's letting me in even though he thinks it might be a line I'm using to gain access to his room.

I glance to my right and then to my left, not seeing any signs of Vivi anywhere.

Then it dawns on me... maybe this isn't a coincidence. Maybe this is my second chance. Maybe my luck is turning around.

I'll be on a flight in less than four hours, headed back to a life built for me. Or maybe it's the life I was built for.

Be brave, Isla.

You can do this.

"Okay, yeah, that would be great," I tell him, taking the steps forward, hoping he didn't bring someone else up here after he left the bar.

If I interrupted his night with another woman, that will top the most mortifying moment of my life.

Possibly worse than catching Collin and Tori together.

His lip turns up on one side while he opens the door wider and then moves sideways for me to enter.

It's the closest thing to a smile I've seen so far.

"Come in," he says.

"Thanks," I say, unfolding my arms and then walking into his room.

When I step into the small entryway just inside the door, I'm surprised to find the suite is two stories with a view of the Strip. Two large sets of windows are stacked on top of each other to make it seem as though the wall is all glass.

The Strip sparkles beyond the windows where a small living room is set up. I take a few more steps in to find a kitchen and bar to my left and a doorway to the bedroom.

The door is open, and I'm relieved to see that only one side of the king bed comforter is turned over. There's no woman asleep on the other side of his bed. As far as I can tell, he's alone.

He left the bar and came up here by himself?

He doesn't turn on any additional lights in the room. The only lights streaming in are from the marquees from the casinos on the Strip.

The dimly lit room gives me the confidence I need to confront him about not asking me to dance.

I take a few more steps and then stop dead in my tracks.

"Whoa," he says, just barely stopping short from running into my back.

I spin around, my long blonde hair, now in a ponytail, swishing into the space between us.

"Why didn't you come out to the dance floor?" I ask.

"What do you mean?"

Is he really going to pretend he wasn't at the bar?

"You watched me earlier while I was out dancing... but then you left. Why?"

He stands there, towering over me like a giant. My five-foot-seven is not doing me any favors when he must be about a foot taller.

"You already had a partner," he says simply, his eyes flashing down to my hard nipples against the silk fabric of my button-up blouse pajamas, but this time, I don't cover them up. I'm braver now that I know he's alone.

His tongue darts out to wet his bottom lip.

"Then why were you watching me?" I ask.

"I asked myself the same question," he says, his eyes fixed on mine. "Now I think it's my turn to ask a question."

"Okay?"

"Did he fulfill what you were after last night?"

"Who?" I ask, still hoping he didn't see Alex.

"The man who kissed you."

Dammit.

"What was I after?" I ask, wondering if he'll say it.

Neither of us likely forgot what I blurted out right before the elevator doors opened, but I wasn't going to say, "Oh, you mean the one-night stand with the first guy I laid eyes on"?

"Did he give you the one-night stand you wanted?" he asks, his hands tightening by his side, almost as if he's preparing himself for bad news.

I shake my head as I stare into his golden-brown eyes. "No, I didn't leave with him."

He takes a step closer, his hands unclenching at his side.

"Are you still looking for someone?" he asks in that low, raspy voice.

This is the moment.

The moment I envisioned when I decided I would spend one night with someone before returning home. And this is who I want to do it with.

I want his hands on my body.

I want his mouth on mine.

"Is that an offer?" I ask, hoping he says yes and puts me out of my misery.

He nods his head. "Let me put it this way. If you're looking for a man to take care of you for one night, I'm the one."

I bite down on my lower lip, and his eyes dart down to my mouth to watch.

He's still staring at my lips when he continues. "But I won't make the first move," he says, leaning slightly back and farther from me.

Is he pulling away?

Why?

"I don't understand," I say, my eyebrows knitting together.

"You're in my room with no way to access your own, no cell phone to call anyone to help you, and I have no idea how much you drank tonight. You're the definition of vulnerable. Besides, no good decisions are made after midnight." His voice is serious, and his lopsided grin is gone... but there's a twinkle in his eye for me. "If you want me, you have to show me. Otherwise, I think we should call your friend, and I'll walk you back safely to your room."

He steps to the left and starts to go around me like he's going to head for his phone.

He didn't even wait for my answer.

"Wait," I say, a little bolder than I intended.

I can't let this moment get past me. I may not get this courage back.

I reach out, gripping his bicep to stop him. Before I can even think about it, I push up on my tiptoes and plant my lips against his mouth and my hands against his bare chest.

The feeling of his lips against mine is an instant dopamine hit. A rainbow of colors flashes behind my eyelids as I kiss him.

No one has ever made me see colors before, certainly not from one kiss.

It's intoxicating, his lips on me. From the very first contact as he presses his mouth back against mine.

He wraps his arms around my back to pull me against his hard, bare chest. His thick cabled forearms keep me tight against his body, his mouth pulling and sucking on mine.

"I'm not drunk," I mutter against his mouth.

"Good. Otherwise, I'd stop this."

His tongue darts out and licks my bottom lip between our kiss and then claims my mouth again.

I moan into our kiss unintentionally. It's just a kiss, but it feels so much better than that.

He still tastes faintly of the IPA beer he was drinking at the bar when I saw him tonight, and of the peppermint toothpaste he must have brushed with earlier.

He walks us a few steps back until my back hits the wall.

His hands hook around the backside of my thighs, and he pulls me up his body, wrapping my legs around his waist as he pushes to get closer.

I can feel him hardening under me.

His basketball shorts don't leave anything to the imagination.

He's bigger than Collin. I can already tell by the hard length rubbing against the top cleft between my legs and how far up his tip reaches against my belly. He presses his pelvis tight against me to pin me to the wall.

I let out a guttural sound as he does. I can't help it. I love the way he takes control.

The way he kisses me has my body breaking out in full-body tingles.

His hands are all over me, pulling me tighter, sliding over my butt and kneading each cheek. His hands demand but also test. I can feel how much he wants me, not only in the growing cock between us but also in the way he touches me.

He pulls my back off the wall and my arms tighten around his neck to keep my place on his body. He turns and heads for the bedroom, carrying me in his arms with my thighs wrapped around him like I weigh nothing.

He makes me feel safe like he'd never drop me. It's in the way he carries me, his arm under my butt to keep me secured around him and the other arm running up my back so his hand can grip around the back of my neck to keep my lips pulled down against his.

Protecting me is his only priority, and he'll do anything to keep me.

But after this is all over... he won't keep me.

And I won't stay.

He walks us through the separate bedroom door, and a few seconds later, I feel his knees hit the bed.

"You're sure?" he asks, pulling his mouth off my lips and working his kisses down my neck.

I can barely focus on anything else besides his mouth against my skin. I know I have to answer, or he'll pull his mouth off me, and that's the last thing I want.

"Positive," I mutter out the words, my head leaning farther to the right side to give him more access to the sensitive skin of my throat.

I'm going to have a one-night stand with this intense man. Yet when it comes to me, he's so careful.

"What's your name?" he says, his mouth shifting to the front of my neck.

He presses kiss after kiss down my throat as he descends. My head falls back, and my eyes close as I focus on his movement until he reaches my collarbone.

He opens his mouth and sucks on the edge of it. My skin senses the feeling of his dark hair brushing against my chin.

I love the soft strokes of his hair against me.

Now, this close to his hair, it smells a little like cigar smoke. He must have lit one after the restaurant and before he came to the club.

He pulls back for a moment after he gets his taste and waits for me to answer. I pull my head back up to face him, my eyelashes fluttering open.

"Can we not exchange names?" I ask.

"No names?"

There's no judgment in his eyes, only curiosity.

"And no personal information," I add.

I can't risk it if there's any chance he'll figure out that I'm Saul Newport's daughter.

My reputation wouldn't come back from the gossip that would abound if someone back home found out that I was having a one-night stand in Vegas.

I've already done enough harm as it is.

He pulls back for a second, but I'm still engulfed in his arms.

"I know this is a little late to ask, but you're not married, are you?" he asks.

I'm not married, and I'm technically not engaged anymore, either.

I texted Collin the minute I pulled into Vivi's apartment garage the day after I left Denver. It was too long of a drive to make it in one day, and I needed the entire nineteen hours to give me the courage to tell him it was over.

I ripped off the ring he proposed to me with and chucked it out the window somewhere between Boise and the Oregon border. That's why he offered to buy me something bigger when I get home. As if I care about the diamond he puts on my hand.

God only knows where it ended up.

But Brutal Bodyguard didn't ask if I have a modern-day arranged marriage situation waiting for me to return to my duties the moment I get back to Denver. He only asked if I am married now... which is no.

"No, I'm not," I tell him.

"Okay." He nods. "Then, if I can't call you by your name, I'll have to come up with a nickname," he says.

"What kind of nickname?" I ask.

"You're about to find out." He smiles back at me.

Oh my God... that smile.

He's so sexy when he smiles.

He bends back down and seals our lips together.

Kaenan

I almost got on the elevator after cigars and drinks with the guys and headed back up to my room.

We had just played a hockey game the night before, and since we won, Coach Bex let us have one night in Sin City. Technically, I shouldn't even be here, so this feels like the pass I never give myself.

I wasn't looking for a one-night stand tonight.

Ever since I brought Berkeley home, she's been my top priority and any nights that I don't have to be away from her for work... I'm not. It's as simple as that.

She's still struggling to bond with me, which guts me.

Not like she is with my mother.

Those two have practically been glued together since we brought her back from Montana four months ago, and I'm relieved that Berkeley has at least bonded with one of us.

But something about this woman I saw when the elevator doors opened... fuck, I don't know how to describe it.

Before I knew it, I was sitting at the bar, trying to find the beautiful woman who turned cherry red the minute her friend blurted out that the blonde was headed to the bar to find a one-night stand.

Jealousy hit me hard and fast.

An emotion I know nothing about when it comes to women. I've never wanted anyone bad enough to be jealous that she might end up with someone else.

Not until tonight, at least.

At first, I figured I'd missed her.

That she had left with someone already or went to a different club. Right up until my eyes locked on her dancing, swinging her hips on the dance floor.

I couldn't take my eyes off her. She was mesmerizing in a way I couldn't put my finger on. I couldn't even think of the last time someone held my attention for that long.

Especially a woman who couldn't get out of the elevator and away from me fast enough.

The words I heard echoed into the elevator before I even saw her angelic face have played on repeat since I heard them.

"Sure, let me just screw the brains out of the first man I see."

She looked so fucking cute when the elevator doors opened. She stood there with her cheeks bright red and her chest splotchy with embarrassment after Brent opened his damn mouth.

I should have stepped up right then and offered to take her back upstairs.

Dammit, I wanted to.

But dinner was already planned, and the pussy-whipped jokes I would have gotten if I hadn't shown up to dinner would have been relentless for the next couple of weeks.

Throughout the entire dinner with the guys, my knee bounced with the uncomfortable idea that she was in the club grinding against some asshole on the dance floor and slipping him her room key.

What kind of asshole would she find out there?

Would he treat her right?

Would he make her come as hard as I could?

Would she fuck his brains out like I wish to God she'd do to me?

Dammit.

My mind couldn't stop racing.

I haven't touched a woman since I brought Berkeley home.

Four months of abstinence is some kind of record for me, but I can't have any distractions from being the father I never had.

This thing between her and I is too fragile to let hookups and one-night stands cloud my judgment.

Keeping my hands to myself hasn't been a problem over the past four months, though. None of the women at Oakley's, the local bar the Hawkeyes frequent after a game, or the puck bunnies waiting at the end of the game, have been tempting enough to break my fast.

But this girl...

Goddammit...

This girl had me physically unwell at dinner with the guys. I could barely keep my ass in the seat, and I don't remember tasting the steak I demolished, hoping to get through dinner as fast as possible.

I'm solid, steady, and unshakable.

It's what makes me one of the top right-defenseman in the league. I don't fidget or squirm, but smoking cigars with the guys, which is usually calming for me, felt more like I took a double espresso shot and couldn't focus on any conversation in our group.

I was antsy or jittery.

I don't know which.

All I know is that this woman makes it impossible to think of anything else.

Dangerous is what she is.

God forbid this woman lives in Seattle and shows up for a game.

If the opposing team ever wanted to fuck with my season, they'd buy her a front-row ticket to every game and sit her on the rival team's side.

I can't even think about her wearing someone else's jersey without clenching my fists.

Nothing gets to me.

Not usually.

I went to the club, found a seat, and ordered a beer. I had to do something to slow myself down from marching through the middle of that dance floor and throwing her over my shoulder like the goddamn caveman she makes me feel like.

I want her.

I fucking can't think about anything else I want more.

I want to taste her on my tongue.

Feel every inch of her against my fingertips.

Watch her tits bounce as she rides me.

Flip her over and watch her come against my cock as I pin her under me.

I want to claim the sounds she makes when I find the spot that has her singing my name.

But then I saw the asshole who got to her first.

I saw him kiss her right in front of me, and I had to leave, or I would have hurt the kid.

He seemed more her type, and I couldn't bring myself to be the dick to scare him off to get what I wanted.

Not that I give a shit about him, but she had to make the choice.

She saw me sitting there at the bar. We stared at each other for long enough that she had to know why I was there.

What I came for.

But she didn't tell him to get lost. She kept dancing with him.

The minute he kissed her, I couldn't watch anymore.

That's why staying celibate until Berkeley and I are in a better place is critical. I can't lose my focus on the one thing more important than anything in this world.

My little girl.

Even if an angel just walked into my life, claiming not to have known my room number.

I'm used to puck bunnies knocking on my door at all hours of the night after slipping the bellboy some cash.

I don't open the door for women who weren't invited up to begin with, though. This is the first time I've gone against my own rules.

But she doesn't seem like a puck bunny.

In fact, I'm not so sure she even knows who the hell I am or what I do for a living.

Maybe that's what has me so goddamn hard.

She's not here because of the zeros in my bank account or the fame I get from the jersey I wear.

She just wants me.

And I'll give her anything she asks for tonight.

One night only.

CHAPTER FIVE

Kaenan

Once we get to the edge of the bed, I drop her legs down slowly until her feet touch the ground.

She immediately attempts to reach her fingertips out around the tip of my cock, still contained behind my basketball shorts and boxer briefs, but I stop her. Once my dick gets involved more than it already is, I'll have a difficult time slowing things down.

There may only be a thin layer of material stopping my erection from springing free, but that feels symbolic of how the rest of me feels right about now. I'm only a thin line away from losing my self-control with her, from thrusting into her until I bottom out, completely inside her, while her tight pussy milks me of every last drop of cum I have left in my body.

I know we agreed to a one-night stand, but I want to give her more than that. I don't want to rush this with her, even if my cock is calling me a liar.

I don't want her to regret this.

Or wish she'd picked someone else.

I want to tease her, make her beg for me, have her dripping wet and ready for what I have in store for her.

"Not just yet," I say, bending down and whispering it against her mouth right before I lay a single kiss against her lips.

She makes a small groan like she's disappointed, and I bite back a chuckle.

"Don't worry... I plan to fill you with it. I promise." I smirk down at her.

She bites down on the inside of her mouth like she's excited but a little nervous about me making good on my word.

Playing with her should be fun.

I reach my right hand up to her collarbone. My fingers slide down over the silkiness of her pajama top until my thumb and index finger glide over her hard nipple.

Her breath catches as I touch her there.

"Can I take this off?" I ask.

She nods slowly, and my fingers work as I unbutton all six iridescent pink buttons that feel like material from a seashell.

I don't rush through it, but it only takes me seconds to unbutton each one.

The second I undo that last one, she pulls her top open with her fingertips and lets the silky material drop over her shoulders and down her arms until it pools around her feet, revealing the buttery soft skin that was covered by that sexy as fuck dress she wore last night.

"Fuck, baby... you're beautiful," I tell her.

Her tits are fucking perfect. Perky like I knew they would be with a slight pear shape and gorgeous mauve nipples. My mouth waters at the idea of laying her out to spend ample time tasting each one.

"Thank you," she whispers softly, her blue eyes glimmering up at me.

She likes the nickname I gave her.

Her eyes flickered the moment I said it.

I wasn't sure what nickname I would end up calling her, but for some reason, baby just feels right.

She seems young for a woman who seems close to my age. Almost like she grew up sheltered.

Maybe it's the slight innocence in her eyes or the way she's giving me the idea that she's peering at me like I get to take full control and use her body however I want.

I've never used "baby" with anyone else before. Primarily because I think pet names are stupid and also because I've had a real name to use. But I have no choice since she won't give me hers.

And her not knowing mine means it's less likely she'll realize that I'm a professional athlete, which serves me as well. Although it does rob me of hearing her scream my name when she comes.

I take a step forward, causing the bottom of my rib cage to press against her full breasts.

I want to feel her mounds in my hands more than I want my next breath, but I want her comfortable with my touch first. I'll settle to feel her hard nipples against my ribs... for now.

I place my hands low on her hips and bend down to kiss her. She responds instantly by lifting her arms to the back of my neck and threading her fingers through my hair.

Jesus, I love how she does that.

My hands smooth back over her hips to the small of her back. Then I lift my hands and trail my fingers over her skin feather soft as they smooth down the valley of her spine.

She quivers under my touch.

She's ticklish.

Of course she would be. How would I not have guessed that?

Every little thing I discover about her makes me want her more.

I continue my fingers' descent down her back until my pinky stops at the top of her crack, her pajama pants riding low enough to allow it.

She moans into our kiss, egging me on.

Telling me I'm on the right track.

I reach my hands down, past the waistband of her pajama pants, and grip her bare ass with both hands, tugging her tight against my erection. She gasps at the feeling of me.

I pull my lips off hers and plant my mouth against the soft spot right under her ear.

"I didn't even taste my dinner tonight," I tell her.

"Why not?" she whispers, her hands pulling out of my hair and wrapping tight around my neck to keep me close.

"I couldn't stop thinking about devouring you instead."

"You're going to devour me?" she asks, her voice shaky with need.

"I plan to taste every inch of you until I've rung out every orgasm I can from your body, and you can barely stand tomorrow," I tell her, pulling back and staring into her eyes.

Her eyes dilate instantly.

She likes it when I talk to her like this.

Good... so do I.

I push down her pajama shorts to find her completely naked for me except for a pair of full-coverage flesh-toned underwear.

I think women refer to these as granny panties, but I don't care what she's wearing underneath her clothing.

What women don't understand is that men don't give a fuck about a woman's underwear as long as they end up on the bedroom floor.

I love that she planned a one-night stand while getting ready and still decided to be practical with her underwear choice.

Just another thing to add to the growing list of things that set this woman apart from anyone I've ever met.

I'm used to seeing red panties, black lacy thongs, and even assless stuff, when a woman is expecting to spend the night with me, but this is probably a first time her panties have been so sensible.

I pull back just a little to stare down at the nude underwear with only a couple of inches of space between us.

"I like these," I tell her, reaching down and gliding the back of my index finger over the top of her panty-covered pussy.

She jerks toward my touch and a quick exhale leaves her lips.

Oh... is that how responsive you're going to be to me?

Fuck yeah.

"I... I... didn't pack anything cuter," she tries to explain, glancing down at her own underwear.

Is she embarrassed?

She sure as shit shouldn't be and if she could feel the pulsating of my cock in her hand, she'd know better than to think I want her in anything else.

"Here let me take them off," she says, hooking her thumbs into the side of her panties.

"No." I stop her. "Let me."

She pauses at my instruction and then pulls her thumbs out of her waistband.

I press my hands on her shoulders, directing her to sit on the bed.

Her eyes watch me carefully but there's trust there that I wasn't expecting.

I ease her all the way down until her back is lying on the white duvet of the hotel's bed. She pulls up her heels and rests them against the bed's wooden side frame. She's too short to have her feet flat on the ground.

Her long blonde hair looks like spun silk, splayed out on the bed from her ponytail. I want to reach out and run my thumb and index finger over a few strands just to see if it feels as soft as it looks. She looks like an angel... an angel I plan to do wicked things to.

I take a step forward and part her thighs with my hands. She doesn't hesitate to open for me as she watches from her position. Then I nudge them further apart as I wedge my legs between hers.

She watches me carefully as I hook my index fingers into the side of her elastic band. I can smell her arousal as I bend down closer, my mouth watering with anticipation to get my tongue on her.

Her panties are drenched between the apex of her thighs.

"You're so damn wet," I mutter, my tongue darting out to lick my bottom lip.

I pull her panties off her hips with experienced finesse, unwrapping her like a present on Christmas morning.

The second I uncover her, I have to stop for a moment and admire her. Her pussy is fucking perfect. Everything about her body is.

Even in the dark, the Vegas lights from the window show her pussy glistening for me.

I remove her panties all the way to the bottom of her feet as she watches, her eyes locked on me. I crumple them into my right hand, savoring the feeling of their wetness in the palm of my hand and my fingertips.

I did that to her.

My chest puffs with accomplishment.

"I'm on birth control but do you have protection?" she asks softly, staring at her panties in my hand.

I've always been responsible, even with Mia... except for the last night we were together. I bought cheap condoms from a minimart.

Rookie mistake.

It broke during intercourse without me knowing, it must have been toward the end. Since she was on birth control neither of us worried about it and being that I never heard from her after, I assumed it all turned out fine.

What a goddamn idiot I was.

Ever since that condom broke, I make sure to buy high-quality condoms and always keep one on me just in case. I never go without one and I never buy condoms from gas stations anymore.

I nod to confirm. "But we won't be needing that right now."

Her eyes flare up to mine and I see the faint movement of her gripping the comforter underneath her at my words.

Oh yeah baby... you're going to need to hold on to something for this.

Just as I'm about to discard my new favorite panties, I make a last-minute decision. I tuck the pair of underwear into the pocket of my basketball shorts when her attention is on my face and not on what I'm doing with my hands.

I've never done this before... stolen a woman's panties, but desperate times call for desperate measures and I need something to remember this woman by when I return home to my abstinent lifestyle.

My vision roams over every inch of her bare skin, laid out and ready for me, her body like a treasure map begging to be discovered. There's so much I want to do with her and so little time to do it in. One night isn't enough, but it will have to be because she's not looking for more than one night, and I have responsibilities back at home waiting for me too.

Isla

I watch as he kneels down on the carpeted hotel room floor, his shoulders hovering above the end of the bed. He grips around the back on my knees, tossing my legs over his shoulders and bringing my bum to the edge of the bed.

"Are you going to let me do whatever I want to you tonight?" he asks, his eyes hooded with a look of lust so intense that it has me wondering if anyone has ever wanted me like this.

"What are you going to do?" I ask.

I'm not afraid of his answer. I'm more concerned that I'll orgasm at the faintest touch from him and this night will be over sooner than I want.

I'm desperate to be touched by someone who looks at me like this man does. He seems as though he's been starving for physical touch as long as I have.

"I give you my word that whatever I choose to do will have you begging me not to stop."

My breath hitches at his promise.

I want that.

I want to lose myself in pleasure tonight.

I nod, glancing down at his face between my thighs.

His eyes glide back down my body and settle between my legs.

"You have a beautiful pussy and I bet you taste just as good. Are you going to let me taste you?"

I nod again as more arousal heats low in my belly and coats my center, dripping onto the bed sheets.

"Good girl," he says.

And then he bends closer, his finger gently running through my folds until it reaches my center. Then his mouth opens against my pussy as his tongue dives in between, and he takes a long lick.

The feeling of his hot mouth on me has my toes curling, but the way he flicks my clit with his tongue has me arching off the bed.

"Oh..." I say breathlessly.

He pulls his mouth off me for a second.

"That wasn't near loud enough," he says, kissing the inside of my thigh. "We should be testing out the soundproof walls when I'm between your thighs. If you don't scream, I'll have to suck on you harder. Now nod like a good girl and tell me you understand?"

My eyes latch closed, and I nod.

He's going to suck on me harder?

The idea has my head spinning already.

His mouth returns to my center but his tongue reaches lower at my entrance.

He starts by applying teasing strokes against it, but I need so much more.

A small moan escapes my throat.

"Not loud enough, baby. If you want it, you better give me more than that," he instructs.

His thumb presses against my clit and starts a circular motion as his tongue continues to tease, entering me.

I squirm under his fingers and tongue.

I need more pressure. I need everything he can give me.

"Please," I beg, louder than before.

I reach down and thread my fingers in his hair, pulling him tighter against me.

"That's better," he says, his mouth reaching higher and covering my pussy again.

His tongue swirls through my folds, sparking nerve endings until I can't take it anymore.

"Oh God, please," I say louder than I have before.

He responds by dragging his teeth down my center and lighting me up like a Christmas tree.

"Fuck me!" I beg him, my fingers pulling on his hair harder.

"That's how I want to hear it," he praises.

His thumb comes back to my clit and circles, and his tongue digs down and presses against my center.

He's fucking me with his tongue, and I can't keep myself still. My back arches again and my fingers dig deep against his scalp.

I'm getting closer and closer the more his tongue presses into me.

"I'm so close! Don't stop!" I beg, just like he promised I would.

At that moment, he does exactly that.

He pulls his mouth off my body, pulls my legs back down his shoulders, and steps into me so that my thighs wrap around his waist.

"What are you doing?" I ask.

He pulls me off the bed and then kneels onto it, carrying me with him.

He drops me on the pillow and then reaches for his wallet on the nightstand.

"I'm a greedy asshole," he says, pulling two condoms from his wallet and then tossing the wallet back on the nightstand. "And I want to feel you grip me when you come."

I want that too.

He drops the condoms on the opposite pillow and then drops down, settling between my legs, and kisses me.

I can taste myself on him.

And something about it is so sexy.

"Are you going to milk my cock like I know your sweet little pussy will?"

"God... I need you," I beg again.

I love the way he talks to me in bed.

Collin didn't like talking during sex, and now I don't want to go back to quiet sex for the rest of my life.

I want to be told what to do.

I want to be praised when I do what he asks.

And I want to know when it feels good for him like it does for me.

He sits up a little, his eyes glued to me as he reaches down and pulls his basketball shorts down his legs, along with his boxer briefs.

Then he kicks them off his feet and onto the floor.

"You're wet enough to take me now," he tells me, picking up one of the condoms and ripping the wrapper open with his teeth.

He reaches down, and I watch in the small sliver between us as he pushes the condom over his tip and then all the way down his shaft. He runs his hands down it a couple of times to make sure it's secure.

Looking down, I can't help but lick my lips at the size of him. He's a lot bigger than Collin, and the anticipation of feeling him stretch me has my legs shaking with need.

Next, he doesn't line himself up with my opening like I thought he would. Instead, his right-hand reaches between us, and his index finger glides through my folds again.

I'm even wetter than I was before.

"Jesus..." he says, his voice breaking off as his jaw clenches like he struggling to hold on to his self-control.

I wish he'd let go.

I don't want him to hold back anything.

He starts kissing a line from my neck to my left nipple, and then his finger enters me.

I buck at the feeling of penetration from his finger and the sharpness of his teeth against my nipple.

I whimper with need as I wrap my hands around the back of his neck.

"I won't last much longer," I warn him.

My knees shake harder, and my clit vibrates with an impending release.

He pulls his mouth off my nipple and stares up at me, his fingers pulling out and gripping his cock.

His mouth crashes down on mine, and then he lines up to my opening and rocks against me once.

"Oh..." I moan loudly into his mouth, and he consumes my cries.

It feels so much bigger than I thought it would.

He rocks into me again, easing himself in slowly. But with every inch, I can feel my orgasm building quickly.

"Hurry, I'm going to come!" I beg again.

He presses into me harder, and now I know why he's trying to go slow. He's big, but it feels so damn good.

"Goddammit, baby. I'm going to end up coming at the same time if you beg like that," he admits.

He rocks into me again and again until he's fully seated inside me. The fullness of him inside me as his pelvis rubs back and forth sparking my clit has my body finally giving out and letting loose. I fall into the hardest orgasm of my life.

My body erupts, squeezing his cock as my legs tremble uncontrollably.

He pulls me tight into his arms as I come while he keeps his rhythm, rocking in and out of me to keep my orgasm going as long as possible.

He makes a guttural sound.

"I'm about to come inside you. Tell me it's ok," he says, his voice on the edge.

I nod, words clogging my throat at how much I want to feel that.

It's all the permission he needs.

He thrusts a few more times and then buries himself deep.

He groans out as his cock pulsates, and he releases as deep as he can, thrusting as he unloads inside me.

Over and over again until he empties completely.

He collapses on top of me and peppers kissing at the apex between my shoulder and neck.

I love how sweet it feels to be kissed there.

It's comforting in some way.

His hand sweeps over my hair, back to my ponytail, as he peers down at me, still under him.

Our eyes latch on to each other as we breathe through our orgasms.

Then he slowly pulls out and turns over onto his back next to me.

I wait a moment until the silence feels right.

"Can we do that again?"

He chuckles.

"Yeah, baby, we can do that as many times as you want." He turns to look at me. "Just give me a minute to *reload*."

I laugh, and then he pulls me closer, guiding my head to lay against his chest.

I don't want to leave this bed.

I don't want the sun to come up this morning.

I'll have to leave in a few hours, and this will all feel like a distant dream one day.

Will he dream of me too?

Chapter Six

Isla

My eyes strain to stay open as I lie against his chest, his fingers gently running over my back. He's practically lulling me to sleep after everything he just did to my body.

I shouldn't feel this comfortable lying in this stranger's arms, but I do.

He shifts under me slightly and breaks the silence we've enjoyed for the last few minutes. With only two condoms, it limited us, but we made use of other ways to enjoy each other.

"Are you going to explain the stuffed giraffe?" I ask, glancing over at his nightstand to a plush toy I didn't notice when we first started since it was so dark in here.

"I think it's my good luck charm. I've had a couple of wins over the past few days. Call me superstitious," he says, looking over at it too.

Wins?

What kind of wins?

But we said no personal information, so I can't ask, even though I'd like to know.

"Do you like stuffed animals?" I ask, not sure how I'll feel if he has some enormous collection.

"No. I bought it a few nights ago. Figured I'd give it to a special girl," he says.

To me?

Is he planning on giving his lucky charm to me?

I could certainly use all the luck I can get.

Although knocking on his door this morning was pretty lucky. Maybe I'm back on a lucky winning streak too. Not that I won't accept it if he offers it to me.

"Hey, listen," he starts, shifting farther to face me better. "I know we agreed to remain anonymous but—"

"No," I say, sitting up instantly.

"Hey, whoa. Don't jump out the window, I'm sorry," he says, trying to pull me back against him, but I don't go easily. "Shit," he mumbles to himself, almost as if berating himself for attempting to step out of our agreement.

Is he really that worried that I would walk out on him now after we already had sex? Isn't that what he was expecting out of a one-night stand?

"I thought maybe since things went well, we could exchange numbers, and I could call you if my job ever takes me near where you live. I didn't mean to change the arrangement if you're uncomfortable with it," he says, his eyes honest as they peer back at me. "Just forget it... and don't go yet."

I meet his eyes. I feel like I could crawl into him and get lost for days. But I'm not that girl.

And I have no idea what life is like for him either.

Could I really see myself with a bodyguard who travels around putting himself in harm's way to defend someone else?

Would he even want me waiting at home for him to come back?

We agreed to a one-night stand and maybe that's how we should leave it.

Tomorrow, I head back to Denver and start the life I was conditioned for.

No more running.

No more wishing for things I can't have.

"I thought you were okay with us not sharing anything personal about ourselves?" I ask.

"In theory, that works great for me. But I'll admit, this is a first. I've never had anyone ask for anonymity before."

"Is it really that unusual?"

I've never had a one-night stand before, but it can't be that odd of a request.

"For me, it is," he says.

"Why? Are you a bodyguard for someone famous or something?"

I am curious, I'll admit.

He chuckles for a second, and I love the sound of his deep timbre laugh. "I've never thought of it like that... but sure, I guess my job description entails guarding a few famous people."

"Then it's settled, no personal information."

His eyes settle on me again, and his thumb rubs up and down on a small section low on my back. It's almost like he felt me tense during the conversation of exchanging information and is trying to soothe me back down.

The weirdest part... it's working.

His calming strokes are actually bringing down my anxiety over this conversation.

How does he do that?

Running is usually the only thing that soothes me when I get tense. Now I can add the stranger from Vegas who I'll never see again.

"You don't want to see me again?" he asks.

Do I want to see him again?

Yes!

I don't even have to think about the answer.

The problem is that once I return to Denver, I'll have to go back to the life my father expects, and there's no room for Brutal Bodyguard.

Not unless I told my father that I need a bodyguard being the daughter-in-law of the mayor.

But I don't, and having him so temptingly close wouldn't be good for the faithful, dedicated wife role expected of me.

Not that I've agreed to marry Collin yet. I still need to see what happens when I get home, but I don't see how my father will let me keep my business unless I do what he asks.

Honestly, even though it hurts, it's what I have to do.

There is no possibility for me to see him again.

"I'm heading home after this. I wanted a one-night stand with no messy strings after," I say.

"... fine, I understand," he says, staring up at the ceiling. "My life isn't simple either. You're right."

I hate being right in this instance.

"The sex was fucking incredible. I just wish we could do it again," he says.

My cheeks redden at his admission, mostly because I know exactly how he feels. I wish we could do this again, another time.

"It was," I say, reaching over and gliding my hand over his jaw.

His eyes lock with mine, and he bends toward me, softly pressing his lips to mine, and kisses me.

The kind of kiss I'll never forget.

A goodbye kiss.

He pulls me tight to him, and before I know it, I drift off in his arms.

CHAPTER SEVEN

Isla

I'm just barely awoken by the movement behind me. A satisfied groan rumbles through the intoxicatingly sexy man sleeping on the other side of the bed behind me.

My brain is still foggy as I'm only half awake, but falling asleep next to him came so easy.

I feel safe with him.

And maybe that's because he spent more time holding me between sex than we spent on the act.

Collin never gave me after-sex cuddling or wanted to talk before or after. Sex has always been scheduled if he had a sliver of time in his eighty-hour workweek.

My eyes dart open at the realization of what's happening. My one-night stand has shown more interest in being in bed with me than my fiancé ever did during our four years together.

I hear another satisfied groan from him as he shifts again to the other side of the bed.

He's talented, I'll give him that, and as much as I'd like to stay here until he wakes up to get one last experience with him before I leave Las Vegas, this moment of bliss is over for me.

I glance up at the clock on the bedside table. It's almost five in the morning. Panic starts to build low in my stomach.

I wasn't looking for cuddling and talking late into the morning.

I didn't ask to be with a man who I'd want more from if my life was different.

I can't allow myself to want something else. Otherwise, I won't be able to get in that Range Rover and drive home.

I need to leave before he wakes up.

It's difficult in the dark to find my clothes all over the hotel room floor, but with the soft light of the Strip still beaming through a crack between the curtains, I find my silk shorts and shirt...but no panties.

Dammit!

I always wondered how men ended up with women's underwear after a night like this. I mean, really... who leaves their panties at his place by accident and goes commando? Well... I now have my answer... and they're my favorite pair too.

What a bummer.

Now I sort of wish I had his number so I could text him tomorrow and ask him to ship them to me if he finds them before checking out of the hotel. Except I wouldn't do that because then I'd have to explain why I left like a thief in the night.

Note to self...

Next time you decide to have a one-night stand with someone you plan on skipping out on, make sure to ask him to leave each of the articles of clothing he's pulling off your sex-crazed body in a nice, neat pile for a quicker escape later.

I quietly pull my shorts over my body and then slip on my top, buttoning it quickly, not bothering myself with whether I have the right buttons.

I just need to get out of here.

Something catches my eye on the nightstand.

The stuffed giraffe.

It's so cute, and he said it was his lucky charm and that he was going to give it to me... or something like that.

He squeezed me when he said it, but sneaking out of his hotel room without saying goodbye might have forfeited my rights to it.

If he was seeing me off this morning instead of me leaving without saying goodbye, wouldn't he be giving that to me?

I'm about ninety percent sure, and since a part of me wants a memento from tonight, I tiptoe over and pick up the giraffe, clutching it to my chest.

I pull the soft, fuzzy material up to my nose, hoping it smells like him. It mostly smells like chlorine and the signature hotel smell that this place has, but a little of his essence is in there somewhere.

I know there's a ten percent chance he wasn't going to give me the giraffe before I left, but the thought that he might give this stuffed animal to another "special girl" has my heart cracking a little.

He offered to see me again.

To exchange numbers and keep in touch.

I'm the one who can't do messy.

I need to forget about the what-ifs and stop thinking about a life I could have if I don't go back to Denver.

I'm just not in a place to take this on, even if it also feels like a mistake to sever ties completely.

I guess if we're supposed to be in each other's lives, fate will bring us back together. Just like it did this morning when it brought me up to his room.

An elevator ride and a few moments later, I arrive at Vivi's and my room.

My heart thumps wildly as I check over my shoulder to make sure there's no tall, hulk-sized man in pursuit of me, asking for an explanation for leaving without a word.

I knock on the door, checking the room number three times before I do.

...for good measure.

"Vivi... Vivi, are you in there?"

After a few seconds, I hear Vivi's footsteps heading toward the door.

She opens it, and I barrel through it as quickly as I can.

"What the hell happened to you?" she asks, dressed with her bags on the bed as she packs for our flight.

"It's a long story," I tell her, heading straight for my own luggage.

A story that can wait until I'm safely on a plane and can no longer second-guess if not leaving him my number was the right decision.

Or whether I just made the biggest mistake of my life.

CHAPTER EIGHT

Kaenan

I run up the stairs of the private jet, taking three stairs at a time. With my height and a running start, it isn't hard for me to sail up the staircase of the aircraft. I know what I'll find once I reach the top of the plane; four of my teammates are staring back at me, already seated and ready for takeoff. All of whom will be wondering why the fuck I almost missed our flight.

I'm usually not tardy for things.

I take my responsibilities seriously, and I respect other people's time. But my morning got turned upside down when I woke up to find the sexy blonde from last night left without saying goodbye.

What the fuck?

I know it was a one-night stand.

She was clear about that.

And the one-night stand rule doesn't exactly come with a list of decorum to be followed.

She even went as far as to demand we didn't exchange information. I just didn't expect she'd split without saying goodbye.

And I sure as hell didn't think she'd steal the stuffed giraffe I bought for Berkeley a couple of days ago at our first weekend game in Nashville.

I did steal her underwear, I guess. I almost threw away the pair of nude panties this morning when I woke up to find the giraffe and the woman gone.

I hovered over the bathroom trash can with the two used condoms inside from earlier in the morning, but I couldn't bring myself to do it.

I'll keep the panties as a reminder.

Women are a distraction I can't afford right now.

Keep your eyes on what's important—Berkeley and being the father you never had.

"Where the fuck have you been?" Lake Powers, the team's left wing, hollers at me from one of the six captain's chairs in the main part of the private plane.

"I thought I forgot something," I say back, keeping my head down but not giving any emotion.

Yeah, I forgot something... something like an explanation from the woman who left me to wake up alone this morning in the suite's king-sized bed. The same bed we did things that are now permanently branded in my spank bank for life.

I may be pissed off by the way she left things, but my cock won't forget the way she felt last night. Or the way she followed every instruction I gave her.

The minute I woke up and realized she was nowhere in the suite, I threw on a pair of sweats and a T-shirt and scoured the entire lobby level floor of the hotel, which included but was not limited to, the restaurants, shops, casino and outdoor pool and cabanas, before realizing the woman had, in fact, vanished.

With no name and no origin story to help track her down, I stood in the lobby of the hotel for a solid ten minutes, staring at the large glass automatic doors.

She's gone, and I'll probably never see her again to ask why she left the way she did and why she took my daughter's stuffed giraffe. I told her it was for someone special. Sure, I didn't tell her it was for my daughter, but she was adamant that we didn't share details of our lives.

I'm tired of being walked out on.

I'm tired of finishing last.

Between the father who didn't stick around, to high school coaches who didn't believe I'd make it to the NHL, to Mia, who kept Berkeley from me until she had no other choice. And now, finally, to the blonde who got what she wanted and then left.

Not that I had anything more to offer her. My life is chaotic, but this is the first time I've ever woken up looking forward to seeing the woman in my bed from the night before.

"Why are you wandering around? Just take a damn seat," Brent Tomlin, our left defenseman, says.

"Jesus, Altman, you're making Tomlin anxious. You know he's a nervous flier." Lake jabs at Brent.

"Fuck off, Powers. Spare a brain cell for his history with planes," Ryker Haynes, our captain and fearless leader, says.

Lake sobers, clearly remembering too late that Brent's parents died in a plane crash when he was younger.

He's the most sensible one on our crew, which is why we all respect him, but I've seen him get buck wild when he wants to.

"Why can't we just fly commercial again? Those don't go down near as easily," Brent says, glancing longingly out the window at the solid ground.

Brent is a fucking animal on the ice, and he's one of the first to jump in and defend a teammate in a fight, but when it comes to flying, well, he clams up.

Although, if you didn't know that about him, you probably wouldn't guess since he sits quietly in his chair with his eyes shut and noise-canceling headphones blaring some kind of Swedish rock band he's gotten into.

The toilet in the bathroom located at the rear of the aircraft flushes, and then the door opens with Briggs Conley walking out. He's our right wing, the man who plays directly in front of me. He's the teammate I'm the most in sync with out on the ice.

"Shit, there you are. I was five minutes away from calling hotel security and asking them to check your room for a man tied up to his bed with a gag in his mouth and his wallet and his kidney missing." He smirks, walking down the aisle of the captain's chairs. "Whatever chick you ended up with last night must know how to suck some morning wood for you to almost miss your flight. You're never late," he says, setting down his backpack by a chair and then flopping into one of the other six captain's chairs not currently occupied by Brent, Lake, or Ryker.

Brent pulls his headphones off while Lake and Ryker gawk at me.

"Did you find that woman from last night?" Brent asks, his eyebrow rising with interest as he leans forward in his chair.

"What girl?" Lake asks, his interest piquing as he leans toward Brent for the answer.

He knows sure as shit that I won't be giving up any details.

A bunch of fucking gossips.

"No one," I tell Lake with a threatening stare.

"I wouldn't say she was no one," Brent smirks up at me. "She was hot as shit, and her friend was parading her around for a one-night stand. You should have seen Kaenan in the elevator."

"Shut your mouth before you regret it, Tomlin," I threaten, but Brent knows me well enough to call my bluff.

"Kaenan was acting like a dog in heat. I half expected him to bend her over in the elevator and fuck her right there, in front of me and her friend."

I stomp off past him, dropping my heavy ass backpack in his lap.

He wasn't expecting my titanium, Hawkeyed-issued water bottle hitting his crotch first.

"Fuck..." he mutters, pushing the backpack off his lap.

My backpack hits the private jet's floor with a loud thud as Brent cradles his jean-clad crotch for a moment.

"Shake it off, Tomlin. He warned you," Ryker says while Lake chuckles.

Turns out that wasn't an empty threat after all.

The guys know I've been abstinent since I brought Berkeley home, and they've all been waiting for the moment I break.

That moment was this morning.

Even before Berkeley, I started slowing down on the frequency of random hookups.

Those days of chasing women are reserved for your rookie years when you think you'll never get older and have to actually work at your job.

After eleven years in the league, I can no longer wake up twenty minutes before the morning skate with a hangover while scarfing down an entire cold pizza left in the fridge from the week before. And then wash it down with a six-pack of beer and play at championship-winning levels.

Nowadays, half of us are just striving to stay relevant in a sport that retires you young, leaving you with bad knees, fucked-up shoulders and ankles, broken facial bones, and memory loss from all those damn hits to the cranium.

For now, we play for the love of the game and all those goddamn zeros whenever we look at our bank accounts.

The camaraderie from teammates doesn't hurt either. But not every player is lucky enough to land a group of guys who you see as brothers.

The Hawkeyes are the best team I've ever played for, and I hope I get to retire here.

A ringtone goes off and has all of us reaching for our pockets.

I pull mine out, and the last thing I want to read displays against my screen.

Mia's Lawyer calling...

What the hell?

"I have to take this," I say, glancing up from my phone at Ryker.

Ryker at his watch.

"Wheels up in five. Make it fast," he says, looking back up at me and nodding, letting me know I have a little time.

I turn around, hitting the green answer button, and sail back down the stairs of the aircraft to the tarmac.

"Hello?"

"Mr. Altman."

"I'm just about to get on a flight to head home. Can this call wait until I get back?" I ask.

"I think you'll want to know this information as soon as possible," she says.

"Okay, I have five minutes. What is it?"

I prepare myself for bad news because what the hell else could it be?

"I just received information on my desk that Ms. Logan, Ms. Wallace's mother, has hired legal representation and will be taking you to court for the custody of Berkeley."

"What the fuck?" I yell over the phone, my free hand pinching at my hip. "She can't do that. Tell me she can't do that."

"I'm afraid she can. Although it doesn't mean that the courts will side with her. I think you should be prepared because her legal team is citing that due to your criminal record and the amount of time you travel away from Berkeley, you are unfit and unprepared to take care of her."

"That's bullshit!" I counter.

"I agree, Mr. Altman—"

"You're going to fight this, right?" I ask, cutting her off.

Mia was the one who made her will ironclad to ensure that I got Berkeley.

"I will be involved in the suit, but Ms. Wallace's trust has me on retainer to ensure that Berkeley's and Ms. Wallace's interest is represented in the courtroom."

"Right. Berkeley being with me is what Mia wanted."

"That's true, but I represent Berkeley and Mia in this case... not you. And should the claimant lead the court to believe you are unfit, they will have final say in who they grant guardianship to."

"But that's me! They can't take her from me. I'm her father."

"Mr. Altman. I will do everything in my power to see that Ms. Wallace's wishes are brought to the courtroom's attention. Ms. Logan will have an uphill battle seeing as you can financially provide for Berkeley and since Ms. Wallace has strict instructions that you become Berkeley's legal guardian. And since Ms. Wallace put you on the birth certificate and in her will, they will have to bring a lot to the court in order to rule against you. But I should warn you that I've seen a will overturned for the good of a child before. You should seek legal counsel and make Berkeley's day-to-day as well supported as possible."

"What do you mean 'well supported'?" I ask.

"You should take that up with your defense team, but think in terms of her support system at home. Who does she have around her besides just you? Is she well taken care of, and do you have a solid plan for her when you're away at games? What does her home life look like? Who can vouch for you as a father and as a person?"

"Like a character witness?" I ask.

What the hell... why would I need that?

"That's right. We pulled your criminal record before we contacted you about Berkeley—"

"You pulled my record? For what reason?"

"It's standard procedure..."

I already know what they found.

It's not good.

"And..." I ask.

"You have a misdemeanor that was dropped from a felony assault charge two years ago against another player. Noah Sinclair. I believe this happened off the ice."

"He hit my right wing after the buzzer during that game and then came after Conley again in the parking lot. I took the second swing. Sinclair took the first."

"Unfortunately, that trial is over, and the courts did drop your sentencing. This isn't an argument anymore, and it's part of your record. A record that will be brought up during this trial to poke holes to make you seem unfit."

Jesus Christ.

"I can't lose her," I say, staring out across the Vegas casinos all lined up near the airstrip.

"I know. Retain the best lawyer you can and make sure they've won a suit where the father won."

"Where the father won?"

"Just trust me," she says.

But trust when putting my daughter in the hands of lawyers is tough for me.

"What are my odds here?"

"We'll have a better idea once they assign a judge. And I would take the letter that Ms. Wallace wrote to you to your lawyer meeting. It was in Berkeley's luggage when you picked her up from the funeral."

That's not reassuring.

And a letter from Mia? Even if I had seen it, I wouldn't have read it. There's nothing Mia can say now to make this right. She couldn't have done anything worse to me than what she's done.

"I have to go. I have a client walking in for an eight o'clock meeting," she says. "Get a lawyer, Mr. Altman... today."

Then she hangs up.

I have the urge to get on a flight right now to Montana and tell Mia's mom to eat a dick.

She sure as shit is not going to take my daughter from me. I won't let it happen.

I'll sell every asset I have, quit hockey, and move us to a corner of the world where she'll never find us before I let Mia's "recovering" drug addict mother take my daughter from me.

I see the pilot climbing the stairs after doing his final checks and heading for the cockpit. I'm out of time and need to head back up.

I take the stairs to the top and take a right into the cabin.

"The self-induced celibacy has finally expired. Welcome back, buddy," Lake says, looking up from his phone as I walk to the back of the plane, taking one of the captain's chairs at the end of the row.

"I'm not back, Lake. It was one girl," I say.

Even though the blonde from this morning couldn't be further from my mind. I wish that getting skipped out on and a stolen plush toy were still the worst things that happened to me today.

I'd take that problem over this any day.

Now I have real fucking problems.

I walk back to the last row on the left side of the aircraft.

Briggs gets up from his right seat in the middle row and switches to the seat right next to me.

"You okay?" he asks.

I don't usually like discussing my personal shit, but Briggs is a good guy, and he's had his own problems this year.

Though he doesn't talk to any of us about it.

We're kindred spirits in that way, I guess.

I glance over at him, about to tell him it was nothing, when he interjects first.

"I heard you yelling at someone. And you said Berkeley's name a couple of times."

I peek down at my phone still sitting in my lap, remembering the call from hell I just had.

I suck in my lower lip, debating what to tell him. The truth is all I have.

"That was the lawyer for Mia's will." All the guys know enough about what happened and how I found out about Berkeley. "Mia's mom wants Berkeley."

He leans over the armchair closer to me, his piercing stare on me and his eyebrows stitching together.

"Mia gave you full rights in her will, didn't she? And you're her dad."

I nod, looking over toward Ryker, Brent, and Lake. There's so much that I still don't know yet. I'd prefer to keep it close to the vest until I get the facts.

I see them all texting on their phone with their headphones on, so I know they're not paying attention to our conversation back here.

"Yeah, Mia did. But her mom thinks she has a case."

"But she doesn't... right?"

I let out a sigh. "She might."

"You're fucking kidding me?"

"No," I say, turning to stare out the window to clear my thoughts for a second.

The cockpit door opens and the pilot sticks his head out. The guys pull their noise-canceling headphones down to hear him.

"You gentleman ready for takeoff?" he asks.

"Get us out of here before one of us ends up in jail, or married by Elvis," Brent says from the front.

"Which one would be worse?" Ryker asks.

"Married... obviously. Now let's get this rattle can in the air," Lake says in Brent's general direction.

"Shut the fuck up, Powers!" Brent yells, keeping his eyelids shut and lacing his fingers together, squeezing tightly enough that his fingertips go white, the blood draining from his hands.

"What are you going to do?" Briggs asks once we've taxied out to the runway.

I turn to him and look him dead in the eye.

"I'm going to spend every last dollar I have to make sure Trisha Logan doesn't fuck with me or my daughter again."

Then I pull my phone back up in my hand and dive into searching for the best lawyer in Seattle.

I'll pay anything to keep my daughter.

There's no price tag on Berkeley.

CHAPTER NINE

Isla

"Well, I for one am really glad you decided to stay," Vivi says as she tosses a pillow that she pulled from the linen closet onto the spare bed I've spent the past month on.

"I'm glad to be here too."

I sent off a text to my father the second we landed in Seattle.

> **Isla: I need more time before I come back to Colorado if you expect me to agree to your terms.**

I ignored his attempt to call me and then watched for twenty minutes as the bubbles jump on the text screen.

He hates texting and I'm sure he had to rewrite over the things he wanted to say to me.

It ended up coming out like this...

> **Dad: You have ninety days and then you make up with Collin. Otherwise, I'll have the board remove you from Newport Athletics and you'll lose your house, your car, your cell phone, and anything else the company owns that you've had the pleasure of using.**

Harsh, Dad.

"I just couldn't bring myself to get back in my car when we got back to your condo. Are you sure you can get me temporary employment for the next three months? I can't keep mooching off you, and Dad won't send me money."

"Isn't that illegal?"

"No. He'll just say that I'm not working since I'm on "sabbatical". And the end-of-year disbursements for next month goes directly to mine and Collin's joint account."

"It's not mooching by the way. The longer I can shield you here, the better. Stay forever if you want and send Dad the middle finger. Start a new business. You're far too talented to let Dad strong-arm you."

I want to believe what Vivi is saying but my dad's right. Newport Athletics would be nowhere without his money and connections.

"Then I'll need a bus pass and a pay-by-the-minute phone if I tell Dad off."

"What? Dad owns your Range Rover and your cell phone?"

Vivi lifts a concerned brow at me.

"Don't look at me like that V, I already know, okay? I set myself up for this," I say, focusing my attention on pulling back the fitted sheet towards the headboard and hooking it over the mattress.

Vivi never would have let Dad get his hooks in her like this. She's smarter than me... or maybe it's just that she's never craved my father's good opinion as much as I have.

He conditioned me this way since childhood and I see that now. Vivi's told me this for years but I always thought she was being overprotective.

"Don't be so hard on yourself. Dad is a master at this. He has a few decades on you of being a class-A manipulator, but you see that now, right?" she asks, pulling her corner down over the corner of the mattress.

The fitted sheet is now in place, and I don't know what it is about a bed with only a crisp white fitted sheet that makes me want to lay on it immediately to take in its 'just out of the dryer' warmth and its clean fabric softener smell.

I nod. "But he's not a monster."

She takes a deep sigh and her shoulders sag a bit.

"I know that. I wouldn't speak to him anymore if he were. One shitty, deadbeat dad is my max and my sperm donor of a father already fills that role. But I've established my boundaries and hard lines with Dad and you need to too. He needs to add to your life, Isla, not try to live it for you."

"He doesn't," I say, walking down to the edge of the bed and grabbing the opposite side of the comforter that Vivi just picked up to finish making the bed.

She gives me a "did you forget I've been around for twenty years," look and I know she's right.

"I don't understand how you and I have such different relationships with him," I tell her.

"I rejected his little school."

"You mean Princeton," I say, giving her side-eye.

She knows it's no *little* school.

She rolls her eyes back at me but she knows I'm right.

"...and then I moved two thousand miles away from him and told him that I'll only endure his presence once a year during Christmas as long as he buys me a new pair of Prada shoes." She winks, and I know she's kidding.

Although, I think there is some truth to that.

My father respects Vivi and brags about her around the country club that she's making it out here in Seattle without his help.

Once the comforter is in place, we both pick up the pillows that Vivi already put new covers on and flop them on the bed.

"I'm going to start running again," I blurt out of nowhere.

Running has always been my hobby, my release, my happy place. I mean, after all, I built a tiny little empire with my passion for the lightest weight fabrics on the market and trend-setting designs that set us apart from the big box athletics wear brands.

"That's a great idea. There are a lot of cool places to run around here and a good community of outdoor enthusiasts.

Maybe branching out and meeting new people will be good for you, too, while you're here," she adds.

"Yeah... we'll see," I say, bending down and tossing my bag up on the spare bed and unzipping it to pull out my phone charger to plug it in. The battery is half dead after traveling this morning. "Have you lined me up for a nanny position yet?"

"It's not always easy to find a family that only needs a nanny for a couple of months. Most people are looking for someone long-term, but I know something will come up."

"Thanks, Vivi."

Her phone starts ringing and she glances down. "It's the calling service. They're probably patching over a client; I should take this. Want to order takeout tonight?"

"Sounds good," I tell her over my shoulder as she starts walking out the door of the spare bedroom.

"Something greasy and cheesy?" she asks,

"How did you know?"

"Pizza coming right up," she calls out while walking down the hallway.

"Stuffed crust!" I yell after her. "I'll run it off tomorrow,"

She chuckles at my empty promise.

I hear the faint sound of her answering the phone and her voice goes up an octave. Sounds like a potential new client.

Good for her.

I love that Vivi's business is doing so well these days. She works hard to ensure her employees are supported in their roles and that the families she selects are a good fit for each nanny.

It affords her this gorgeous three-story condo that's located downtown and I know it must cost a small fortune.

My phone rings on the nightstand and I walk back over to grab it.

Collin calling...

I take a second to debate whether to answer but after ignoring his calls for the last four weeks, curiosity is starting to get the better of me.

"Hello?"

"Finally, you answered. Are you going to be at Thanksgiving dinner tomorrow? We need to talk."

I'll miss the Country Club's annual Thanksgiving dinner. A dinner I haven't missed since I was seven years old.

"No, I'm staying in Seattle. And discuss what exactly?"

"About you coming home. We can fix this. What you saw is over. It was unfinished business but it's over now."

"It didn't seem like unfinished business to me. It looked like it was just getting started," I say.

"I said I'm sorry. Can you please come home now? The line your father is giving people that you're at some spa retreat to decompress and relax before the wedding is starting to get some whispers."

I turn and glance out the window at the Seattle skyline.

"My father is an expert at deflecting. I'm sure he'll think of something. And he'll need to come up with something new anyway because my father agreed to another Ninety days."

"Ninety days?" he asks, raising his voice louder than I've ever heard him before. Not a lot gets to Collin. He's usually cool and calm under pressure. I'm glad he's sweating it a little. "My father's going to shit a brick. We're supposed to be rubbing elbows with voters as a couple around town to help with his campaign efforts. And what are people going to say when you're out of town for another three months?"

"Tell them that I rented a cabin in Washington and I locked myself away until I finish next summer's collection. It's not that far from the truth."

I hear him sigh on the other side of the line and the sound of his leather office chair groan as he takes a seat.

"And are you working on the summer collection?" he asks, with a tone like he doesn't believe me.

"Yes. Of course, I am. The product we put out is a direct reflection on me. I'm the face of the brand." I remind him. "If it flops, everyone will blame me."

"You know the seamstresses need the new drawings by New Year to get the prototypes done."

I fold my arms over my chest, annoyed by him thinking this information is news to me.

"Collin, do you have anything to say to me that I don't already know?"

"I told Tori that I'm going to make it work with you and that if she doesn't keep her distance, then I'll have to let her go."

Let her go?

"Do you mean to tell me that she still works for us?"

And walks by Collin's office every day on her way to the warehouse for packaging?

"If I fire her, she might go public with what happened between us."

"What happened between you two?" I ask.

I guess it's time I actually ask the question even though it makes my stomach physically sick to think about.

"I don't think that will make things better."

How did I not think he'd follow in his father and my father's footsteps?

Naïve.

So naïve.

The embarrassment of thinking Collin and I were going to have one of those rare marriages in our circles where the husband and wife are in love has my eyes welling with tears.

I don't see why he's complaining about me being gone for three more months. He should be happy to have the house and the business all to himself while he plays house with Tori or whoever he's been sleeping with now behind my back.

It would be stupid of me to believe him when he says he's not seeing her still. He'll just get better at hiding it.

Like my father did.

Up until my father didn't care anymore and having affairs almost became part of his brand.

"I figured it would be easier with me out of the way."

"How is that? We're supposed to be out in the public, strengthening my father's voter polls. He needs the "in love couple" image to cover up the scandal of his mistresses from last year."

Oh, the irony.

Now, instead of being embarrassed for thinking I was going to get the princess fairytale that we were all sold as kids, I just feel plain stupid.

"Why me? Why not just pick someone else to do this with?" I ask, wishing he'd just let me off the hook.

Maybe if he could talk some sense into my father and tell him that an unhappy participant in this scheme isn't the best idea.

"I love you, Isla."

I make a scoffing sound instantly.

"I do. Maybe not the way you think I should, but I swear that I've had your best interest at heart since we met."

"Collin—"

"Just hear me out, okay?" he asks quickly.

When I don't answer quickly, he continues.

"I've had your back ever since the beginning. Even in the business when you wanted to try some less popular designs or spend more funding on trying out more expensive wicking material. The board shot most of those ideas down, but I went to your father and asked him to push them through because I believed in your vision," he says. "When you wanted to open up another international offering, but the market didn't show promise, I backed you and got your dad to give us start-up funds to do a trial run," I wondered why my dad approved that so quickly. "When your dad wanted to outsource the designing to a company overseas, I told him that I would quit if he took that from you."

"Wait! What?!" I ask.

My father tried to push me out of designing my own products.

How could he do that?

How did I not know about this?

"Why didn't you tell me any of this?"

"Because your father isn't always right, and in this case, I knew how to diffuse the situation and make him see. If you had found out, it would have been a blow-up."

He didn't want me to do what I finally did when I found Collin with Tori...

He didn't want me to leave and mess up everything.

"He wanted to replace me?" I ask, the sting is almost unbearable.

Here I was finally thinking I had an unmatched marketable skill, designing cute and trending, yet functional running wear.

"Not because your designs are bad. He just thought an international company with more years of experience in the commercial sector would create designs that would cut down on manufacturing costs. I made him see that this company is what it is because of your designs. Our brand is social media driven, with your customers want your designs. Without you, it would fail."

"You did all of that?"

"I believe in you, Isla. We make a good partnership. Can't that make us happy?"

"A faithful husband would make me happy," I tell him, almost shocked that I spoke out loud what I need from this relationship.

"This has been a business deal marriage from the beginning. I thought that your father explained this to you?"

"Well I guess I didn't get the memo. I thought we were different," I say.

He lets out another sigh.

"Just come home. I'll give you anything you want. You have to know that," he almost pleads over the phone, "Kids... how about kids? I know you've always wanted them. I'll give that to you. Just come home, Isla, and I'll get you pregnant the minute you walk through that door if that's what you want."

He's not getting it.

"I want monogamy."

"It's not as if I'm out looking for an affair, but I can't promise that they won't ever happen. Tori was the first woman since you and I started dating, I promise you. I showed up one day and you had hired her without telling me. Our past caught me off guard. I didn't plan it."

I want to shake him senselessly.

Doesn't he understand how this is part of the problem in our circles?

Lack of loyalty... of commitment to another person.

"I need some time to think about this," I tell him, about ready to hang up.

"Please consider it. I'll give you anything you want. The biggest diamond ring I can find, kids, a new house, vacations in Dubai. Shopping sprees all over the world. You name it, it's yours."

"Except for the exclusivity of my husband?" I ask.

"That doesn't have to be one sided. Just please no one from the club or any of my business acquaintances," he offers.

"Oh, you mean like don't screw the warehouse manager that your fiancé has to work closely with every single day?"

There's a short silence.

"That was a mistake. We have history. I loved her once and we never got closure."

"Pick someone else to marry, Collin. Please. Convince my father that there's another way to have it all."

"I would if I had to but our fathers are committed to this idea and contrary to what you believe about me, I do care about you, and I don't want to see you lose it all. Just give me a chance to make you happy," he asks, in his CEO manner that always gets a yes from the person he's trying to convince.

Collin is good at what he does, and he even has me considering it.

"I need ninety days to think about it all. If my father can agree to it, so can you," I demand, being far stronger than I've ever been.

Being on the phone instead of in person probably helps give me courage. If Collin showed up on my doorstep, I might cave easier. I know I would if it was my father.

"If you agree to marry me and help my father stay elected, I'll convince the board that your father has to sell his ownership to you."

My ears perk instantly.

"Force my dad out?"

My father would never let that happen.

"Not force him out. We'll make him think it's his idea. And I have friends on the board too, Isla. If you agree to this, I'll do everything in my power to help you get control and the company will be yours. No more strings attached to your father," he says.

I hate how tempting that sounds but I don't know if I can do it.

"A loveless marriage," I say softly, mostly to myself.

I need to hear the stark truth of it off my own tongue.

"I didn't say it would be loveless, Isla."

I need some space to process this.

I don't have a lot of options if I want to hold onto my business. My father won't let this go and the idea of Collin helping me get control is something I never considered a possibility before.

The question is: is the business and my father's good opinion worth my life?

Will I be okay with having a daughter and knowing that Collin might one day convince her to do what my father is making me do?

We end the call and I'm even more mixed up than I was before.

The end result is the same. I have to go back to Denver after these three months are up or else I lose it all.

The business and a relationship with my father.

I exit the bedroom and find Vivi in the kitchen.

"You look like a kid who just realized her mom ordered her a birthday cake sweetened with Splenda. What happened?" Vivi says.

"I just talked to Collin."

"Oh," she says, leaning against the kitchen island. "What did tiny dick want?"

I shake my head. He's somewhere within the national average, but after this morning with the sexiest man I've ever been with, Collin falls short in so many other ways that can't be measured with a ruler.

"He wants me to come home for Thanksgiving, but I told him no."

"Oh, speaking of which, I should call the best Chinese restaurant down the street for reservations tomorrow. Their spread is better than the county club's. It's hard to get a spot usually but the owner likes me."

I nod, sadly.

The only thing I've ever been able to count on in my childhood are traditions and since my father is a creature of habit, I've looked forward to the few we always keep.

"Why does Collin want you home for Thanksgiving?"

"He wants to talk... about an open marriage," I say, cutting to the chase.

No sense in prolonging the story.

It's pretty cut and dry.

"Well... he is a by-product, right? His dad's a tool too," She says, setting her phone on the island. "Did you tell him no?"

"It's not that simple. Dad isn't going to let me out of this and keep the company. I don't have a choice. I have to go back at some point," I say.

She takes a deep sigh and then shrugs her shoulders.

"It's your life, Isla. You know what I would tell Dad to do with that company, but it's your call. I'll wear the ugly ass bridesmaid dress, or be your getaway driver, you just tell me which shoes to wear and if I should pack snacks for our long drive to the Mexican border."

"Thanks, V."

"Anytime," she says, and then clicks on her phone to wake it back up. "I'll call out for pizza and then I need to send this new client's information to my office manager to send his background check through. He might be a good fit for you but I need to make sure he's not a serial killer first."

"Jeeze, thanks for looking out for me," I say sarcastically.

Vivi puts her phone up to her ear after dialing her office.

"Hey Paula, can you run a background check on a potential new client? Yeah, he's going to complete the application and send it to you... last name is Altman... I spoke with his mother so she'll be the one sending in the application... Perfect, let me know when you get the results back... He wants to start services as soon as possible... Great, thanks."

She ends the call and then pulls up a new number to dial the pizza place right down the street.

"Extra cheese?" she asks.

"I'm in hiding... not dead. Tell them to triple it. I need to drown my sorrows in pounds of mozzarella."

"Sure... that's healthy. Coming right up," she says, right before the restaurant answers on the other line.

Forty-five minutes later, we're eating pizza and streaming one of my favorite old movies, Serendipity.

Maybe I should have written my name and number on a five-dollar bill and told the sexy man from room 2509 that he can call me if he finds it.

Why can't love stories be more like our favorite films?

I sit on the couch with Vivi and reflect on my conversation with Collin.

I have to go back or else my father will force me out and probably disown me. I don't have as thick of skin as Vivi to wait out several years until Dad decides to come back around.

I don't have a supportive mother like Vivi. Aside from sending me the occasional gift when my mom wants her husband to think she's the doting mother, our correspondence has all but died out.

She loves her new life in Italy and I'm just the child whose existence required my father to pay a big enough child support payment to afford her lifestyle. At least until she could bag a husband richer than him. She would never have settled for less.

So maybe my father is controlling, but at least he's present for me and Vivi. And in his way, he thinks this is the best match for me.

Kaenan

"Mr. Altman, good afternoon." A man in a dark navy suit stands with a door open to a hallway next to the receptionist window.

He waits patiently for me to stand out of my chair in the lobby of their third story office downtown.

Marc P. Salinger.

He looks just like his picture on the Salinger and Smith's law office website.

I'd guess he's a little older than my mother based on his peppering short hair. A pair of thin black glasses frame his blue eyes, and he's smiling at me as he stands with the door open for me.

A light chocolate brown labradoodle stands at his side, waiting to greet me as well.

I'm not used to doctors or lawyers escorting me to an exam room or office, let alone a dog. Usually, a receptionist or nurse does that. Yet, here he is. The best damn custody lawyer money can buy on the West Coast and I'm lucky he so happens to live in Seattle.

His slobbery mutt too.

I stand out of my chair, gripping my water bottle and take the steps towards him, passing by the fake Christmas tree already erected in the reception area and decorated within an inch of its life.

"Thank you for agreeing to see me the day after Thanksgiving," I say, walking towards him, while he keeps the door open for me in the hallway.

He waits a few more seconds until I'm through and then closes the frosted glass door behind us.

I wait for him to walk past me and lead me to his office.

"Not a problem Mr. Altman. I'm a huge Hawkeyes fan and your case intrigued me. Did you and your family have a nice Thanksgiving?" he asks, walking in front of me, past four other offices.

The office smells like hot off the press ink and paper, dark roast coffee, Christmas pine tree and sadness.

I assume that's what most law offices smell like during Christmas. Though this office seems cheerier than I would expect, with bright lighting, Christmas music streaming through the lobby speakers and a welcoming receptionist who asked me countless times if I wanted something to drink. I finally accepted a bottle of water to make her happy.

I'm glad I could make someone happy today.

"Yeah. My mom is living with me during the season to take care of my daughter, and she made too much food as usual. How about you?"

"It was great, thank you. I have two grown daughters a few years older than you. They brought their husbands and my grandkids to visit from Arizona. We lost my wife to cancer six years ago so being together is important."

"Oh...I'm sorry to hear about your wife," I say.

That can't be easy during the holidays, especially.

"We'll be right in here," he says, offering a hand towards an identical frosted door and into a small conference room with another Christmas tree, just as well decorated.

An elongated oval table sits with six chairs.

A woman sharply dressed, with a platinum blonde pixie cut, gelled to perfection, and probably in her mid-forties, sits on one side of the table facing me with a yellow legal pad and a file folder next to her. I've seen her picture on the website as well. She's a lawyer at this firm and is probably here to help Marc with the case.

Another woman in a Christmas sweater dress sits at the end with a laptop. Probably an assistant here to take meeting notes.

"Mr. Altman— "

"Kaenan... please," I tell him.

This whole situation is cold and heartless enough that formalities make it worse.

He nods.

"Well, as you can see by the looks of my dog Willabee and the Christmas explosion, we are quite relaxed around here," he says.

"Thanks," I say, taking a seat across from the other lawyer where he instructs.

"Let me introduce you to the team. Corrin Taylor, a junior partner and amazing lawyer here with years of experience in family law, will be here to assist us in every step of the way. And our legal assistant, Sherry Lentz, who will be taking care of a lot of the behind the scenes and aiding in the research needed to win our case."

I nod at each and say hello.

They each smile back and Sherry gives a quick wave.

Sherry's black hair is pulled back into a bun and she appears to be about my mother's age.

"And I'm Marc Salinger, one half of Salinger and Smith, and your lead counselor. You can call me Marc. I assume you've read my bio on the website and that's why you selected us. So unless you have any questions, I say we dive into our meeting," he says and then points at his dog to lay down on a Serta mattress dog bed in the corner of the conference room.

The northwest and their dogs is something I've had to get used to. As well as their penchant for hiking in any and all weather conditions.

Marc walks around and takes the conference chair next to Corrin, a notepad and pen waiting for him.

"We received Ms. Wallace's will via email yesterday and Corrin had time to get through the documents. Since we don't have anything from the plaintiff in this case, that gives a small advantage to prepare ahead of time."

"Yes," Corrin says. "Our first act of business is for you to show that Berkeley is in a safe, loving and well-organized household considering your travel schedule."

"Right, Mia's lawyer mentioned that to me."

"Great!" Marc says, folding his hands over the notepad and leaning in. "You mentioned your mother is the caretaker for your daughter when you're out of town?"

I nod. "Yes. She's a retired high school counselor. She and Berkeley are glued at the hip. But we just found out two days ago that my grandmother broke her leg and needs to be moved to a long-term memory facility. My mother already reached out to a live-in nanny service to fill her spot."

"This is going to be crucial- to get a nanny in the house and show a consistent support system. A live-in nanny that can keep Berkeley's life as unaffected by your line of work as possible. Make sure to select the most reputable nanny service in town," Corrin says, jotting down a note.

I nod, understanding the assignment.

My mother poured over reviews and called the top three. I trust her more than I would anyone else to find the right person for the job.

"We may need some character witnesses, and the courts will want to dive into who Berkeley surrounds herself with. These can be positive influences, but you'll want to make sure there aren't negative influences that the plaintiff can bring against you."

"Like who?"

"Like friends. Teammates, coaches…" Marc suggests.

"Women…" Corrin shoots out.

"I don't bring women home. Berkeley has never seen any of that," I say, narrowing my sights on Corrin.

I can see in her eyes that she thinks I might be a player off the ice. I get it's her job to play devil's advocate, but that doesn't mean I won't fight back when I'm wrongfully labeled. My "player" days are in the past.

Corrin nods. She's happy with my answer and writes another note.

"Good, we just want to make sure that none of the sides of hockey aren't represented in a bad light. That's all," Marc says.

We talk through Berkeley's schedule and Corrin offers up some things I should pull together to make Berkeley's home life look happy and fulfilled.

"Keep in mind that you will likely be served at some point," Marc informs. "We need to know the minute it happens. Then, we'll take it from there. Day or night—text me."

We say our goodbyes and Marc escorts me out.

"Keep in touch and use the group email on the business card Corrin gave you if you have questions. It will go directly to me, Corrin and Sherry. Whoever sees it first and has the answer, will email you back as quickly as possible."

"I appreciate it."

He nods and then I walk out of their office.

The list Corrin gave me is comprehensive but I'm lucky to have my mother here to help me get through this.

This battle hasn't even started yet.

And waiting like a sitting duck to be served sucks too.

Not knowing when they'll show up… or how.

Will the media witness it?

Or worse, will Berkeley?

CHAPTER TEN

Isla

It's been two weeks since I came home from Vegas, and my bank account is almost zeroed out.

Vivi comes barging in through the front door of her condo as I make us spaghetti for dinner.

Or more like I boiled noodles and bought premade sauce from the store. I didn't learn to cook as a kid since both of my parents had chefs who prepared all of our meals. Either that, or we would eat out. I learned a few things from Libby, my dad's personal chef that he's had since I was little. She'd pull up a barstool and let me watch her if she wasn't swamped with hosting a large dinner party like my father did frequently.

"I have good news," she sing-songs, practically skipping into the gray U-shaped modern kitchen. "I have the perfect family for you to nanny for."

"You do?" I ask, glancing over my shoulder at her.

"Yep. We just got back the background check from that new client, and he's not a serial killer."

"How reassuring," I tell her, turning back to the dinner that looks as though I slaved away over the stovetop today.

"Only one assault charge but it was dropped to a misdemeanor," she says quickly like she's trying to slide it in there fast enough that I won't notice.

"V! What?"

"I know, I know, but I called his employer, and there is some gray area there."

"His employer? He hit someone at work?"

"He's a professional athlete, and it happened after a game with another player. The guy had it coming... or so the woman on the other line said. I think her name was Penelope. You can't not trust a girl with a name like that."

"So naturally, you thought of me?" I turn back to her, crossing my arms over my chest and lifting a brow.

"I can't give him to any of my other nannies because they are all booked up, and my insurance won't cover the liability of placing an employee with someone who has priors. None of the other nanny services in town are probably going to take him either because of this. He needs our help, and you should have heard his mother rave about Berkeley. She's two years old, and she sounds perfect for you."

"I don't know..."

"Isla, I promise you... this is going to be a really good fit for you. I wouldn't put you in danger if I hadn't called his references and felt that this is sort of typical for his line of work."

"His line of work? What is he? A boxer?"

"No, more aggressive... a hockey player." She laughs.

"Why are you laughing?"

"Have you ever watched hockey before?" she asks.

"No... why?"

"The Hawkeyes are really big around here, and if you knew anything about hockey, you'd probably be shocked he only has one prior on his record."

If that's supposed to make me feel better, she missed the mark entirely.

"Is his wife normal at least?"

"No wife. He's a single dad, which is why he needs you during the season. When I called him this morning to tell him his background came through, I told him you could only commit to ten weeks since you're leaving, and he said he'll take whatever he can get. He's desperate at this point," she says, pressing her lips together and staring back at me.

She knows I have a soft spot for someone in need.

"You're sure that I'm the only fit?" I ask.

I shouldn't be trying to get myself out of it.

Vivi has already pitched me to a few new clients, but they all need someone who can at least commit to a year. If I want funding to stick it out for the next ten weeks, I need this.

Funds are bone-dry now, and I'm too proud to ask Collin to send money.

"I just know you'll be the perfect fit for this family," she tells me, an odd glimmer in her eye when she says it.

"Fine," I huff, turning back around to stir my sauce again. "I'll meet him tomorrow."

"Great! I'll tell my assistant to text you his information once he agrees to a time."

"Okay," I say, not turning back to look at her.

"I have a good feeling about this," she says, but I ignore it.

"Dinner will be ready in five minutes," I offer.

Vivi spins around and heads for her bedroom to get out of her suit from being at work all day.

I know she means well, and I know that she is really good at what she does, but she didn't exactly sell him in the best of light.

I guess tomorrow I will meet the hockey player and his little girl.

CHAPTER ELEVEN

Kaenan

"The new nanny is coming today, right?" Briggs asks, watching my hands wrap around the barbell while I lay on the bench press.

"Yep," I say simply, pushing up on the barbell and taking the full weight that Briggs added to the ends.

The new nanny, damn.

I've been dreading this day since the day I got home from Vegas when my mother said that my mamaw is getting moved into a new memory loss ward and will need physical therapy after her surgery.

My mother doesn't believe that the centers will care about my mamaw's care as much as my mother will, and she's probably right. She wants to be nearby in case she needs to rush to the care center while they try my mamaw on new meds and therapy.

I still haven't been served by Logan's lawyers yet, and maybe I'll get lucky, and it won't happen. And even if it does, maybe it won't come until after my mother returns. I just have to make it until then.

I offered to move my mamaw to Seattle, but her doctors don't think she's in a good place to travel from Tennessee to Washington. Not only because of the hip surgery she's getting next week but also because new places aren't usually encouraged for people already struggling to know where they are in the first place.

I finish my first reps, and Briggs's hands hover over the bar in case I need help getting it back in place. I can already feel perspiration start to coat my hairline. He added more today than yesterday. I can feel it.

I take a second to breathe before starting up my next reps when I hear the door open to the stadium's gym. Ryker and Brent walk in and head for the treadmills.

"You checked, and this place is reputable?"

I nod. "It's also the only place that will give me a live-in nanny with Sinclair's assault charge still hanging around," I say.

"Fuck, man, I'm sorry about that."

"It wasn't your fault, and I'd do it again if given the chance," I tell him. "Although I would have hit him harder if I knew the pencil dick was going to press charges."

I didn't throw the first punch, but that's the only thing that got caught on camera by a fan... a fan of the Blue Devils.

Convenient.

"What a fucking whiny prick," Briggs says.

I just nod, glancing over at the treadmills that aren't far from us. Ryker and Brent start up their treadmills, and Ryker points a black remote at the TV and turns on the sports channel.

Sam, our general manager, and the Hawkeyes legal team got involved. With enough eyewitnesses seeing Sinclair jump Briggs first, the court proceeded to lower my charge.

We never saw the inside of a courtroom. Sinclair and I have hated each other ever since. Now, games against San Diego aren't just games against San Diego. They're our biggest rival, and with Sinclair on the roster, emotions during that game will always run high.

Briggs is a good friend for asking about the nanny service. All the guys have been protective of Berkeley since the day I found out that I have a daughter and was bringing her home.

The team broke into the backyard of the new house I had bought while my mother and I were back in Montana picking up Berkeley. They built her an impressive play structure on the large lawn.

She's still a little too small to play on it now, but the sentiment meant a lot to me. Her eyes lit up when she saw it.

After a long plane ride with almost non-stop tears, I was happy to offer her a little bit of sunshine on her otherwise cloudy day.

These people are my family, so I appreciate him looking out for my daughter. He knows how unsure I am about letting a stranger come into my home and have access to her.

"When does she move in?" Briggs asks.

I reach up and wrap my fingers around the cold barbell for my next set of reps.

I swallow hard when he says the words "move in."

Nothing about this feels good, but I have no alternative.

Mia isn't here, I don't have a wife to look after Berkeley, and my mother is headed back home to Tennessee to take care of my mamaw.

"Hold on. The nanny is going to live in the house with you?" Ryker asks from across the gym.

I guess they can hear us even over the whistling sound of the treadmill belt and television broadcasters.

Before I can answer, Brent chimes in.

"Whatever you do, don't fuck the nanny."

Briggs lets out a snicker and shakes his head. I abandon the weights for a second and stare back at Brent.

"No shit. Thanks for that groundbreaking advice."

It's not Brent's fault I'm on edge. I'm riled up about the impending first meeting with the new nanny today.

And he's not wrong. Getting involved with Berkeley's nanny would be a huge mistake.

Maybe pushing my muscles to the brink of collapse is exactly what I need to do to take my mind off things for a couple of hours.

"Is she hot?" Ryker asks, glancing over at me.

What kind of fucking question is that? She's the damn caregiver to my child.

But goddamn it... I hope she has the face of a donkey and a body that resembles a hunched-back turtle. The last thing I need is to be attracted to the woman I pay, whose room is down the hall from mine.

"How the hell should I know? The service didn't exactly send over her *Playboy* centerfold with her résumé," I say sarcastically.

"What if she ends up being one of those video girls who does it on the side while you and Berkeley are sleeping?" Brent asks with wide eyes and a grin.

I shake my head and try to ignore it.

"Hey! Doesn't your bedroom share a wall with the spare room upstairs? It might be worth brushing up on your Morse code." He winks.

Jesus! Really?

I blow out a frustrated breath.

"Does anyone have any athletic tape I can slap over Brent's mouth?" I ask.

"This is going to be a long-ass season," Ryker mutters to himself as he turns up the volume on the TV to end this conversation.

It's already hard enough to let someone watch my daughter who I've barely bonded with myself, let alone leaving for long weekends to play away games. Now these dumbasses have me worried about what else the nanny is doing for side money?

Not that I care what she does with her own time. I'm just not ready for Berkeley to be exposed to any of that. Not until she's at least... eighty. And with this woman living in our home, it makes her *own time* a little trickier. Additionally, I don't want her second job to potentially come out in court if I have to use her as a character witness.

I never thought to ask Vivianne whether the nanny makes a side living doing anything else.

When she told me that the nanny was twenty-eight, I liked the idea that the nanny was young enough to chase Berkeley at the park and keep up with my wiry two-year-old.

Playdates at the stadium with Penelope, our general manager's assistant, and Tessa, the PR manager for the team, have been great. I appreciate them always offering to let me drop her off at their offices when I have a coaching meeting or an appointment with the physical therapist, but Berkeley needs more consistency, and I need to prove to the courts that I'm not just dropping my kid with anyone who has an hour or two to keep her.

I'm still concerned that bringing in a new person will disrupt the progress she and I are making toward bonding.

My instinct is to protect it...

Guard it...

To be the defenseman I'm known to be on and off the ice to shield my daughter from something that might upset our current norm. But I still have a couple of years on this contract with the Hawkeyes, and providing for Berkeley is still a priority. At least my ability to financially provide for Berkeley won't be in question with how much I earn.

Berkeley will never want for anything.

She'll always have what she needs.

I'll make sure of it.

Briggs can see the frustration on my face.

He sets a hand on my shoulder. "He's just fucking with you, man... It's going to be fine, I promise," he says.

"Yeah, don't stress so much. People hire nannies all the time," Ryker says over the loud treadmills and the TV.

"Yeah," I say simply, though I don't feel any better than I did before I walked into the Hawkeyes gym today.

At the end of the day, it doesn't matter how I feel.

I have to make it work with whatever nanny that Little Stars Nanny Services sends me.

Isla

"You've reached your destination," the navigation on my Range Rover tells me.

I stare at the large wrought-iron gate of this gated community through the misty windshield as I pull up to the security building perched just in front of it. It hasn't stopped raining since we returned from Vegas two weeks ago, but I can't complain... beggars can't be choosers. This is typical October weather for Seattle, and I'd rather be here than in Colorado.

A man in a security uniform steps out of the small enclosure and waves me forward, his hat and jacket starting to dampen while he waits for me to roll down my window.

"How can I help you, miss?" he asks politely, one hand resting on the window seal of my door while he bends down to get to eye level with me.

"I'm here to meet with…" I pull up my phone and scroll to the text from Vivi. "A Mr. Altman? 1913 Valley Way? I'm the new nanny," I tell him, hoping I have the right address.

"Sure thing, miss. He said you'd be coming through. Go ahead."

He steps back toward the security enclosure and pushes a button to allow the gate to open.

I roll my window back up and drive toward the gate, rolling open on a set of tracks.

I follow the directions as my navigation system gives them to me and head for 1913 Valley Way, passing mansion after mansion of homes.

Vivi said that this is where the rich and famous of Seattle live, and I can see why. This community looks a lot like the one I grew up in. Huge mansions on every street.

I pull up to the curb of a large two-story home. It's more traditional in design than I would have pegged for a pro sports player. It's a tarnished terracotta color with black shutters, four matching dormers across the second story, and white trim work throughout.

I just assumed he'd live in a home with a modern style. Something with a lot of cement and glass to show off.

Maybe it was his ex-wife's taste?

Or at least, I assume there's an ex-wife.

Vivi didn't tell me any details. She said the client will fill me in on everything I need to know.

In theory, I guess letting the nannies do the switch-off would be better than parents having to do it every week. My mom relished the drop-offs and pickups with my father. She used it as her way to show off her new plastic surgery or fillers, hike her boobs up to her chin, and try to make my father come groveling back to her.

He never did.

My father gets bored too easily to stay with one woman. It was only when my mother moved to Italy with a rich Italian dressmaker ten years ago that she finally gave up hoping my father would come back.

I haven't seen her since her wedding, and I'm not surprised or disappointed. I get the occasional gift, like the pajamas, but I'm never sure how to interpret them.

I always felt like a pawn in her war against my father up until the moment I aged out of child support payments. Suddenly, it seemed I had become obsolete.

Maybe that's why life has me here.

Maybe I'm supposed to help this sweet little girl for the short time I'm in her life.

I climb out of my car, then run my hands down my black jeans and pull my puffy hooded jacket tighter around me as a gust of wet wind comes swirling past.

I'll probably have to buy a warmer jacket for the ten weeks I'll be here since I left Colorado with only running clothes, and I've been borrowing clothes from Vivi ever since I arrived in Seattle.

I push my door closed and hit the lock button on my key fob as I walk around to the front of my car and take a step up onto the sidewalk.

I check my phone before sliding it into my back pocket and see that the time says I'm five minutes early.

Being a little early is better than being late. I just hope who-ever is expecting me wasn't planning on using those last few minutes to stow the skeletons in the closet.

Okay, maybe not great timing to bring up skeletons in a strange person's house.

I know Vivi did a thorough background check on this client. She probably went as far as she could, short of conducting her own cavity search of the guy.

Vivi takes the safety of her staff very seriously. Still, serial killers have to have their first kill at some point... right? And these cute heeled boots I borrowed from Vivi's closet aren't exactly designed to outrun a professional athlete.

I walk up the pebbled concrete pathway and scan the well-manicured lawn. A For Sale sign still leans up against the side yard fence with a Pending sign plastered over it.

Did he just buy this place?

So he didn't buy this house with his wife or ex-wife?

Now I'm curious to see what sort of millionaire jock buys a home that seems like the quintessential sitcom family home.

I walk up the few concrete steps to the front door and notice a wreath decorated in fall leaves on the door with a small "Wel-come" banner on it. My intrigue starts to peak.

I ring the doorbell once and wait. I don't have to wait too long before I hear the loud footsteps of someone approaching the door from inside the house.

I hear the door handle engage, and the front door swings open.

The moment our eyes meet, my heart drops to my stomach, and my lungs forget how to expand.

"Oh..." I say instantly, my eyes widening in shock.

How in the hell...?

Chapter Twelve

Kaenan

In my line of work, it's been hard-wired into me to prepare for the unexpected. I've learned to adapt at a moment's notice, whether it's different players coming on and off the ice, distractions in the stands, or fights breaking out at any second.

Nothing in my career could have prepared me for this.

Nothing could prepare me for her.

Her long blonde hair is pulled up in a ponytail like it was the night she showed up at my hotel room. Her casual jeans and Patagonia jacket are a stark difference from the pink second-skin dress or the silk pajamas that I saw her in last.

Actually, the last time I saw her, she was bare-naked and laying on my chest in a king-sized bed in Vegas after I had just thoroughly fucked her.

But the biggest difference from when I last saw her two weeks ago...?

That angelic smile she wore the entire time she spent in my suite is gone, replaced by a look of pure dread. She seems almost more shocked to see me than I am to see her.

Highly unlikely since she's the one who showed up at my door.

How the hell did she find me?

And why is she here?

Did she come to apologize for leaving without saying good-bye? Or maybe her guilty conscience kicked in and she's here to return the giraffe? Either way, how did she figure out who I am?

Did she know who I was the entire time and thought that agreeing to not exchange names was her little game? I bet she had a good laugh about it at my expense.

I peer over her shoulder to see if the new nanny is about to walk up on this bizarre encounter.

"What are you doing here?" I ask, my voice low and threatening.

If she thinks I'm going to let her into my home to screw with me and my daughter, she can turn that tight ass right around and head back from wherever she came from.

"I... I..." She leans back to read the house number again on the right side of the front door.

Deja vu all over again.

Then she peers down at her phone, her eyes moving back and forth wildly as she reads something on the screen.

"How did you know I live here? Are you stalking me?" I ask, closing the door tighter around me so that my mother doesn't see her standing on the front porch.

She immediately abandons her phone, and her eyes flash up to mine.

"What!" Her look of shock turns into sharp eyebrows and a frown. "No, of course, I'm not. I'm looking for 1913 Valley Way."

"You got the right address. Now why in the hell are you on my porch?" My eyes narrow down on her.

She takes a step back, correctly sensing my irritation.

My eyes dip down to her pillow-soft lips quickly before I force them back up. My mouth waters at wanting to taste her again.

Are you sick, man?

She fucking found out where you live and showed up on your doorstep after convincing you that exchanging information was a bad idea.

I should be calling the police and issuing a restraining order, not imagining pushing her up against the side of the house and diving my tongue between her lips.

...All of her lips.

She stole Berkeley's stuffed giraffe. Remember that?

But I do remember.

The problem is I remember *everything*.

Including the little whimpers, she made when I nibbled down on her neck as I thrust inside of her.

This is bad fucking news.

I need the woman from Vegas to turn around and leave before the new nanny gets here and hears about my one-night stand with the kleptomaniac, serial stalker.

The last thing I need the new nanny to think is that I'm a player with a violent past, and now have a crazy woman following me.

The owner of the nanny service barely had anyone available to work on short notice and with a short-term contract. Not to mention the mark on my criminal record, that barely got me the nanny I have.

I can't afford to miss the opportunity to have someone help me while my mother is back in Tennessee, getting Mamaw back in good health.

"Are you mute now?" I ask when she only stares back at me.

"Uh... no," she stutters. "I'm the new nanny for the Altman family. Vivi must have given me the wrong address. I... I'm so sorry to have disturbed you," she says, starting to make slow steps backward and towards the few stairs that lead up to the house. "I'll be leave now."

Did she just say that she's the nanny for the Altman family?

Goddamn it.

This can't be happening to me.

There's no way this is a coincidence.

Banging on my hotel room door in Vegas at two in the morning was as far a stretch to an unlikely event as I'll allow.

This?

This is something different.

"Wait. Did you just say Vivi? As in Vivianne from Little Stars Nanny Service?"

She nods. "It's my sister's company."

And now the memory of her warning her friend "Vivi" on the elevator comes flooding back.

Did they plan this?

But how? My mother is the one who called Vivianne and it was the day after I got home.

I looked up her sister's nanny company and it's been operating for the last fifteen years here in Seattle. It's not as if they concocted this whole business overnight.

Still, I don't believe in fate.

This feels more like a nightmare.

The kind you wake up from in a cold sweat.

Except... I'm not waking up.

"I'll just call her and get the correct address. This was an unfortunate mistake. I'm sorry again," she says, and then spins around to retreat.

Her blonde ponytail swishes as she turns.

The smell of mangoes and vanilla swirls towards me.

The second her essence hits my nostrils, I take a deep inhale in. My brain flashes to the image of her lying on the hotel bed, her hair splayed out for me, her eyes closed and her mouth open as sweet sounds came from her mouth every time I advanced deeper inside of her.

It's a damn good thing she's leaving on her own.

Then I feel my front door yank back out of my hand.

"My goodness Kaenan, are you planning on letting that poor girl freeze out here?" my mother asks with her drawl cranked up to 1000%.

She's been in her Southern hospitality mood all day, knowing that the nanny is coming over. She wants everything to be perfect for "our new guest to feel right at home."

She rewashed all the guest sheets, even though they were already clean. She fluffed every damn pillow in this house, and then she made fresh gooey pecan pie bars.

My mamaw's recipe.

I'm not sure how I'm going to tell my mother that the nanny isn't staying, without divulging the details of why.

My mother has seen the tabloids. She knows I'm no saint, but I don't want to tell her that my cock knows intimately how the new nanny's pussy grips tight when she comes.

My mother shoves me a little with her shoulder as she pushes past me and grabs the "nanny" by the hand.

"I'm Sunny and this is my bonehead son, Kaenan. You must be Isla."

She nods.

"Isla," I whisper to myself.

I say the name out loud by accident and when I glance up Isla looks past my mother and over to me.

She heard me test out her name on my lips. Knowing her name now makes what we did in Vegas feel more real. It makes *her* feel more real.

My mother received more details about the nanny than I did since she set most of this up. I couldn't have been less interested if I tried. This whole thing feels even more of a mistake than it did before.

"Come on, darlin', let's get you inside and get you some hot cocoa. I made it special with homemade marshmallows," my mother beams at her.

"Uhh... okay," Isla hesitates.

But it's not as if my mother would have given her a choice.

My mother spins back around and heads straight for me. I take a step out of the way to give her a wide berth. It's not that I fear my mother, but... okay, maybe I do a little.

She was a single mother and raised me by herself, with the help of Mamaw. Those southern women know how to plaster on a smile, but you cross them, and they'll put the fear of God into you if you so much as forget your manners.

Yes ma'am... no ma'am, or Lord have mercy on you.

Southern mommas aren't to be trifled with.

She pushes past me, Isla in tow, seemingly against her will as she looks up at me with wide eyes. I don't think she can believe this is happening. But I won't save her.

You knocked on *my* door, baby. Remember?

And now you've done it twice.

But this time...

You'll get a lot more than you came for.

Isla

Kaenan... his name is Kaenan.

Kaenan Altman.

Why does that name sound familiar?

Sunny continues to lead me down the hallway that opens up to a large space at the back of the house. I try to use the time to rack my brain at how I know the name Kaenan Altman.

I stare down at my hand wrapped in Sunny's as she pulls me happily behind her down the hall. I don't want to pull my hand out of hers. Her skin is so soft and she smells delicious, like a bakery and clean linens. Holding her hand feels like a warm hug and I could use one right about now.

She can't be more than 5' 4" or maybe 5' 5". She's at least a couple inches shorter than my 5' 8" and it has me wondering how something so small could produce the giant man following behind us like the grim reaper.

"I apologize for my son's behavior. He was raised with better manners than that, I can assure you."

I heard her southern drawl when she introduced herself and now it has me trying to recall if I heard the drawl in Kaenan's voice the night we spent together.

I'm sure I would have remembered if he had whispered all those dirty things in my ear with a sexy southern voice.

"I didn't take offense. His reaction is understandable. I'm a little surprised, too," I say, shooting a look over my shoulder at him.

His jaw clenches slightly and his hands dig into his pockets as he follows a few feet behind us, keeping his distance like I carry the plague.

He seems anything but happy to see me and I can't blame him.

This isn't what I had in mind for today, either.

"You were surprised?" Sunny asks as she continues down the hallway. "How so?"

I swallow hard, realizing what I just did.

I just segued myself into telling my new boss's mother what her son and I did in Vegas.

"We met briefly on an elevator in Las Vegas a couple of weeks ago. I don't think either of us expected to see each other again," I tell her.

I hear Kaenan clear his voice behind me. It sounds more like a threat to dissuade me from telling her anything about how we met, rather than him having a clog in his throat.

"What a small world," Sunny beams.

"Microscopic, as it turns out," Kaenan mutters.

I can feel his eyes searing into the back of my head as if he wishes for me to vanish into thin air.

For both of our sakes, I wish I could.

However, Sunny has me glued to her hand, and I'll be honest: It's been a long time since I've felt this warm connection with a mother figure.

Is it shameful that I'd like to hold onto it for a few moments longer?

"Well, then, it's kismet. You were meant to find us," she says and then gives my hand a reassuring squeeze.

Kaenan grunts in disagreement. "You don't believe in that garbage."

"Oh, you hush, young man. No one asked you," Sunny says.

I hold back a chuckle. There's nothing funny about this situation but the way Sunny dishes it out to a man twice her size is comical. And the way Kaenan takes it from her without much rebuttal is equally entertaining.

I follow her through the arch at the end of the hallway and into the large, vaulted space with a large family room to the left and a chef's kitchen to the right.

A long L-shaped couch divides the family room from the kitchen/dining space. A TV far bigger than any human should ever need sits against the far wall facing towards the kitchen. Children's toys are all stacked in a large pile in a bin in the corner of the family room.

I imagine Sunny cleaned up before I came over, but it does have me wondering where Berkeley is if we're all here.

I haven't heard the little pitter-patter of tiny feet yet.

Sunny pulls me to the right and towards the open-concept kitchen.

Walnut-stained cabinets and black granite countertops give this more family-friendly house its first masculine feature.

I peer out of the big bay windows to the backyard as Sunny leads me toward the island. An impressive kids' playset has been erected outside, and a hot tub sits under a covered patio just beyond the sliding glass doors.

My muscles ache at the sight of steam billowing from under the hot tub's cover, begging me to soak after my long run this morning. Unfortunately, I won't get the opportunity to use the hot tub since I imagine Kaenan plans to kick me out of his house the second he gets the chance. There's no way that he'll agree to keep me on as his nanny based on the way he looked at me the moment he opened his front door.

If his mother hadn't interrupted us, I'd already be back in my car headed back to Vivi's.

Speaking of Vivi... she's going to get an earful from me about not giving me a fair warning that the guy from the elevator is the single dad that she sent me to meet.

Sunny leads me to the island and then releases my hand.

"Are you hungry, Isla?" she asks.

I'm about to say no when my stomach speaks for me and lets out an embarrassing growl.

"I just ate, actually, but whatever you made smells amazing. My stomach must think so, too," I tell her.

"Good, I made plenty. And my son barely eats any of the sweets I make. He's worried about his figure." She winks.

Little does Sunny know that I'm very familiar with her son's figure. I've touched just about every inch of it.

She moves over to open a drawer, pulls out a paring knife, and begins slicing squares of caramelized pecan bars still sitting on the cooling rack.

The bars remind me of Liddy's cooking for the holidays and it's the first time I'm a little homesick.

Not for home per se, but for the times I've sat in the kitchen with Liddy while she concocted delicious meals. Not unlike these yummy-looking pecan bars.

I missed Thanksgiving dinner at the Country Club, and she usually designs the menu every year.

"Here, you should eat something. You look like you haven't eaten in days. Doesn't she look like she hasn't eaten in days?" Sunny asks Kaenan while the tip of the knife presses into the gooey deliciousness.

My eyes reluctantly break away from the confection to find Kaenan sulking at the opposite side of the kitchen. He's leaned up against the floor-to-ceiling dark cabinets that probably make up some kind of pantry space.

His thick forearms cross over his chest, and I flashback to a couple of weeks ago when I was wrapped up in them.

He sees me staring at him, his eyes connecting with mine.

That intense stare of his reminds me of the moment I first laid eyes on him on the elevator.

The night we spent together in his suite, he was a totally different person.

Less guarded, I guess.

But I get how this is an unusual circumstance and he's not sure what to make of me showing up on his doorstep.

I don't know what to make of it either.

But I do know that my sister has a lot of explaining to do.

CHAPTER THIRTEEN

Kaenan

I watched from behind as Isla took in our home.

It's an open concept and it's the reason I bought the house.

That, plus it was the only house in this gated community that was for sale and move-in ready by the time I brought Berkeley home.

Architecturally, it wouldn't have been my first choice but the owners were motivated to sell and took a cash offer and agreed to vacate in four days.

As far as the house for Berkeley... It's ideal.

She has over five thousand square feet of house to run back and forth through. Especially when it's dumping rain outside, which is 150 days a year. It's exactly what my rambunctious toddler needs.

Growing up without a father, my mother and I lived with my grandparents when I was little, until my mother finished her degree in child psychology. After she got her first job as a high school counselor for a private school in Tennessee, she saved up enough to buy us our first home.

It wasn't big but it was ours and that was something I wanted to give Berkeley the minute she came home to Seattle.

Stability.

Belonging.

I didn't care what house we moved into as long as it was ready the day we flew home. This one just so happened to be in the same neighborhood as Brent Tomlin's house, which sold me instantly.

When people see the large space, they usually respond with an "Ow" and "Aw," but Isla only peers around as if she's simply observing.

My house doesn't impress her.

Should that offend me?

I don't know. But it has me wondering where she came from if a house this size doesn't do anything for her, and she showed up in a brand-new Range Rover.

There's something more to her situation. I don't know what... but I sure as hell plan to find out. Even though the smart thing to do would be to kick her out and never speak to her again.

I want to be a goddamn child and tell my mother that this crazy lady doesn't deserve a bite of my mamaw's perfection, but it would lead to more questions. And no matter what this stalker did to me in Vegas, my mother would never send her away without a Ziplock of snacks to go and a mug full of steaming hot cocoa.

My mother asked a question that I didn't hear since the alarms going off in my head must be too loud.

"I said... doesn't she seem like she should eat somethin'?" she asks again.

I give Isla a quick once over.

I mean, my mother just asked me to comment on Isla's figure, so naturally, I have to look at her body.

"I think she's perfect the way she is," I say back.

I didn't mean to just compliment the woman, but I can't lie either. As much as I want this woman out of my house... her body is perfect.

And I should know because I've seen it naked and up close.

The corner of Isla's mouth pulls up slightly.

It's not the full-fledged smile that reaches her eyes like I saw in that suite when we spent hours in bed together. Before she snuck out.

Fuck, that smile had me in a damn chokehold that morning. I think I would have done or said anything to get her name and number if she hadn't skipped out on me.

Then I woke up and that interest turned to irritation when she left without saying goodbye and took Berkeley's stuffed toy. Now that irritation has turned into distrust.

What is she doing here?

And what does she have to get back to that has her leaving Washington in ten weeks.

Not that I care.

There are only a few people that get my good side and she won't be one of them.

My mother, Mamaw, Berkeley, and on occasion, my teammates.

"We're certainly lucky to get you for the time we do, Isla. I can't tell you how relieved I am that you'll be here to look after Berkeley and Kaenan while I'm gone," my mother says to Isla.

"I'm an adult, Momma. I don't need a nanny. And she's not staying," I say.

Isla's eyes flash up to mine from her plate of pecan bars that my mother just handed her. To her credit, she doesn't look the least bit fazed. Like she was already expecting this to be the result.

"Why not? She just got here!"

"It's just not going to work out," I tell my mother, shaking my head.

I pull my hands out of my pockets and cross my arms over my chest. The kind of body language to cue my mother into the fact that I won't be budged on this.

"That's just silly," she says. "May I remind you that Isla is the only available option you have and she's agreed to help you on such short notice? Not to mention that my flight leaves in three hours."

"I'll find someone," I say quickly, even though we both know that I can't keep asking Penelope and Tessa to fill in for what my mother has done for me.

They both have lives and work full-time.

"Oh really? How has that worked out so far?" my mother asks.

She doesn't look up at me as she continues to cut bars but I can see that "you can run but you can't hide" glint in her eye from here.

"I told you, I'll figure it out," I say, trying to avoid Isla's line of sight as she watches my mother calling me out. She always knows when she's got me backed into a corner. And she's fucking good at it.

I guess she should be now after thirty-two years of getting the jump on me. My mother is book-smart and incredibly clever. A deadly combination for a man trying to assert his dominance in his own house.

I don't even know why I try anymore.

I should just say yes ma'am and save us all another thirty minutes of a pointless argument that my mother will win anyway.

"If you don't keep Isla, you will end up shifting Berkeley back and forth to whoever has the ability to take her at that moment. You'll burn out your friends and, most importantly, you'll shake Berkeley's already delicate stability that we've spent the last three months cultivating," my mother says, cutting a bar out for me and then hands the second plate to Isla with her warm southern bell smile. "And let's not forget what the lawyer said."

My eyes squint at her to warn her not to continue.

The last thing I want Isla to know is that I'm fighting for custody of my child and that she's my only option.

"Isla, dear, will you hand this to my ungrateful son?"

Isla snickers but tries to hide it by covering her mouth with the back of her hand. She takes the plate from my mother and then does as she's asked, walking around the island and heading for me.

I don't like how my biceps flex when her eyes center on me as she walks over. Or how my abs tighten as she draws near as if I'm trying to impress her. Like one of those gorillas who beats on their chest to attract a mate.

You damn idiot. You want her gone, remember?

But I also want to toss her over my shoulder and haul her up to my bedroom to pull out more of those desperate whimpers of need she made for me in Vegas.

Pull your shit together, Altman.

My primary focus should be on bonding with Berkeley and winning my case, not screwing the gorgeous nanny in the hot tub.

Have you forgotten that the woman stole your daughter's plush giraffe before she left your hotel room without so much as a "thanks for the fuck" note?

Of course, I can't forget because the panties I put in my back pocket that night are now in the cupboard of my master bathroom.

"Now offer her some southern hospitality, like I taught you, and show her to her room," my mother demands in a soft tone, but I know a threat when I hear one.

My mother's reminder that what's best for Berkeley is the right course of action, is true. Though this might be the biggest test of self-control I have ever had to endure.

My cock doesn't care that those two coincidences seem like two too many. He only gives a shit that the woman I haven't stopped thinking about for two weeks is in my kitchen and she looks even better than I remember.

Our eyes lock as she hands me the plate and then she backs up, puts space between us immediately and heads back to her spot next to my mother.

I can't help but wonder if she's trying to get space because she's worried, she's about to jump me too? Or if the scowl on my face is doing its job and she's retreating to get as far away from me as possible.

When I get lost in my thoughts about whether Isla can still feel this pull, my mother's voice breaks my attention.

"Pay him no mind, Isla. He must have forgotten his manners back in Tennessee. I'll show you to your room," she says, setting down her pecan bar that she just took a bite out of and wipes her fingers with a napkin.

Isla responds immediately and follows my mother, leaving her own plate behind and scurries out behind her, anxious to get away from me, I suspect.

When Isla and my mother leave the kitchen, I take a moment to pull my shit together.

As much as I hate to admit it, my mother's right. I don't have another option. I'll be out on the road by next week. Even if I could convince Penelope and Tessa to watch Berkeley during home games, I can't take Berkeley with me on away games. It just isn't an option. I need Isla at this point even though it kills me to admit it.

I have no idea how we're going to live in the same household for the next ten weeks. Or how I'm going to keep my hands to myself.

Isla

"Please excuse my son," Sunny says.

I watch her open the child gate at the end of the stairs and then I follow her up the stairs to the second story. "Give him some time. He'll come around. In the meantime, you'll love Berkeley. She's a little spitfire and will keep you entertained for hours. And I already can sense that you two are going to hit it off."

Entertain me for hours? Isn't entertaining her my job?

"How do you know?" I ask.

"I can sense your energy," she says glancing over her shoulder with a quick smirk and then turns her head in the direction we're walking.

"My energy?" I ask.

"You have a bright soul. And a soft heart. You love in the worst of circumstances. Even when it brings you pain."

How can she tell all of that just from meeting me?

"How do you-"

"People aren't hard to read. I should know. I've been a counselor for so many years that I've learned to read people the moment they walk in my door. Most people have an energy about them and that energy dictates a lot about them."

We continue down the hallway a little ways. It's mostly blank walls painted in a dark beige color and a couple of commercial replica paintings hung up on the walls. No family photos to be seen but then again, he's a guy. They also just moved in, judging by the recent for sale sign still outside.

She points to the right. "There's the bathroom that Berkeley uses."

She continues further down and points to the first room on the left.

"This will be your room," she says, and then takes a step back so that I can glance into it.

I peer in quickly. It's just a place to lay my head, assuming Kaenan doesn't kick me out as soon as Sunny leaves, so it doesn't matter much what it looks like.

It's a large room with a cherry wood four-poster bed against the left wall. A beautiful dark green comforter covers the bed with more pillows than I will know what to do with.

Sunny must have picked this out because I don't peg Kaenan as the throw pillow type.

Against the right wall is a matching dresser to the bed set.

A small desk and cushioned chair sit under the window.

This will be a good place to hide out when Kaenan wants me out of their hair. And with the desk, I'll have a place to work on my designs.

"This looks nice," I tell her as she waits for me to get a good look at the room.

"There's a small bathroom in here as well so you won't need to share. This is the room I usually stay in but you'll need your privacy. There's also a small walk-in closet. Feel free to unpack and make yourself at home."

Make myself at home?

Not likely.

I'm already not wanted here, based on what Kaenan said downstairs. I'm torn though, between wanting to stay in order to have the funds to pay for the ten more weeks of freedom and wanting Kaenan to kick me out, releasing me from this job.

"That was thoughtful, thank you."

She points at the bedside table and I see a baby monitor perched there.

"That monitor goes to Berkeley's room. Kaenan has a monitor to her room as well. He'll fill you in on his schedule so you two can work out when you'll need to be available."

She continues walking back down the hall and I turn to follow behind.

She walks up to another door to the right and pushes it open.

An adorable room painted in pink with a Beauty and the Beast bedspread over a twin-sized white frame with a crown design headboard. A matching lamp, nightlight and any other Beauty and the Beast memorabilia in existence covers every inch of this room.

It's a perfect little girl's room and if I ever have a daughter, I think this is exactly how I'd design it.

A full-size decal of Belle and the Beast dancing is plastered on the opposite side of her wall.

This can't be Kaenan's design. It just doesn't seem like his taste. Although the Beast and Kaenan might be kindred spirits.

"This is Berkeley's room. A couple of the ladies who work for the Hawkeyes did it before she moved in. Isn't it adorable?"

I turn to her and smile. "It's perfect."

Sunny turns but doesn't move any further. She just points down the hall a little further.

"The last room on the left is Kaenan's and there is another small guest room that I will stay in if I'm able to come back to check up on everyone," she says. "And that concludes our tour upstairs. I'll ask Kaenan to bring your things up to your room so that you can get situated before Berkeley gets home from daycare."

She smiles back at me and then turns again, passing me, and heads back towards the stairs.

I stand there for a second, staring at Kaenan's closed door and realizing that our rooms butt up against one another.

We're sharing a wall?

This can't be good.

She closes the child gate behind me as we get down the stairs and then I follow her back to the kitchen.

She points to the glass double doors that we passed on the way into the house.

She stops briefly in front of them. "That's Kaenan's office. The couch is quite comfortable if you're looking for a quiet place to read when you're not on the clock with Berkeley. I'm sure Kaenan won't mind if you use it when he's not."

Want to bet?

I just nod. "Thanks, I'll keep that in mind."

It does seem like a nice place for drawing my stretch designs but I'll keep to my room when I'm off the clock. Or maybe I'll find a nice coffee shop somewhere in Seattle.

Vivi's taken me to a few and there's one that I love. It's quaint and has the best bakery items made fresh.

Serendipity's Coffee Shop I think it was.

"My son is a little gruff around the edges sometimes but he's really easy to love once you get to know him."

Love?

I'm not looking for love. I'm just looking for an escape.

"I'm sure he is Sunny. But love isn't a requirement for the nanny position, last time I checked. "

Sunny spins around to face me before we make it out of the hallway and into the great room.

She pulls my hands into hers.

"It's not, but give him a fair chance, will you? For me?" she asks, almost pleading with me not to write her son off.

He already hates me so I don't see any sense in arguing with her over it. If Kaenan doesn't kick me out the minute Sunny has boarded her plane home, my best hope is that we can co-exist under the same roof until Sunny comes back.

"I'll give it my best shot," I tell her honestly.

"That's all I ask," she says, releasing my hands and then leading us into the great room again.

The large bay windows show that the sun is starting to set. It gets dark much earlier this time of year. The backyard is illuminated with solar lights around the perimeter.

"Oh right! I almost forgot my favorite place in the house. The hot tub is also a nice spot to relax with a glass of wine."

Well, at least there's one perk I can see myself using in this house.

"Momma," Kaenan says, hearing us from the kitchen. "Did you just tell my nanny to drink on the job?"

She looks over at me and rolls her eyes.

I let out a chuckle.

These two couldn't be more different and I wish she were staying longer.

"Use the hot tub when you're off the clock and text me if he gives you trouble," she whispers.

We walk back into the kitchen and Kaenan is still standing where we left him. He hasn't touched his pecan bar and his scowl almost seems permanent at this point.

Except... I've seen him smile.

I know what it feels like when those honey-brown eyes sparkle back at me and that perfect smile stretches from ear to ear.

Maybe I do understand a little bit of what Sunny means. I caught a glimpse of Kaenan's sweeter side in Vegas. But it doesn't matter, the damage between us is done and in less than three months, I'll head back home and marry Collin. Or, at least, I think I will.

"Now that she's well acquainted with the house, you should help her with her things. I'm going to go get Berkeley down the street while you two have a chance to talk and Isla can settle in."

Kaenan doesn't object this time. He just stands where he has the entire time, his arms still crossed over his chest.

Sunny grabs a set of keys off the counter and a small brown leather purse and then turns towards me and sets her hand on my shoulder.

"Thank you for showing me around," I tell her.

"Any time, dear."

Then she walks out of the kitchen and Kaenan and I stare at each other as we listen for his mother's footsteps down the hallway. The front door opens and a chime sounds with a voice.

"Front door open," a pre-recording says.

"The security system in case Berkeley tries to get out," Kaenan informs me, though I already guessed that.

"That's smart," I say back.

My eyes wander around the kitchen again, trying to find something else to settle on other than him.

"I don't plan on sleeping with you while you're under my roof," he says, catching me off guard.

My attention darts back to him and I can't hide the shock on my face as my eyebrows turn up in surprise.

"I didn't think we'd—"

"I don't know how you found me or why, but if I had another option for someone to care for my daughter while I'm working, you wouldn't still be standing in my kitchen."

"I understand." I nod, crossing my arms over my chest and mimicking his stance.

I fight the urge to tell him to stuff his nanny job up his ass and storm out the door but I still need this job for the next ten weeks. And his mom begged me to try with him. Why can I not turn down the plea of a mother asking me to help her son?

I've heard of people having daddy issues, but my mom issues are evident in my inability to disappoint Sunny.

"We won't be repeating Vegas so don't bother showing up at my room in the middle of the night saying you got locked out of yours. I fell for that once but I won't a second time. My daughter has been through a lot and she's my priority. The last thing I need is a distraction that takes away from Berkeley bonding to me."

I bite my tongue to keep from saying something snarky. My upbringing mostly consisted of my father and mother telling me to look pretty and only say pretty things.

What I want to say to Kaenan isn't pretty at all.

But also, what does he mean by Berkeley still needing to bond with him?

Wouldn't that relationship already be established? Vivi told me that she's two years old. It seems a little old to still be establishing a relationship with your two-year-old daughter, doesn't it?

"You don't have to worry. You've made it perfectly clear that you won't be sleeping with me under your roof, and I'll be more than happy to make sure you don't slip up," I say with my best debutant-like poise.

His eyes flare, as if me using the phrase "sleeping with me" incites something akin to interest.

His stipulation is more than fine with me.

I have zero interest in him laying another finger on me with the way he's treated me since I knocked on the door. Even if the man is incredible with his fingers.

I'm just as shocked to have landed on his doorstep. Although I suspect the one person in this arrangement who isn't shocked by this is Vivi. I can't wait to rip into her as soon as I get a minute to call.

"Good. We're in agreement," he says, and then unfolds his arms and trudges over to a calendar magnetized to the stainless steel fridge. He points to the writing in blue.

"My momma wrote out the calendar for the next two and a half months for you. The blue is all of Berkeley's scheduled events. She has daycare during the day and ballet twice a week. You'll need to handle drop off and pick up, then ballet on Tuesday and Thursday, unless I'm here to take her. You'll have her for the afternoon until the evening. Once I'm home, you're off duty and you can have the rest of the night to yourself until daycare drop off the next morning."

"Does that mean I can go for a run in the mornings?"

"You run?" he asks.

"I'm training for a half-marathon."

He stares at me for a second like he doesn't know what to do with this new information.

"Yeah... sure. I'll take care of breakfast. You'll just need to get her to daycare at eight am."

"If you're making breakfast, do you want me to make dinner for you two if I have her in the evenings?" I ask.

I'm not sure why I'm offering to do something I'm not good at. Neither my mother nor father ever cooked. I grew up with a chef and all of my friends did too.

He eyes me for a second like he's trying to imagine if I have any culinary skills to speak of. I don't have many, but I've helped

Liddy in the kitchen before, and I'm sure she could send me a couple of easy recipes.

"I want that time with Berkeley, and I eat a lot. I'll make dinner," he says and then focuses back on the calendar.

What am I going to do with all the time during the day then?

"The schedule changes during the weekends." He points to the area on the calendar written in red dry-erase marker. "These are my games and where I'll be: home or away. On away weekends, you'll have her 24/7. When I'm home, I want to do bedtime if I can make it home in time and I'll have her in the morning before I have to leave for the stadium."

"Seems like you'll have her a lot. Are you sure you even need me?" I ask, looking past him at the calendar.

He turns to me.

"Trust me, Isla. If there was any way I could eliminate you from this situation entirely, I would have already done it the second I saw you on my front porch."

Ouch.

I can't hide my frown at his inability to at least conjure up the least bit of kindness towards me. I know that what I did in Vegas has him thinking the worst of me, but I am the one bailing him out right now.

I stare back at him. I have no idea what to say at this point. If I wasn't so desperate for funding to keep me from driving home and marrying Collin right now, I'd have already turned around and slammed the door on my way out.

His eyes shift between mine for a moment and then he lets out a sigh.

"I'm an asshole Isla. And I have enough people reminding me of that fact daily. If you haven't come to that conclusion already... you will."

I'm not sure how to respond to that.

Great. Thanks for the heads up?

"Duly noted," I say, trying to give him zero emotion.

If he's hoping to get a reaction from me, he won't.

I've been trained by the best to hold everything in and never appear weak.

My father would be disappointed if he saw my pageant girl façade falter in the least. He paid far too much money to my coaches to create the ideal daughter.

Two of those coaches added to his collection of wives. Wife number three and wife number four.

"I just need you for ten weeks until my mother gets back, as per my agreement with Vivianne. Then we'll be free of each other, and we can both forget this ever happened. Can you handle that?" he asks.

I'm not sure if he means to be condescending or if it just oozes out of him naturally.

"Well, when you put it that way, how could I possibly say no?" I ask sarcastically and then run my hand through my pony-tail.

"My daughter lost her mother, Isla."

My attention snaps back to him. Berkeley's mother died?

Vivi didn't say anything about that. She told me that the client would tell me what I do and don't need to know.

That poor little girl.

Does that make him a widower?

"The last thing she needs is for there to be friction in this house. If you have any issues with this arrangement then-"

"Her mother died?"

His eyes darken to a deeper chocolate than before.

I touched on a subject I can see I shouldn't have but I didn't mean to. I just blurted it out without thinking.

"I won't be discussing Berkeley's mother with anyone. I've kept it out of the media to protect my daughter and that's how it will stay."

I nod quickly.

I didn't mean to overstep about something as sensitive as the death of Kaenan's wife...or girlfriend... or whoever she was to Kaenan besides just his daughter's mother. She must have meant more to him than just Berkeley's mom.

"Right, of course."

His eyes break from mine. "Let's get your things so you can unpack. My first away game is in three days."

His tone is short and if things could get any more awkward than this, I sure as hell can't think of a way.

We've reached max capacity at this point.

I follow him as he leads us back down the hallway, out of the front door and down the small, cobbled steps that lead us down the path and to the street curb.

I stare at my Range Rover parked against the curb in front of the house. If I'd known then what I know now when I pulled up to the sidewalk earlier, I wouldn't have stopped. I would have hit the gas and I'd be a little over an hour closer to Colorado about now.

But now I'm here and Sunny is counting on me. Not to mention that hearing that Berkeley doesn't have a mother sort of hit a nerve with me.

In some way, I can relate to this little girl in a way I wasn't expecting.

We walk to the back of my car, and I hit the automatic gate. The door opens, and I have two small backpacks in the back. I reach down and unzip one, pulling out the stuffed giraffe that I've slept with every night since I left Kaenan. It still smells like him. That used to bring me comfort, but now it doesn't.

"You brought that with you? And you expect me to believe that you didn't know that I was the client?" he asks, his eyebrows drawn together.

Okay, maybe this wasn't a good idea but I want to give it back hoping that it somehow rectifies one of our many compounding issues.

"I swear I didn't know that you would be on the other side of that door. I can honestly tell you that if I had known that you were the client, I wouldn't have come."

"Then why did you bring the giraffe?"

The truth might sound worse, but I have to give it a try because the klepto thing isn't winning me any favors.

"I sleep with it at night," I say, bracing for impact.

"You sleep with the stuffed giraffe you stole from my room? Why?" he asks, shaking his head like he can't understand.

I glance down at the stuffed animal and rub my hand over its head and down the backside of its neck.

"Because it reminds me of..."

I stop in my tracks.

Shut up, Isla.

This is the moment he sends me away.

He's going to think I'm insane.

"Me?" he asks in the softest voice he's used since I arrived, though it's still guarded.

I look straight up, his eyes locking with mine.

It isn't what he said that has my attention... it's how he said it.

Before I can answer, I hear a car pull up behind us and into the driveway. We both turn around to see who it is. It's the same lifted Suburban that was here when I pulled up.

The driver's door swings open and Sunny jumps out with a smile.

"Someone is very excited to meet you," Sunny says to me then turns back towards the car.

She opens the side door and bends in, messing with the car seat. Then she twists around and I get my first look at Berkeley.

This adorable little girl with chocolate brown curls, long black eyelashes and honey brown eyes that rival Kaenan's, squeals at something in my hands.

She's the spitting image of him. My heart squeezes at the similarities.

Sunny puts her down and Berkeley comes barreling towards us. All hair, a puffy vest, jeans, and rainbow-colored rain boots.

I glance down at what she sees and I realize I'm holding the giraffe.

"For me? For me?" she yells as she runs straight for my legs and wraps both arms around my right thigh.

Her big brown doe eyes and lashes flutter up at me and I'm a goner in that moment.

"Hi Berkeley," I say, squatting down to her level and handing her the giraffe.

As much comfort as it has brought me, the only memory I'll have now is of a grumpy asshole. It's time the giraffe goes back to its rightful owner.

Her sweet little arms put the giraffe in a tight choke hold and she pulls it to her chest.

"Mine! Mine! Jer-gaffff!" she squeals, twisting side to side and squeezing the giraffe tighter.

She steps between the space between my bent knees and releases her left arm around the giraffe to wrap it around my neck.

"Aww," I hear Sunny say as she starts walking closer to us but I keep my eyes on Berkeley and her wild eyes as she admires every inch of the stuffed animal.

She's the cutest toddler I've ever seen. Maybe I'm a little biased since I don't think anyone has ever greeted me with that much excitement before.

"I'm Isla," I say, wrapping my right around her to solidify our hug.

"Lala," Berkeley says back, still staring at her giraffe.

"I guess you have a new name," Sunny giggles. "I was supposed to be Mamaw but Berkeley calls me Meemee so that's what I get. It turns out... they name you."

I glance up at Kaenan, who's watching his daughter with a lopsided grin and those light honey brown eyes that I saw in his hotel room in Vegas. The ones I got lost in that night.

When he catches me staring up at him, his eyes meet mine. My belly flips at having those beautiful eyes back on me once more.

He loves this little girl and for some unknown reason, I swear my uterus tingles at how attractive Kaenan is as a doting father.

I've always wanted kids but I've never had that baby fever that women usually talk about. Maybe the idea that I'm doomed to repeat the same life my parents have led makes me worried about bringing a baby into that world of unrealistic expectations and a life not your own.

But wrapped up in Berkeley's arms, I'm not sure how I'll leave in ten weeks' time and leave her behind.

"Brrr, it's cold out here. Let's get your new giraffe inside and warm her up," Sunny tells Berkeley.

She and Berkeley hold hands as they trudge through the grassy front yard, and then she turns abruptly to Kaenan. "Grab Isla's things and she can get unpacked while Ms. Berkeley here takes me to the airport."

Kaenan pulls my two backpacks out of the back of my car and then closes the door.

"This is it?" he asks of the two small bags carrying my only possessions in this city.

"I pack light," I say simply.

He doesn't ask a follow-up question and then turns to head for the house. I'm relieved not to have to explain why I have so little for someone moving in for two and a half months.

I follow him as we enter the house and go back up the stairs.

He drops my things on the bed and then turns to leave.

"I'll be back in a couple of hours. The fridge is stocked, just don't steal any more stuffed animals while I'm gone," he says. "Can you handle that?"

I want to cover my cheeks, which are probably flaming with embarrassment.

"I think I'll manage," I say, cutting eye contact from him and walking over to my backpacks.

"Good."

Then he turns and leaves the room.

I listen for when Sunny, Berkeley, and Kaenan leave.

Once I hear the door shut a half hour later, I stare out the second-story window, watching as Kaenan backs out of the driveway and then I dial Vivi immediately.

I listen for the minute she picks up and I don't bother to wait for her to speak first.

"What in the hell were you thinking?" I demand, starting to pace the large guest room.

Although it's more like a smaller second primary bedroom.

"Hello to you too. How was your meeting with the client?" she says, playing coy.

"Are you really going to pretend you didn't know?"

"Didn't know what?" she asks.

Oh please.

"That the guy from the elevator and my one-night stand from Vegas is also the client. I know you knew!"

"Yes, I knew—"

"Vivi! Not only is this completely awkward, but it's completely unprofessional of you. He almost kicked me out of his house, but his mom warned him that I'm his only option. Now

I'm stuck living under the same roof with him, and he hates my guts."

"Wait... why does he hate you? You wouldn't stop smiling the whole drive to the airport, and you said that he asked for your number."

I never told Vivi that I left without saying goodbye... or that I stole something from his room.

"I might have taken something from his room."

"Oh my God, Isla! What did you take?" Vivi's voice is now the one elevated.

"It was a giraffe stuffed animal. Nothing crazy, I swear. I thought he wanted me to have it... but I snuck out before he woke up, so I took it with me."

It sounds worse than it felt at the time.

If she had heard the way he said who the stuffed animal was for, I guarantee she would be on my side.

"You snuck out?" She pauses for a second. "Wait a second, what grown man has a teddy bear?"

Oh, why did she have to ask this question?

Now I sound like a terrible person.

"It was for his daughter Berkeley." I squeeze my eyes shut, waiting for her to berate me.

I know it's bad... It's so bad.

She just gets quiet for another second.

"Why didn't you tell me any of this?"

"I don't know."

"You liked him... I could tell. You were glowing on the airplane and blushing whenever I asked questions. Then when his background check came through and I googled him, I knew why I recognized his name. It just seemed..."

"Don't say it..." I warn.

"Serendipitous."

"You freaking said it," I say, shaking my head and picking up my pace across the floor.

"I knew you wouldn't go if I told you who he was, but I thought if you could just spend some time together, you might realize that going home and marrying someone you don't love is a mistake."

She thought that I would nanny for Kaenan and that we would somehow fall in love, and then I'd be willing to leave everything in Colorado behind. Does she think I'd give up my company that easily?

"So this was a setup! I knew it!"

"Yeah, well, I knew that without me giving you a little push, you'd run from this like you run from everything."

"I don't run from everything."

"Come on, Isla."

Maybe she's partly right, but that doesn't make what she did okay.

"God, this is such a mess."

"How bad could it really be?"

"He thinks I'm a thief, and he thinks you and I came up with this scheme and that I'm a jersey jumper."

Is that what they call it?

I have no clue.

"I can't believe you stole his daughter's teddy bear. You're more cold-hearted than you let on."

"Oh, shut up." I snicker. "You're not going to change the subject and put this on me."

"It sounds to me like you need him, and he needs you right now. Ten weeks won't kill either of you, and I'll call him and straighten this all out. Then you can go back to dumb and dumber back home. Neither of them are going anywhere."

"I wouldn't call Kaenan just yet. It's all still a little fresh. Wait until he calls you, or at least give it a day or two."

"Fine. I'm sorry I put you in this position. I didn't know you stole his beloved giraffe. Next time, maybe don't steal things from strangers."

"Oh... this experience solidified that there will never be another time."

"Just be open, please? A lot can happen in ten weeks."

We make plans to get together for lunch later in the week, and then I hang up, returning to getting my things in order.

I have no intention of unpacking my things.

There's still a chance he'll kick me out, but I have to try to make this work because I don't want to go home any sooner than I have to.

CHAPTER FOURTEEN

Kaenan

Something wakes me out of my deep sleep. Then I hear the sound from the kitchen that I never want to hear at five o'clock when everyone under my roof is asleep.

"Front door open."

I sit up in bed faster than I have in my entire life and grab the baby monitor. Berkeley is still sound asleep.

I walk to my window and peek outside and see Isla jogging in place down on the sidewalk by her car, with her watch up to her face as she clicks on it, probably bringing up a running app or something.

There's a lot about Isla that doesn't quite make sense, including her running half marathons. Not that she doesn't have a great body... she does. It just has me wondering what other things I don't know about the beautiful blonde sleeping on the other side of the wall from me.

She didn't say that she runs in the dark. It's still pitch black outside now that daylight savings has passed.

I reach for my phone on the nightstand and draft up a quick text asking where she's headed and when she'll be back... just in case, but I hear the chime of her phone coming from her room. It's a faint sound between the walls, but I still hear it.

I can't sleep knowing she's out there running alone without a way to call for help if she needs it. When she said that she's training, I assumed that meant she runs on a treadmill at the gym, not running in the dark with no way to defend herself.

Five o'clock is earlier than I usually get up, but there's no way I'll go back to sleep with her out there.

I head to my bathroom to take a shower to get ready for the day before Berkeley wakes.

Last night, Berkeley and I took my mom out to dinner and then dropped her off at the airport to say our goodbyes while Isla unpacked and settled in. It tore me up to see Berkeley cry and grip onto my mom like a lifeline.

My daughter has had to say too many goodbyes in her short life.

Her mother vanished from her life.

Her grandmother and aunt when I picked her up at Mia's funeral.

And now my mother, who Berkeley bonded with instantly the moment we left the funeral. Berkeley didn't leave her side that whole first week.

Getting comfortable with me took longer.

I know I'm not the most inviting-looking guy on the planet. I'm told that regularly too, but it has me wondering if Mia ever had a boyfriend or any male role models around for Berkeley.

Since Berkeley took a minute to warm up to me, I'm lucky that my mother and Berkeley had an instant connection in order to make the transition for Berkeley a little smoother.

An hour and a half later, there's still no sign of Isla, and I'm tempted to load Berkeley up and go looking for her. Having a nanny was supposed to make me worry less... not more.

While stirring eggs in a skillet for our breakfast, I stare at my wristwatch every few minutes. Where could she be?

Is she hurt?

Did she get lost and can't find her way home?

I know she's not a damn dog that got out of the backyard and can't find its way back. She's capable, I'm sure, but it doesn't make me any less concerned.

Finally, I hear the door chime.

"Front door open."

My heart thumps in my chest at the sound of the front door closing and her footsteps down the hallway. I know we'll be face-to-face soon, and I can get confirmation of life.

My eyes dart between the eggs and the opening of the hallway, waiting for Isla to show up, and within seconds she does. Relief hits first as my eyes set on a red-faced, sweaty Isla.

She's home.

She's safe.

Now, where the fuck did she go?

She takes a few more steps into the family room, and I get a clearer view of her.

Tight pink leggings that show off her beautiful glutes, calves, and ass, her hair pulled up in a messy bun, a darker pink scoop neck racerback running shirt that exposes the top of her breasts, and a black jacket scrunched in her hand.

"Good morning, Berkeley," Isla says, her head turned to look in the opposite direction of me and toward the family room where Berkeley is playing.

I get a moment with Isla not watching and give her tight body in her running gear another full scan.

Even from here, I can see the perspiration across her chest and neck. Sweat glistens off the mounds of her breasts, squeezed tight together from her sports bra.

I fight the urge to walk up to her and push her deep into the hallway where Berkeley can't see us and lick her tits clean of her salty sweat and up her chest and neck until I've had my fill of her.

I shake the thought when I realize my cock is starting to think that idea is a good one.

The half-chub starting to form might be a mixed signal for Isla, considering I warned her yesterday about how I wasn't going to fuck her under my roof.

"Lala," Berkeley squeals and jumps up to greet Isla.

Isla bends to one knee in preparation for my daughter to tackle her.

"Did you have good dreams last night?" Isla asks her.

Berkeley nods, partially listening, partially more interested in the dog cartoon she's watching.

It shouldn't matter to me how fast Isla and my daughter are bonding, but something about it just does. I don't know if it's a relief that Berkeley is taking to a new person in our life so easily, helping to lessen the burden of my mother's departure, or if I like the idea that Isla fits in seamlessly without trying.

I add sliced strawberries to Berkeley's plate and call her over.

"Berk, breakfast," I call out, rounding the kitchen island with her plate, heading for the eat-in kitchen table set in front of the large windows.

Berkeley likes to watch the birds in the morning catching worms while we eat our breakfast, and I just like watching her.

Her curiosity fascinates me, and being her dad is a gift I never realized I needed. Spending time with my daughter makes me a better person, that I'm sure of.

Berkeley races over to the table and climbs up into her chair with a booster seat strapped down to one of the kitchen chairs.

I set her plate in front of her, along with her fork and a sippy cup with milk. I head back to the kitchen to get my food.

Isla stands back up from her kneed position and then takes steps toward me as I head for the kitchen.

"You were gone for a while. Where did you run to?" I ask over my shoulder.

"I don't really know. I just ran past the gates until I hit five miles, and then I ran back," she says, eyeing my plate of food.

I want to ask her why she didn't take her cell phone, but I'm trying not to seem overbearing or overprotective.

She can do whatever the hell she wants.

And it's better if we spend as little time with each other as possible.

I can't allow myself to get distracted by the beautiful woman living under my roof. I spent too much of last night convincing myself not to leave my room, head down the hall and knock on her door. I imagined picking her up off her bed and hauling her back to mine last night. It would have been a bad idea, I know that.

But goddamn, Vegas wasn't enough I want another taste.

"Want some?" I ask.

I made a lot more than I usually do. Maybe I was expecting her to show up and be hungry, or maybe I just didn't measure it out right.

I'm not going to think too far into it. The point is that I have more than enough to share.

And if she's caring for my daughter, she should have the energy to do it.

Though what I'd like to feed her...

is something else entirely.

Isla

The second I walk in the door, I can sense that Kaenan is not happy with me.

Did he wake up like that, or did I do something this morning without even being here? Or is this just how things will be for the next two and a half months?

I watch him set a plate for Berkeley on the kitchen table, then prepare one for himself.

He walks back into the kitchen and assembles another plate.

He sets the plate up on the island of the kitchen over the top of a barstool.

"Here. Eat something," he says without making eye contact, his voice low and gruff.

He walks back to the kitchen table with a gray plaster shaker cup full of a protein shake he just made. He sets down his shake before lifting Berkeley into her booster seat and then sits beside her.

On his plate is a mountain worth of eggs, a stack of thick crispy bacon that I could smell permeating out on the porch when I got back to the house, and practically half a loaf of sliced bread toasted and slathered in butter.

I turn to study the plate of breakfast he set out for me. Sure, he set me at the island instead of at the table with them, but this arrangement is awkward enough not to have to force ourselves to pretend we want to be in proximity to each other.

He served me a heavy helping of eggs, sliced strawberries, a piece of toast, and a few strips of that thick-cut bacon that has had my stomach growling since I opened the front door to the house.

"Thanks," I say to him, but he doesn't acknowledge it.

We're close enough that I know he heard me, and I see his eyes reflect at me from the glass pane of the bay windows that frame the backyard.

It's only a moment and then his attention gets drawn else-where when Berkeley becomes enamored by the red robins hopping around in the dawn light.

The frosty morning dew coats the tops of the blades of ever-green grass.

"Look, Daddy! Bird! Bird!" Berkeley squeals with a piece of bacon in one hand and her sippy cup of milk in the other.

"Whoa, Berk. Is that bird eating breakfast just like us?" Kae-nan asks.

His voice is more animated than I've ever heard before.

He's so sweet with her. His interest in what she's thinking and saying is obvious with how he watches her carefully, not to miss a single wide-eyed look or funny facial expression she makes while she watches the few dozen birds hopping around in the grass searching for worms and bugs.

I take my seat and spear a strawberry as I watch them both.

I finish my breakfast quickly and then head for the kitchen to get a jump on cleaning up before I have to take Berkeley to daycare.

"You don't have to do that. I can do it when I'm done," Kaenan says.

He already loaded a lot of the bowls and utensils he used to make breakfast into the dishwasher, but the pans still need to be hand-washed.

"It's not a problem. That's what I'm here for."

He doesn't respond. He just stares for a second while I wash the pans until he finally turns back to his breakfast and his entertaining conversation with Berkeley, where she tells Kaenan which birds are the mommies and daddies and which ones are the babies.

Berkeley's family tree becomes more and more fascinating as she progresses through the flock. Her toddler voice is still something I'm trying to train my ear to. I don't quite understand each word, but I could listen to her talk all morning.

I finish wiping down the range while Kaenan rinses off his and Berkeley's plates. After he loads them into the dishwasher, he starts to walk out of the kitchen back toward Berkeley.

"Thanks for cleaning up," he says.

"Thanks for making breakfast."

"Sure. I'll get Berkeley's shoes, and then I'll drive you to Berkeley's daycare this morning so you know where it is for pickup."

"Okay, can I go like this?" I ask, turning toward him, giving a flick of my wrist toward my body to indicate my workout outfit.

He gives my body a long scan and then clears his throat quickly.

"That's fine," he says, and then turns toward Berkeley, helping her out of her booster chair.

They head down the hallway together in search of her shoes. Berkeley skips in front of Kaenan.

Within twenty minutes, we're all set in the car and headed down the street. The butt warmers on my side of the car are already heated and toasty compared to what the tan leather seats would usually feel like.

Kaenan must have turned them on when he walked out to heat the car after he got Berkeley's shoes on. When I study his control on his side, I notice that his isn't on.

"You didn't turn on your seat warmer?" I ask.

"I don't mind the cold. Professional hazard."

I've never met a hockey player before, but I suppose that makes sense.

And why is that so freaking sexy?

Because he'd have to be either physically or mentally strong enough to handle this morning temperature in the thin long sleeve base layer with no jacket that he's sporting in thirty-two-degree weather.

Sure, that could be it.

It's only a short ten-minute drive to Berkeley's daycare, and he spends the time pointing out the closest gas station and grocery store, as well as Berkeley's ballet studio that's on the way.

When we arrive, Kaenan introduces me to the owner of the daycare.

"This is Isla. She'll be bringing Berkeley in and picking her up sometimes over the next ten weeks," he tells her.

The woman smiles up at me and asks me for my contact information so she can add me to the approved pickup and drop-off list.

A few minutes later, Kaenan and I are back in his SUV and headed back to the house.

The silence stretches on until Kaenan pipes up.

"Where did you run to this morning? I should know, just in case you don't return in time to take Berkeley to daycare."

"You asked me that already. Like I said, nowhere in particular, just past the gates until I hit the miles and then turned around."

We pull up to a red light at an intersection, and I see Kaenan's hands twist around the steering wheel slightly.

"I don't like the idea of you running alone, in the dark, without your cell phone. What if something had happened to you?"

The light turns green, and he eases back on the gas pedal.

He's concerned about me?

Wasn't it just yesterday when he was ready to kick me out on my butt?

Now he's worried about me?

Or is this about control?

With the current state of the men in my life, I can't be sure I know the difference anymore.

"I'll be fine. I've been running most of my life."

Vivi's words come back to me about how I use running to cope with the life I have no control over.

In one way or another, I've used running as an escape. Maybe that's one of the reasons I'm pushing so hard to prepare for this half marathon, after having given up on running in more recent years to build my company.

The first thing I did when I caught Collin with Tori was run. And now, I'm still running from the life I'm bound to.

I turn and watch out the passenger window as we pass by homes near his neighborhood. My hands flatten against my thighs, covered in Newport Athletics running leggings in cherry blossom pink.

The new spring addition color gets released in early March, but I just so happened to have the box of prototypes in my car when I left Vegas.

At least I can say that one thing in my life is going right.

Our spring launch is our most highly anticipated release to date, with our first day of pre-orders crashing our website.

Collin was a mess that day trying to get our website host to work as fast as possible to get the website back up.

We posted like crazy on social media, thanking our loyal customers for their support.

"There," I say, pressing my pointer finger against the SUV's window to indicate the sidewalk.

"There what?" he asks, quickly glancing out my window but misses it.

"That's where I stopped this morning."

Kaenan grabs the rearview mirror and angles it in an attempt to see where I was referring to.

He glances back and forth between the rearview mirror and the road ahead of us to keep us from wrecking.

"You stopped there and then turned around?" he asks to clarify and then settles back into place once he seems to have mentally GPS'd my stopping point.

"Yep," I say, smacking my lips together and rubbing my hands down my leggings.

He turns on his blinker and then turns right, back into his gated neighborhood.

Driving up to the guard's station, he points up to a camera device off the corner of the building.

"That monitor senses the magnetic code on the window sticker," he says, now pointing at a small metallic sticker in the left-hand corner of his windshield. "I have one at the house for your car."

We drive past the sensor, and the gate starts to slide open.

A moment later, we're through the gate and headed down the street toward Kaenan's house.

"Take your cell phone next time."

"Ask nicely and I'll think about it," I say, closing my arms over my chest.

I'm not sure where this braver version of myself comes from. Maybe I'm taking it out on Kaenan because I'm struggling to stand up for myself in front of my dad and Collin.

Or maybe because Kaenan has resented me since the day I showed up on his porch, so I don't care what he thinks of me anyway.

Kaenan pulls into the driveway, and as soon as the car stops, I open the door and slide out of the vehicle.

"Berkeley has ballet today. I'll do pickup," he says out the window.

I just nod and head for the front door.

I hear him back out of the driveway but then he stops in the road.

Feeling his eyes on me as I march along the pebbled walkway up to the house has me consciously aware of how I look from behind.

Once I input the code to the house and twist the door handle to open it, Kaenan puts the car back in motion and leaves for the stadium.

Good, he's gone.

Now I just need to think of what I'll do for the rest of the day to earn my paycheck.

I can tell that Sunny kept the house immaculate, so there won't be much to do immediately.

Making Berkeley's bed and putting all the toys away in the living room took up a small chunk and unloading the dishwasher from running it earlier. I start Berkeley's laundry since I didn't ask if Kaenan would like me to do his, and then rounded it all out by spending the afternoon scrubbing out the oven when I internet-searched the most commonly forgotten places to clean.

No wonder because no matter how many times I scrubbed, the grease kept coming.

It's just past five o'clock when I hear them pull up to the house.

The front door chime sounds and then Kaenan's steady steps and Berkeley's toddler gallop come down the hallway.

I'm still on a stepladder wiping down the bay windows with window cleaner when Berkeley busts through into the living room.

"How was ballet?" I ask her, but then meet Kaenan's eyes.

"That place is organized chaos. How that woman wrangles twenty toddlers, I have no idea." His eyebrows shoot up and his nose flares as he shakes his head. "We got her tutu for the recital, though."

He drapes a royal blue heap of tulle stuffed in a dry-cleaning bag over the back of the couch.

"A recital?" I ask Berkeley with an excited expression to gauge her interest in it.

She just keeps twirling in her leotard without giving me an indication if she even knows what a recital is.

"It's their Christmas program. Ages two to twelve. Each age group has a performance," he says, studying the window behind me. "You cleaned the windows?"

"Better visibility for the birds. I think they like watching Berkeley eat her breakfast."

A small lopsided grin emerges on Kaenan's face and then it disappears just as quickly.

"It looks good," he says, straightening his lips, and then turns and walks to the kitchen. "The kitchen smells like oven cleaner. Wait...did you clean the oven?"

He walks over and opens the oven door to peer inside.

"I had plenty of time on my hands," I say simply.

He nods and then closes the door.

"I'll take it from here. The rest of the night is yours."

He's quick to get rid of me, but it's better this way. After yesterday's event, I'm still not sure how many eggshells I'm walking on with him.

"I'll just be right upstairs if you need anything."

"Thanks, good night."

"Night," I call out.

He's already turned his back to me while rifling through the fridge, pulling out ingredients I assume for dinner.

I could ask Vivi if she wants to get a drink at the bar down from her condo, but it's so dark tonight, and the rain is pouring harder than it was earlier.

I turn and head upstairs to work on my sketches for Newport Athletic. Something about going upstairs while Kaenan and Berkeley are down here feels... a little lonely.

Not that my first choice of companionship would be Kaenan Altman.

My phone dings, and I pull it out of my back pocket.

Vivi: How did day one go?

Me: No one died.

Vivi: That's literally the bare minimum requirement of your job.

Me: He banished me to my room like Cinderella as soon as they walked in the door tonight.

Vivi: It will get better. I know it will.

Me: I think I'll try sketching at Serendipity's Café tomorrow for a little change of scenery.

Vivi: Good idea. Text me tomorrow to let me know how day two goes.

Me: I will. Night.

Vivi: Good night.

An hour later, I hear Berkeley's chitter-chatter as Kaenan follows her up the stairs and heads to her bathroom for her bath time.

A little while later, I hear Kaenan's deep voice as he reads her a bedtime story.

Before I know it, there's silence from her room beside the slight sound of Kaenan breathing heavily in his sleep.

A sound that lulled me to sleep in Vegas while he held me against his chest.

That morning with him almost feels more like a dream. Like something I imagined one night after too many drinks with Vivi in Vegas.

I wish I could convince myself that he and I never happened. It would certainly make the next ten weeks a whole lot simpler. Yet deep down, I can't deny the truth. Those fleeting hours with him made me realize what I'll give up if I marry for privilege.

I'll give up marrying a man who looks at me the way Kaenan did in his hotel suite.

CHAPTER FIFTEEN

Isla

The next day, the morning repeats itself.

I go for a run and show up to breakfast on the island. Only this time, my eggs are accompanied by two pancakes with chocolate chips cooked into them.

The pancake smiley face made with sliced bananas and blueberries on Berkeley's plate looks a little lopsided, but I smile at the thought that he puts this kind of effort in for her.

"I didn't know you were an artist," I tell him as I take my seat on the barstool and squeeze a dollop of ketchup next to my eggs.

"Berk wanted pancakes, and I need to carb load today."

I glance over to find a not-so-short stack of pancakes, void of chocolate chips and syrup on a plate, next to a heaping pile of eggs and bacon taking up a whole additional plate.

"You weren't kidding when you said you eat a lot."

"I'll burn all of this off during drills this morning. Then I have weights in the afternoon."

As a runner, I understand that food is fuel. I've just never seen anyone besides a competitive eater put away so much in one sitting.

Now I understand why he says it's easier for him to cook for Berkeley and himself. I wouldn't even know where to start with portion sizes for him, let alone how to cook almost anything besides spaghetti.

I finish my breakfast first, again, and start to clean while Kaenan and Berkeley discuss the tooth fairy and her exchange rate.

Berkeley's too young to lose any teeth as far as my limited knowledge is on the subject, but her curiosity is boundless. I can see Kaenan chuckling at something she just said. Seeing him with her reminds me that there are two sides to Kaenan.

The side that the world gets.

And the side that Berkeley gets.

But what I don't understand is why.

"I'm taking off," Kaenan says, rinsing off his plate and then dropping it in the dishwasher. "Daycare by eight, pick up at four."

I nod. "I remember. Berkeley and I have it under control."

"Okay, thanks. I loaded her spare car seat in your car when we got home last night. I stuck the sticker in your window too," he says, and then bends down to kiss Berkeley on the head.

"I'll be back tonight for dinner, Okay? Be a good girl today."

She gives him a hug and then runs off to get her shoes, so we can leave for school.

Kaenan leaves a few minutes before us, and he's backing out of the driveway as we exit the house.

It's a chilly morning.

Even more frozen than yesterday, and this morning's run had my throat burning a little.

I see my car parked against the curb still from yesterday. It's already running and looks warm from here, thank God.

Even with an automatic start button on my key fob, I always forget to do it.

Kaenan must have grabbed my keys and started it for me when I wasn't watching.

I walk Berkeley to her side of the car and notice that he scraped all the ice off my windshield and side windows.

I know it's probably just because he wants to ensure that Berkeley makes it to daycare as safely as possible. He could have just left the ice scratcher for me to do it, but he didn't. My cheeks warm in the cold November breeze at the sweet gesture.

Collin is always rushing from one place to another. It's not as if he wouldn't do it for me. I just don't think he would think of it with his brain clamoring with spreadsheets and sales projections.

...And Tori.

I let out an exhale at the memory of what brought me here, and a cloud of steam flutters out of my mouth.

I load Berkeley up, and we head for school.

After dropping her off, Serendipity's homemade chai spice latte and scones are calling my name.

I head into town, a little worried about the traffic since it was crazy when Vivi drove us around, but I make it and find a parking spot only a block away.

Pushing through the apple-red door, the smells of Serendipity's Coffee Shop pastries hit me immediately.

The line is relatively long, so I head to find a table first.

A little one close to the cashier is open, so I take it, deciding to start sketching while I wait for the line to die down.

"Oh my gosh! Are those the new Newport Athletic running leggings for the spring line?" a woman asks.

Oops.

I glance up to find a woman, maybe a couple of years younger than me, with long platinum blonde hair and striking bluish-gray eyes standing in front of me.

Her bright white smile is on full display as her diamond studs glint in the café's lighting.

I didn't even think about wearing these outside of the tight-knit community that Collin and I live in. Everyone who lives in our gated community knows that I own Newport Athletics, and I only wear the prototypes around our neighborhood for just this reason.

I don't get this sort of reaction from them.

"Hi, uh... yes, actually, they are," I tell her, keeping my voice lower than hers and scanning the area to see if anyone else can hear our conversation.

A few people are looking in our direction but more toward her excitement than understanding the reason for her excitement.

It's not that I mind if people know what I own, but I like flying under the radar more than my father and Collin do... even though I am the social media face of the brand.

I often forget how recognizable our brand is until I venture out of Denver, where people are used to seeing me.

"Tessa! Come here right now," she says over her shoulder, waving over another woman to my table.

Tessa seems closer to my age, with gorgeous dark curled hair and stunning hazel eyes.

"Look, she's wearing the Newport Athletics spring line."

Tessa smiles and then laughs at her friend.

"You'll have to excuse Penelope. She's obsessed with this clothing line."

"Oh please," Penelope says. "You have a pair of leggings from every season."

Tessa stares at me and then nods as if she's been called out and is fine with it.

I don't usually tell people who I am unless they put it together, and since they haven't...I'll let them assume that I got my hands on the leggings early.

"I'm glad to hear that you enjoy them too. I'm Isla."

Penelope stares at me for a second like she's nervous to ask a question.

"Can I... touch your leggings?" she asks. "I preordered them in all eight colors."

I laugh. "Sure. I don't mind."

"Just don't feel her up. This is a family establishment," Tessa teases.

Penelope runs her hand over my thigh thickly and then her eyes widen.

"You have to feel this, Tessa. They're like butter," she says.

"Don't worry. I have no intention of making this encounter any more uncomfortable for you," Tessa tells me.

Penelope's peacoat opens slightly, and I get a glimpse of the name on her shirt.

Hawkeyes hockey.

"Are you a fan of the Hawkeyes?" I ask.

"I guess you could say that. We work for them," Penelope says, motioning her hand to include Tessa.

"Do you watch the games?" Tessa asks.

"No, I've never seen a game... but I know one of the players."

"You do? Who?" Penelope's eyes sparkle, and her eyebrows lift with her question.

"Kaenan Altman. I'm helping watch his daughter—"

"You're Kaenan's new nanny?" Penelope's eyes widen to the size of saucers.

"It sort of just... fell into my lap."

"Will you be coming to any of the games?" Tessa asks.

"Oh, uh, Kaenan hasn't asked me to. I'll have Berkeley when he leaves town, but I haven't watched her for home games yet."

"If you come, tell us, and we'll get you a pass to the owner's box where we hang out most games," Penelope offers.

"Okay. If he wants me to bring Berkeley to a game, that would be nice."

"And if you need help with anything, I live at my brother's house down the street from Kaenan's in the same neighborhood. Brent Tomlin is the left defenseman on the team."

"The what?"

They both smile.

"We'll teach you when you come," Penelope offers.

"If you need a sitter for a doctor's appointment or need help with Berkeley when Kaenan's at away games, you can drop her by my house or the stadium," Tessa says.

"I might take you up on that if I get into a pinch."

"Penelope, dirty chai latte. Tessa, vanilla latte," the barista yells over the noise of customers and the milk being steamed.

"Oh, that's us. We have to get to work, but it was really nice meeting you, Isla. I'm sure we'll be seeing you around," Penelope says.

"It was nice to meet you both." I wave as they both give a little wave back and then head for the pickup window.

They leave shortly after, and I can barely believe my luck to have met two people who work for the Hawkeyes and seem really sweet.

Finally, after the rush dies down, I get my chai latte and a cranberry-orange scone.

My juices seem to be flowing in this café, and I make great progress on my new racerback design.

I head home and find a few things to clean and then head to pick up Berkeley at four o'clock.

When we get home, Kaenan's car is already in the driveway.

The second we step through the door, a delicious aroma has me licking my lips. I take off her wet coat and hang it off the coat rack while she runs down the hall toward the kitchen.

"Daddy!" she yells when she makes it to the end of the hall and sees Kaenan in the kitchen.

"How's my little ballerina?" he asks.

"Good."

I head for the kitchen as well.

"How was pickup today?" he asks me when I come into view.

He bends down to lift Berkeley off the ground, her short arms already wrapped around his leg.

He's standing barefoot in a pair of steely gray athletic sweats and a white Hawkeyes T-shirt pulled tightly across his pecs. The arm that holds Berkeley up to his chest flexes as it keeps her suspended against him. The white cotton material stretches almost beyond what it can handle.

I remember feeling just like that T-shirt sleeve while under him in his hotel room with every thrust that entered me.

Chills run down my arms at the thought, but I try to shake them loose.

He wishes I wasn't here.

He has said it enough times.

Usually, I would tell myself not to take someone's bad attitude as personal.

But this is personal.

It's as personal as it gets.

"It was seamless, and I got in and out of the gates without a problem."

"I'm glad it worked," he says, turning away from me toward the bubbling pot of what appears to be spaghetti sauce on the stove.

He stirs it and then puts a lid over it.

I think about what he did this morning, scraping off the ice for me.

We may be in a weird place, but that doesn't mean I shouldn't thank him for his thoughtful act.

"Thank you for this morning. The ice and warming up my car."

"It was freezing this morning. I didn't want you out in the cold having to do it," he says, adding a pinch of salt to the pot of noodles in the water.

"I just wanted to tell you that I appreciate it."

"I take care of the woman living under my roof. It was how I was raised, and since you live here now, you're under my care."

I'm not exactly sure if I should swoon or feel like the act I found so generous was out of duty and obligation.

"Either way, thank you."

He just nods and then opens the oven to set a loaf of garlic bread wrapped in tin foil inside.

My stomach begins to rumble at the savory smells coming from his cooking.

Then I remember who I met today. I don't know how well Kaenan knows Penelope and Tessa, but it must be well enough since Tessa is the sister of a player.

"I ran into a couple of Hawkeyes employees today at Serendipity's Coffee Cafe."

"You did? Who?" he says peering over his shoulder at me.

"Penelope and Tessa."

He smiles and then turns back to stir his sauce. "Those two love that place. How did you find it?"

"It's down the street from Vivi's office. We go there together sometimes."

"What did they say?"

"That if I ever take Berkeley to a game, they'll get me a guest pass for the owner's box."

That must have gotten his attention because his entire body turns around when before, I could barely even get a look.

"You would want to come to a game and watch me play?" he asks, searching my eyes as if he's searching for the answer before I speak.

"Yeah, it could be fun. If you want me to bring Berkeley to one of your games, I mean. They said they'll teach me the ins and outs."

A little smirk shows across his lips for a second and then he turns back to the dinner.

What was that?

He seemed interested in whether I wanted to come to a game.

"Down, Dadda," Berkeley finally says.

She runs straight for the living room, and I watch as she unpacks everything I packed up last night, but that's to be expected.

"You're off for the rest of the night," he says.

I turn toward him in the kitchen and find him watching me... watching her. His butt leans up against the countertop and he holds a pair of noodle tongs, his right ankle crossed and resting over his left foot.

"You can go out and get dinner with friends or whatever. You don't have to stay here in the house with us."

He almost says it as if there's something about being here with them that shouldn't appeal to me.

I'm not looking for a way out of this house, and with how well I did today with the sketches, I want to keep working until I run out of inspiration.

"Thanks, but I think I'll stay in and sketch."

"Okay," he says and then turns back to the stove.

He shuts off all the burners and then pulls the big pot off the stove and walks it to the sink to strain the noodles.

I turn to head down the hall and up to my room.

"You can use the office if you want," he says right before I enter the hallway and out of sight.

The idea of sketching in the office instead of upstairs alone feels really nice.

"That would be great, thanks."

I remember that I left my sketch pad out in the car.

Dammit.

I slip on my shoes and head outside to my car to retrieve it. It's freezing out now that the sun has gone down. I grab the sketch pad and race back to the front door, closing it and the cold behind me.

The minute I set my sights on walking back down the hall to the office, I barely catch Kaenan walking out of it. When I get to the double French glass doors, I see a plate of spaghetti, a slice of garlic bread, a pile of green beans, a fork, and a napkin waiting for me.

I smile to myself and then set up on his desk, keeping the doors open so that I can hear Berkeley's little voice during dinner.

But also so I can hear Kaenan's answers to her questions. Sometimes his answers are just as entertaining.

I get lost in my sketches until I hear a knock against one of the open glass doors.

"Hi," I say, glancing up from my sketch pad.

My empty plate sits off to the side, completely devoured where spaghetti used to be.

"Berkeley's ballet recital is next week. You're not required to come. I just think that Berkeley would really like it if you came."

Of course, I'd love to see Berkeley up on stage in her tutu with all her cute little friends.

"Yes," I say quickly. "I'd love to come."

"Great. She'll be happy to hear it."

He gives a quick smile and then reaches for the plate sitting on the desk.

"You don't need to—"

"It's fine, I don't mind. You've been doing most of the dishes anyway," he says. "And I leave for our away game tomorrow. You'll be on your own for a few days in a row. Save your energy."

There's a glint of teasing in his eyes when he says it.

I let out a chuckle.

Berkeley can make me feel a little bit like the house in caught in that tornado in *The Wizard of OZ*, but being with her has been the escape I need mentally to Collin's "proposal."

Are Kaenan and I starting to get along now?

It would definitely make this arrangement a lot easier.

He offered his office, made me dinner, and now invited me to Berkeley's recital.

The next week flies by with Kaenan out of town for half of it.

When he does return, he and I keep mostly to ourselves. His pithy comments have stopped, and there's an occasional smile, but we don't spend any more time together than we have to.

That's how it should be.

We don't need to be friends, but I'm at least happy we can live under the same roof and be a good team for Berkeley.

Even though the idea of leaving her is getting harder and harder to stomach.

CHAPTER
SIXTEEN

Isla

The night of the recital, I help Berkeley into her tights and the cutest royal-blue tutu with tiny violet silk flowers adorning the bottom of the bodice where the fabric meets the tulle.

I pull her hair back into two even buns on the top of her head like two little bear ears, and then I tie two royal-blue ribbons around her dark-chocolate curls. Next, I slide on her ballet slippers, and she's all set.

I snap a photo and send it off to Sunny.

Kaenan's footsteps echo through the hallway as he exits his bedroom and heads toward us in the hall bathroom. He's dressed in dark jeans, a button-up paisley shirt, and cowboy boots, similar to how he was dressed in Vegas. His masculine cologne wafts toward me, and I inhale deeply.

I wish I wasn't still attracted to Kaenan.

I wish he hadn't made me feel things that night in Vegas that I've never felt so intensely with anyone else before.

Wanted.

Gorgeous.

His.

"You look perfect, Berk," he tells her, bending down as she runs to him and does a twirl to show off her complete outfit.

"It's a tutu!" she tells him.

"Yeah, baby, I know. I love it."

The word baby coming from his lips zips through me.

I remember the way he whispered it against my ear as he pushed inside me. And the way he said it as I came hard on his cock.

I've dreamed of the way Kaenan Altman says baby when you belong to him. And I have no doubt that the night we spent in Vegas, he made me belong to him.

His eyes reach up to mine as Berkeley keeps spinning in circles in front of the full-length mirror to check out every angle of her poofy tutu.

"Thank you for taking the time to put her together," he says.

"I used to be in pageants. I know a thing or two about stage presence. Confidence should come from the inside, but it certainly doesn't hurt when you feel prepared on the outside."

His eyebrows furrow for a moment.

"You used to do pageants?" he asks.

"Not in a really long time," I say, waving it off like it was a lifetime ago. But the longer I'm away from home, the further away that life feels. "We'd better go, or we're going to be late," I say, deflecting from the conversation.

It's part of my past, and unfortunately, the future I'm headed back to. Maybe not pageants exactly... but that world. It's a world that I don't want Kaenan to know anything about.

What will he think if he finds out that I ran away from my father's expectations?

"Oh poor rich girl, running away from a home that has given her more opportunities than most people can dream of."

I shouldn't care about Kaenan's opinion of me, but I do.

He glances down at his watch. "Yeah, we should leave before we hit traffic."

"Let's go, Berkeley," I say, grabbing the comb and hairspray off the countertop just in case she needs a touch-up before showtime.

We load up into Kaenan's SUV, and he pulls out of the driveway.

Forty-five minutes later, we arrive at the arts center downtown. Kaenan drops Berkeley and I off in front so we don't have to walk through the rain. I pull Berkeley under my jacket to shelter her from the drizzle as we run for the doors because Kaenan doesn't believe in umbrellas... a Pacific Northwest thing, I guess. But I'll be damned if Berkeley's hair gets ruined.

I managed through two full-blown toddler tantrums and a snack break to get this look together.

Not even the heavens opening up and trying to drown us will keep me from her making her grand entrance with perfect hair.

Kaenan

Getting the car parked was a shit show, but I do it and then race into the center to make sure to see Berkeley before she goes on stage.

I catch up to Isla and Berkeley as Isla delivers her to the ballet teacher.

"Knock 'em dead, Berk!" I yell to her with a thumbs-up before she runs to her friends.

A few of the stage moms stare over at me..

Some with obvious interest.

Some with annoyance.

I've gotten used to getting hit on by the mothers of Berkeley's class. It used to be sort of funny to me, and a little flattering, but then it got to the point where I couldn't focus on watching Berkeley because I had women trying to hold a conversation during class.

Until my mother left, I used to make her take Berkeley so I wouldn't have to deal with it. Now, with the possibility that Mia's mom might take her away from me, I don't let an annoyance stop me from spending the time I get with my daughter anymore.

What if I lose her?

"She doesn't need us from here, right? Should we go find a seat before it fills up?" I ask.

"Yeah, good idea," Isla agrees.

Isla's skintight blue velvet dress, which matches Berkeley's tutu exactly, has me wondering what it would feel like to run my hands down every inch of her curves in that material. If she was mine, I'd find a dark corner somewhere and do it right now.

The dress hugs her figure with just the right amount of cleavage to have my mouth watering, but it's still appropriate for a children's ballet recital.

I see other dads here eyeing her too. Just like all those fuckers in the Vegas club who wanted to take her home that night.

But I'm the only asshole who made her come.

I reach out and grab her hand. The crowd we have to get through to our seats is thick with people. Luckily, I'm a big guy, and most people move out of the way for me if I'm coming through. Like an icebreaker on the front of an Antarctic exploration ship.

It's how I am on the ice as well.

Either get the fuck out of my way or get run over.

I grip her hand behind me to pull her along as I cut through the crowd.

"Kaenan! How good to see you," the owner of the ballet studio says.

Ms. Tully is, from my guess, in her mid-seventies and as thin as anyone I've ever met. I've never seen her dressed in anything but a flesh-colored leotard and leggings, and I'm almost confident that her French accent is fake.

I'll give it to the woman. She runs a successful ballet studio with over ten classes twice a day, three other instructors, and an average of fifteen kids per class. Somehow, she keeps the circus train on its tracks, and I have to give her props for that.

I've never seen the woman frown.

Not even once.

"Ms. Tully, good to see you," I tell her as she makes a beeline for us.

I squeeze Isla's hand in mine to make sure she's still with me, and she squeezes back.

"I thought you might be out of town for a hockey game."

"Not tonight. I'm lucky to be home to watch Berkeley really shine in her true element."

Ms. Tully laughs. "She was born for the stage, that one. Not unlike her father."

Then Ms. Tully's vision cuts sideways to the woman standing slightly behind me but within view.

"Oh, my darling. You are quite exquisite," she says to Isla and then shifts her attention back to me. "You're a lucky man."

I should correct her, but I don't.

She said I'm lucky to have Isla, and I don't completely disagree. Though I don't have her in the way that Ms. Tully thinks.

Before I can introduce Isla as my nanny to disprove any of Ms. Tully's assumptions, another instructor grabs Ms. Tully's arm and pulls her toward her.

"We need to get the program started, Ms. Tully."

"Right, well then, lead the way," she tells the woman, and then turns and abandons our conversation.

I don't glance back at Isla to see how she took that encounter. I decide to ignore it and then head for a set of open seats toward the front.

I pull Isla behind me as we squeeze past people.

I feel a sense of relief to have Isla here. She didn't have to come, and she didn't have to spend the time she did on getting Berkeley ready.

I'm probably biased, but Berkeley looks the most put-together of all the kids I saw backstage.

Isla and I find seats quickly. It isn't long before the program begins.

Berkeley's class is the third up, but we have to sit through the other ten. By the time the program is over, the hard chairs we sat on have my back begging for some time in the hot tub.

As I load Berkeley into her car seat, Isla opens the front passenger door and climbs in quickly to escape the rain.

Soon, we're all loaded up and headed home.

Keeping my hand from reaching over and taking Isla's as I did in the art center when I pulled her through the crowd is really hard to resist. She looks so damn good sitting shotgun in my SUV.

We pull into the house's driveway, and I cut the engine. Berkeley is out cold from the drive home. She danced her heart out tonight.

"I'll change her into her pajamas while you change... if you want?" Isla asks, offering to give me a minute to get out of my jeans and into sweats to read Berkeley a book before bed.

It's too late for bath time tonight, and my back is done. I need a long soak.

"Thanks."

Her little eyes open the second I pull her out of her seat.

I haul her upstairs and then drop her in the bathroom with Isla. She's livelier now, but the second she gets in bed, she'll be out like a light.

I hear Isla and Berkeley giggling together in the bathroom down the hall as I change. Their bond is growing rapidly while Berkeley and I make smaller strides forward.

By the time I walk out of my bedroom, Berkeley is cuddled up in her bed and waiting for me. Isla stands in the doorway until she sees me and then blows a kiss to Berkeley.

"Night, night, sweet dreams," Isla tells her.

Berkeley blows a kiss back, and then Isla turns to head down the hall as I turn in to enter Berkeley's room.

She's probably going to turn in for the night like she always does about this time, but I wish she wouldn't.

Coming home from an out-of-town game, or even just from practice, has me racing back, knowing that Berkeley and Isla are waiting to greet me.

I know Isla's time here is temporary, but I'm starting to wonder what it would feel like if she didn't leave.

Isla

My work here is done for the night.

I head for my room, desperate to get into my swimsuit and head for the hot tub. My run this morning really pushed my limits, especially since I forgot to wear my running brace for my right knee. With everything I needed to get done today, before Christmas, I didn't have time to get in the hot tub after my run.

A few minutes later, I'm downstairs with a towel slung over my shoulder and a glass of some rosé wine that Sunny stashed in the fridge for me. I open the door to the outside patio and close it behind me.

I turn on the jets and the lights at the bottom of the hot tub to see as I step in. The minute my toes hit the hot water, I discard my towel on the staircase.

The vibration of the jets has already put my muscles at ease.

I slide over to the corner, then dunk my body as far into the hot water as possible without getting my face wet.

I close my eyes and let my mind drift off.

Today I experienced some confusing feelings that I thought Kaenan had permanently scared away—but then there they were again.

It doesn't matter what feelings I do or don't have. They are irrelevant because in eight short weeks, I'll be headed back to Denver.

I'm pulled from my relaxation when I hear the glass sliding door open.

Who was that?

I push back up until my shoulder blades are out of the water. My tasty pink wine swishes almost out of the glass, but I don't care because it's the only blunt object in my current possession, and I'm ready to use it if I have to.

When I glance over the hot tub to see my fate, I find a shirtless Kaenan in a pair of swimming shorts headed towards me.

Bare-chested, gorgeous, and, as far as I can tell, unaware that I'm already in the hot tub.

He's also a hot, asshole hockey player with washboard abs, a dirty mouth, and a talented cock to match.

I'm going to need more rosé.

Just bring the whole bottle.

CHAPTER SEVENTEEN

Isla

He must not have seen me at first because when I sit up straight in the hot tub, his eyes connect with mine, and he pauses in his tracks.

"Oh... I didn't know you were out here," he says, standing between the house and the hot tub.

This is his home, and I don't want to be the intruder.

"I'll leave," I say quickly, standing up out of the water. The cool night causes my nipples to harden under the thin material of my bathing suit. "I should have asked if you planned on using the hot tub tonight before I assumed I could use it."

I walk over to the edge of the hot tub, bend to grip the side of the tub, and swing my leg over to exit.

When I glance back up, Kaenan has his eyes locked on my thin aqua-blue bathing suit top. My breasts strain to stay inside the confines as I bend forward.

Is he checking me out?

Excitement bubbles up in my belly at the sight of Kaenan's perusal of my body.

"No..." he says, lifting his hand up to stop me. "Don't leave. There's enough room for both of us."

He starts walking again and takes the first step onto the wooden staircase of the hot tub, discarding his towel in the same place I did. I take steps back to the far corner again and sit while I watch Kaenan's muscles flex as he lifts himself over the edge.

I watch as he steps in and then settles into the opposite side of me.

He leans back and rests his head on the back of the headrest on the edge of the hot tub.

He moves his body so that the jets are hitting a spot on his shoulder blade.

A groan vibrates through his throat as he must have found the spot causing him discomfort all night. It didn't seem like he could get comfortable during the recital.

"Is your shoulder bothering you?" I ask.

I've had some experience massaging out a knot with all of the years of running I've done.

"It's from a bad hit in last week's game," he says, his eyes closed as he presses his shoulder against the jets.

His face scrunches up like it must cause him a lot of pain.

"I could rub it for you... if you want," I offer softly.

Tonight might have been a small breakthrough for us. Just maybe, he'll stop avoiding me during the days, and I won't feel the need to hide out in my bedroom when I'm off the clock, but I won't be getting my hopes up. If he wakes up and it all resets, I'll deal with eight weeks of this.

"Okay, thanks," he says.

He bends forward and pushes out of his corner, heading closer towards me. He's tall enough that he can kneel on the bottom of the hot tub and still have his shoulders out of the water.

I stand up and sit on the edge of the hot tub, giving him room to sit in front of me so that I have better leverage rubbing his muscles from a higher vantage point.

My body is hot and tingly from the hundred-and-three-degree water. The brisk, cold night air feels good against my skin, with the light breeze whipping through the trees in the backyard.

He raises up to his feet and towers over me from where I sit. His hands slide over my knees, and we both watch as he pushes gently on them to ask me non-verbally to open for him so that he can sit between my thighs. I give him what he's asking for, and my thighs separate farther to accommodate Kaenan's wide body.

Kaenan's eyes drift over me, catching on my hard nipples before he turns around, faces the house, and sits down. He lifts his arms and drapes them just above my knees, giving me room between us to access both of his shoulders.

"Which one bothers you the most? We'll start there," I ask.

His right hand comes up over his left shoulder and he squeezes. The ends of his fingers turn white with the pressure as he shows me exactly where he needs it. "This one. Took a hit last week into the plexi."

The moment my fingers connect with his skin, a flash of our night together in Vegas replays in my head. I try to shake the memory loose. No matter what happened in our past... our present is less than ideal. After all, Kaenan can't stand me... even if he held my hand tonight.

A future with Kaenan and Berkeley isn't a choice that's available to me.

In eight weeks, I'll be gone, and that's how Kaenan wants it.

I begin to rub my right thumb into his left shoulder as my left-hand grips around his arm to keep him in place, not that he's trying to get away. In fact, he's pushing against my thumb to add pressure.

The last time I gave a message with this much pressure, I was working out a knot in Collin's back, and he asked me to stop because it was too painful.

This man's pain tolerance is impressive, and I never realized how much of a turn-on that is.

He groans when I hit the most painful spot on his shoulder.

The sound vibrates through his rib cage and against my inner thighs. I attempt to clench my legs together to stop my clit from tingling at the sound he made.

Kaenan must have felt my squeeze because he looks up over his shoulder for a second. "You okay?"

"Yeah, I'm fine," I say quickly.

"Am I hurting you?" he asks.

"I think I should be asking you that."

"If anything, I need it harder."

I smile to myself at the thought of asking for it harder. When I did in Vegas, Kaenan was happy to oblige as I said it in the heat of the moment.

I don't think before I say it. I just blurt it out the minute it comes to me. "I think I'm the one that should be asking for it harder."

The instant I let the words go, I know what I've done.

What I don't know is how he'll react.

Will he kick me out of his house?

Ask me to leave in the middle of the night and not come back?

He made it clear that nothing will happen between us while I'm here, and I agreed to it. This is completely unprofessional, and I won't be surprised if he asks me to leave.

Vivi will take me in, no questions asked, and then I'll be headed back home because I failed to make it on my own for a few more months.

How humiliating that will be when my father says he told me so. I'm basically a bird with clipped wings since I've been dependent on him my whole life.

Kaenan peers over his shoulder at me, and I wait for the moment he pulls his body away from mine and lectures me about crossing the line.

But he doesn't.

He just stares at me.

"Is that what you want?" His eyes search mine.

There's no judgment in them like I expected.

No disapproving side-eye.

He asked me a question, and I already know the answer.

I nod slowly, hoping this isn't a joke he's playing.

"Do you want me, Isla?"

"Yes," I whisper.

He might be kind of an ass to me, but he's an ass who's great in bed, and I'd be a liar if I said I didn't want one more night with him before I have to go back to my life of passionless sex.

Back to a man who is more capable of getting a hard-on for one of our employees than for his fiancée.

Kaenan reaches his right hand over his body, wrapping his finger behind my neck, and pulls me down to his mouth.

He smashes our lips together with force and need.

His full lips devour mine.

He spins the rest of his body around to face me and kneels into the seat where he was sitting.

My thighs open wider to allow him closer.

Now we're eye to eye, and our lips adjust to the new angle.

He releases the back of my neck and uses his right hand to glide under my chin, tilting my head back, and then dips his tongue between my lips.

I moan softly at the feeling of his tongue swiping across mine.

I don't know how far this night will go, but I know that from this day on, whenever I smell chlorine and newly fallen rain on Washington pine trees, I'll think of Kaenan and this night with him.

Kaenan wraps his left arm around my waist and pulls me against him, removing me from the edge, then turns around and sits with his back against the backrest.

His hands reach down and grip around my thighs. He pulls my legs apart, guiding me to straddle him in his seat.

Goosebumps cascade down my back at every inch of skin his fingertips touch.

He sets me right on top of his growing cock, and I feel his length beneath me as he takes my mouth.

I cradle his jaw as I kiss him harder.

His hands grip my waist, pushing and pulling as he rocks them back and forth, creating a rhythm that I pick up on quickly.

He wants me to grind down on him.

My hips keep the rhythm as my aching center rubs over and over his erection.

Hot heat builds in my belly, and no amount of pressure seems enough.

I need more.

He releases my hips, and then his hands dip behind my back and sneak behind the waistband of my bathing suit bottoms.

"I need these off," he says while he grips my ass with both hands, and he squeezes tight, adding more and more pressure against his lap.

I nod and my fingers shake a little as they clumsily mix with his down by my waistband.

We both work to get them off, and within seconds, I no longer have bikini bottoms on. We've removed one of the two layers keeping Kaenan from slipping inside me. This is becoming so real.

A moment I thought I'd never get to experience again.

"Feel how hard I get for you? This is how it is whenever you walk around in those tight-ass leggings all day," he says over the jets.

I push back from him to stare into his warm brown eyes.

How can he tell me that he's always hard for me with how he's acted toward me since I showed up?

"Then why have you been avoiding me?" I ask.

"Because I knew I wouldn't be able to resist you unless I kept my distance. I haven't stopped thinking about fucking you since you knocked on my door."

Since he practically yelled at me to get off his front porch?

"I thought you said you weren't going to sleep with me in your house," I ask, hoping he's changed his mind because if this is just a tease, he's the cruelest man I've ever met.

"We're not in my house. And besides... the hot tub's going to do most of the work."

"The hot tub?" I ask in surprise, but before I can get an answer, Kaenan lifts me off his lap and sets me on top of a jet.

The swirl of the water hits right where he should be.

Right at my center.

Without bathing suit bottoms on, the jets work better than the best vibrator I've ever owned.

He kneels in front of me and then grips my hips to angle me just the way he wants.

"Oh! Oh God," I say as the new position has the jet hitting me right where all my nerve endings meet.

I look down into the water. The jets cloud some of my vision, but the lights in the bottom give me just enough to see the bubbles coming up between my legs.

I reach out and grip the back of Kaenan's neck to have something solid to hold.

"Does that feel good, baby?" he asks.

When I glance up, I find that Kaenan isn't watching between the jets with me... he's staring at the look on my face instead.

I nod.

"How about now?" he asks.

Kaenan reaches down and adds a thumb to my clit, and starts to circle in smooth rotations.

"Kaenan..." I whimper, gripping tighter against the back of his neck.

My eyes flutter closed again as I focus on my body's reaction to what Kaenan and the jets are doing to me.

More tingles shoot from my clit down my legs as warning signs of my body building up.

"Jesus... you're fucking beautiful," he says.

My eyes flutter open to see him still watching me.

"Are you going to come for me?" he asks.

I nod profusely.

I'm already on the edge. The vibration of the jets and Kaenan's thumb have my center pulsating and so close.

"Then be a good girl and lean back for me," he instructs.

He helps me back until my neck hits the neck rest on the back of the hot tub.

I don't have anything to brace my back against with how far forward I'm sitting on the jet, but I'm able to balance like this with my back arched up toward him and my hand around his neck for stability.

Kaenan reaches up for my bathing suit top. His right index finger hooks into the triangle fabric. In one quick motion, he pulls the material over and to the side, exposing my breast.

I gasp and then shiver when my bare nipple hits the cool night air.

I watch him as he bends down, his hot mouth connecting with my breast, and I buck the instant his hot tongue connects with my freezing skin.

My fingers lace through his hair, holding on tight as his tongue swirls and licks.

Without warning, his mouth clamps down hard as he sucks on the hard nub. A bolt of lightning shoots down my belly and hits my clit. A buzzing sensation takes over my body.

"Kaenan," I whimper.

I pull his hair harder, begging him to stay in place.

He pulls his mouth off my nipple. "I like it when you pull my hair. It means you're close."

I groan from the missing heat, and he chuckles.

"Don't stop..." I say, almost incoherently.

His thumb continues to work my clit until I'm now just a bundle of nerve endings firing uncontrollably. I can't control my body anymore as I rock into his hand, needing more friction.

The pressure building up in my center is gaining so much force that I couldn't stop the orgasm nearing its peak even if I wanted to.

"Only because you asked so politely," he says, his voice low and gravelly.

He bends me back down.

But instead of returning to my right breast, his finger hooks into the left side triangle of fabric and repeats the same motion he did with the right.

He takes what he wants from me, knowing what I need before I do.

Now my chest is completely exposed for him, but I don't feel exposed like I should. I feel wanted and beautiful in the way his eyes drift over every inch of me in admiration.

Besides a thin string around my neck and the tie around my back with the material of my bikini bunched at my sides, I'm completely naked for Kaenan.

He bends down finally, his lips clamping down on my left breast harder than before. The sharpness of his teeth slides across my nipple.

I scream out in pain and ecstasy.

My center clamps down, and I come hard and fast.

Almost without warning.

I knew it was coming, but I didn't know that the pain would make me come so hard that my eyes roll back, and I see stars.

My hand grips his hair even tighter as my body's climax rips through me.

"Ride it out, baby. I got you," he says softly, watching me.

A protective arm is still wrapped around me to hold me up as I crumple in his arms while the shock waves continue to roll.

He scoops me up into a cradle hold, my bare breasts against his chest as he twists around, heading to the edge of the hot tub with me in his arms.

"Where are we going?" I ask, in my climax coma.

"Inside. I don't have any condoms out here."

He steps up on the seat in front of us and then swings his leg over the side.

His long legs straddle the edge with ease while still cradling me in his arms.

"Grab our stuff," he instructs, bending down so I can scoop the towels and baby monitor off the wooden teak table.

"We're not done?" I ask, my heart thumping fast at the idea of getting more of him.

This isn't it.

He wants more of me.

"Not even close," he says.

CHAPTER EIGHTEEN

Kaenan

I can't wait another second to get inside her.

My cock is pulsating to the point that it's uncomfortable.

I need that squeeze of her pussy.

That sweet smell of her need for me coated all over my cock.

I need to unload inside her and watch her eyes roll in the back of her head again.

Jesus Christ.

Watching her come for me is an addiction that I don't think I'll ever be cured of.

Wanting her this bad might be poison for my ability to keep all my distractions out of the way.

But tonight, I don't want the antidote.

I carry her toward the glass French doors of the back of the house and lift her high to get my hand on the door handle.

The minute I close the door and lock it behind us, I head straight for the kitchen countertop.

I dropped my wallet there earlier, and I know I have a condom waiting inside.

The steps I take toward the kitchen are rushed, but I have to be careful with my wet feet on the wood floors. It makes this venture a slippery one.

Good thing my job requires incredible balance.

I wouldn't drop her—I won't let myself.

We make it to the kitchen island where I'd set my keys and wallet.

I set her on the barstool, keeping an arm hooked around her back to make sure she doesn't fall as I reach for my wallet.

She's still soaking wet and could slip, but not on my watch.

She's safe with me, and I want her to know that.

I lean into her, gripping the wallet in my right hand.

She bends forward toward me.

Her lips connect with my chest as she peppers soft kisses across my pecs and then trails kisses up my collarbone and the base of my throat.

Her hands trail up my stomach.

Her fingertips run through my happy trail as she goes.

I love when she can't keep her hands off me because the feeling is mutual.

I grip the condom and pull it out of my wallet when I immediately suck in a breath the second Isla dives into my shorts and wraps her fingers around my cock.

"Fuck..." I say, my eyelids fluttering closed at the feel of it.

If my cock wasn't already as hard as it's ever been in my entire life, it would be now.

I have to focus to keep from coming in her hand.

"Are you going to use this on me?" she asks with that sexy-as-shit innocent little eyelash flutter she does.

But she doesn't try— it's part of who she is.

Sweet on the outside but wants to be dirty once I get her on her backside.

"All night," I tell her.

Her eyes dilate at my response.

I push down my soaked shorts to the floor.

A loud thud rings out through the vaulted ceilings of the space, her hand still firmly gripping around my erection.

Before I see it coming, Isla dips her head down, and I feel her hot breath right before her lips wrap around my cock.

"Goddammit..." I hiss, squeezing my ass cheeks together to keep myself from coming in her warm mouth.

As soon as I regain my composure and ward off the first instant orgasm, I open my eyes again to watch her.

She bends over me.

Her tongue darts out to lick me, and her lips gently slide back and forth over my tip. Her hand slides up and down to meet her mouth as she tests me out for size.

"How do I taste?" I ask.

She gives a throaty moan that vibrates through my cock, and my balls tighten.

My fingers slide into her hair as I guide her a little farther down on me.

I'm not forcing it.

She can take me as deep as she wants.

Just having her wet mouth on me is heaven.

"That's it, baby. Be a good girl and suck my cock," I praise her.

She advances and takes me deeper.

My fingers tighten around her hair, ready to pull her back before I come down that sweet throat.

I want to be inside her when I empty every last drop I've had waiting for her since she walked through my front door.

Not that I haven't jacked off in my bathroom with her panties that I took from Vegas wrapped around my cock.

I'm fucking sick, but when it comes to her, it can't be helped.

The sucking noises she makes have my cock begging for release.

Her tongue swirls around my tip and then sucks down on me like a straw.

A burst of nerve endings explodes at the base of my skull, and I react instantly, pulling her hair gently but firmly to get her off my cock.

A pop sounds when she removes her mouth from my cock.

I pull the condom to my mouth and rip it open.

I need to get inside her as fast as I can, or I'm going to come all over her lap.

"Did you not like—"

But before she can finish that sentence, I run my finger through her slit to feel how wet she is.

I bend in and press my lips near her ear.

She moans, gripping my forearm as my finger slides through her wet folds.

"I liked it. But I was about to come in that hot mouth, and I want to come in your sweet pussy instead. Would you like that?"

"So much," she says, her voice breathy.

She's dripping with arousal.

She's ready for me.

Sucking my cock turns her on, and there is nothing hotter than knowing that she enjoys going down on me, as much as I like it too.

I slide on the condom and then step forward, lining myself with her center, but she leans too far forward.

"Lean back against the island," I instruct.

I need a better access point to enter her.

When she does, I watch as that perfect pink pussy glistens for me.

I brace my left hand against the island as I lean in, guiding my cock until my head pushes into her.

She moans at the stretch. Her lips part, and she takes a quick inhale and exhale, her chest filling with air and then decreasing.

I push a little deeper, rocking back and forth, watching Isla's face as each thrust earns me a little whimper.

Her full tits start to bounce with my advances as her arousal continues to coat my cock.

I reach behind her, untying her bikini and letting the minimal material fall to the floor around the barstool.

I groan at how fucking good she feels the farther I sink inside her.

The granite countertop isn't ideal for her, but she takes it like a champ, just like she takes my cock.

I reach my arm back and lay it between her and the granite to block her from the hard, cold edge.

"Is your back, okay?" I ask as I pump harder into her.

"Yeah," she says, her eyes hooded. "Keep going."

I pull her closer, and her arms come around my rib cage until her hands find my back.

Her encouragement eggs me on further as I start bucking into her hard.

More of her wetness coats me, and I can't stop my cock from pulsating inside her tight muscles.

The harder I fuck her, the harder she presses her nails into my flesh to hold on.

She's clawing my back as she moans out my name.

She's close, and fuck... so am I.

I want her to come first but unless she comes in the next half second, I don't think that's going to happen.

"Isla..." I start.

"Yes, I want it," she says, reading my mind.

My jaw clenches as I try to make it a little longer, but after everything we've done tonight, I can't.

I growl out as I come, emptying everything I have as deep as I can inside her.

My cock pulsates as spurts of cum fill the condom.

I rock a few more times to make sure I empty all of it.

But I won't leave her like this.

I pull out of her in one motion and bend down to my knees.

"Kaenan, what are you—"

I pull her ass closer to the edge of the barstool, lifting her legs over my shoulders and then dive my tongue between her thighs.

"Kaenan! Oh God!" she says as I suck down on her pussy and then press my tongue into her center.

She goes off, gripping as best as she can onto the island behind her to keep herself stable, but she never has to worry.

I'll never let her fall.

CHAPTER NINETEEN

Isla

Lying wrapped up in a giant blanket on Kaenan's couch as we watch the electric fireplace pop and fizzle, I can't believe this night just happened.

"Thank you for tonight," he says.

We're facing each other on the long couch.

He brushes his finger over my temple to push back some hair that threatens to fall in my eyes.

"I think you did most of the work." I wiggle my eyebrows at him.

He chuckles and runs the side of his index finger down my jaw.

"Team effort," he offers.

"That's very generous of you, considering what you did in the hot tub."

"Want to do it again?" He grins back at me.

Yes!

"I would love to, but you turned my legs into jelly, and I still have to train tomorrow."

"No rest for the wicked?" he says, reaching his right hand down the side of my body and squeezing.

I squirm in his hands.

I'm too ticklish, and I can't hide it.

"Stop!" I giggle, pushing his hand away, but he doesn't release me, and he's too strong to fend off.

"Why? I like how ticklish you are. It's cute."

"Ever heard the saying, 'You win more bees with honey'?" I ask with a raised brow.

Tickling won't get him between my thighs if that's what he thinks.

"Ever heard the saying 'You break it, you buy it'?"

As in, if he breaks me with that huge cock... he buys me?

The thought is too tempting to consider.

With Collin and Newport Athletics... and the fact that less than twenty-four hours ago, Kaenan kept his distance, I won't let myself run away with ideas of what that could have meant.

If he's hoping for emotional whiplash, he's well on his way. But a part of me springs up with hope.

And sometimes, hope is the most dangerous emotion of all.

"What does that mean?" I ask carefully.

"Something we can talk about tomorrow. You need to sleep," he says.

He leans forward and kisses my forehead.

"Now close your eyes," he instructs.

I do it.

I fall into the sound of his breathing and the light brushing of his fingers over my shoulder and down my arm, and then back again.

I don't know how long he does it because I fall asleep.

Until all of a sudden, I'm woken by the sound of Kaenan cursing.

Kaenan

"Dadda?" I wake immediately, wondering if I heard what I thought.

My eyelids open, and I look around, barely awake.

I glance toward the large bay windows with the morning sun starting to rise.

The windows are icy from the morning frost, the birds are chirping, and the smell of sex still lingers in the air.

"Dadda?!" I hear Berkeley's desperate voice this time.

The fear sweats shoot down my back the minute I hear my daughter's cries for me.

"Dadda!" she screams.

The sounds of sobbing come from the baby monitor.

I had brought it with us when we moved to the couch.

Normally, I wake before Berkeley, but on occasion, she wakes up before me and heads for my bedroom.

"Shit! Shit!" I yell as I realize my daughter woke up and came searching for me, and I wasn't in my room like I always am.

I wasn't in my bed this morning, where I should have been, because I'm butt-ass naked with her nanny downstairs.

"Wha...What's wrong?" Isla's groggy voice wakes to my yelling.

I flip off the blankets between us, lunge off the couch, and head for the towel... since I have no clothing down here. My swim shorts are still on the kitchen floor soaked in chlorine water from last night.

"Berkeley woke up. She's in my room. She can't find me," I say.

I find the towel I brought down to the hot tub last night and wrap it around me.

"I'm coming up, Berk!" I yell up towards the ceiling, hoping she can hear me and it brings her some comfort.

Then I toss the second towel toward Isla, but it only makes it to the back of the couch. And then I notice that Isla is already wrapping herself in the blankets we slept under together last night.

The last thing I need is for Berkeley to see Isla and me naked together and think that she's not my priority.

"I'm sure she's okay. The baby gate is up above the staircase. She's probably just confused about where you are," she says, standing quickly.

I take a quick assessment of everything around me to make sure that whatever Berkeley sees when I bring her down won't scar her for life.

I grab Isla's bathing suit top and grip it in my hand and start heading for the hallway to get to Berkeley whose pleas haven't let up.

She's scared and not sure why I'm not where I should be.

I fucked up.

I took my eyes off my priority, and now Berkeley is awake, upstairs and thinks I left her.

Isla takes quick steps down the front of the couch and then around it like she's going to hurry up the stairs.

"I got it," I tell her, making it to the hall just before her. I hand her the bathing suit top and turn towards the staircase. "This is my fault. I knew better."

"Knew better?" she asks, following me.

I can't see her, but I can hear her quick footsteps and the sound of the blanket that's far too big for her, swishing around her feet.

"I knew something like this would happen if I got involved with you," I say, taking the first few steps up the staircase.

I know the minute I say it that it came out completely wrong.

I should have told her that guys like me don't get to have it all. And that I might lose my daughter to Mia's mom.

But it's for the best for her to hate me.

I can't let this happen again, and history would suggest that I can't keep my hands off her.

"Involved with me?"

I no longer hear her footsteps follow me.

I glance over my shoulder for a second to find Isla at the bottom of the stairs, gripping the blanket up higher over her chest, her eyebrows downturned, and her lips parted.

Now to drive the wedge to make sure she never lets you in again.

"I told you I wouldn't sleep with you again. Last night was a mistake."

"Dadda."

I look back up the stairs to find Berkeley standing at the child gate at the top of the stairs, tears streaming down her face, her little fingers wrapped around the white metal fence.

I take the last few steps toward her and lift her up over the gate and squeeze her against my bare chest.

"Sorry, baby. Are you okay?" I ask, looking over her, but she's fine, just like Isla said she would be.

I open the gate to walk through to get Berkeley and I both dressed. When I glance back down the stairs, Isla's no longer waiting at the bottom of the stairs.

She's gone.

A little while later, Berkeley and I come down so that I can make us breakfast, but Isla isn't downstairs either.

I walk back from the kitchen to the hall and see that her running shoes aren't by the door where she leaves them every morning.

It's just as well.

I need a second to clear my head too.

Isla doesn't show back up until Berkeley and I are putting on her shoes in the entry.

She walks through the door, her body tight as ever in a pair of tangerine orange leggings and a matching razorback, a black hoodie wrapped around her waist, and her hair in a ponytail.

Sweat dripping between her full breasts.

This is going to be fucking torture.

She doesn't look at me when she walks in the door, but she flashes Berkeley that beautiful pearly white smile.

The same one she gave me all night last night.

"You ready to go Berkeley girl?" she asks.

"Yeah, Lala. Let's go," Berkeley says, jumping up with her shoes tied and runs into her arms.

Isla picks her up and then turns her back to me, exiting the house as quickly as she can.

"Wave bye to Daddy," I hear Isla say, pushing Berkeley up her shoulder so that Berkeley can wave to me.

I watch from the door as Isla loads Berkeley into her Range Rover, but Isla doesn't look back in my direction once.

She pulls off of the curb and then they're both gone.

And I'm left knowing, somehow, I'm going to regret telling Isla this was a mistake.

Because it feels a lot like I lied to us both.

CHAPTER TWENTY

Kaenan

"What in the hell happened to you? Looks like you got in a fight with a cougar," Briggs says.

What the hell is he talking about?

"Not a cougar... his nanny's younger than him," Brent tells Briggs with a chuckle.

Shit... I felt her fingernails against my back last night when I fucked her against the island.

I reveled in the feeling, knowing it would leave a mark. I wanted her to mark me, like a badge of honor. I'd wear it proudly in the locker room if I hadn't pushed her away and said what I said.

Now it's just another reminder of what I can't have.

"Get fucked," I say over my shoulder.

"Well, at least one of us is," Brent jabs.

Briggs chuckles again.

If life has taught me anything, it's that I'm not the guy who gets to have it all.

My father didn't think I was worth raising, Mia thought I was only good enough to be a backup parent, and with every day I age, sports reporters and hockey forecasters are waiting for me to trip up.

In the world of professional sports, your worth is measured by the success of your next game.

So you'd better fucking smash it.

I hear the sound of my phone vibrating in my duffel bag.

Coach Bex doesn't let us have cell phones out on the ice for drills, even though it should be an obvious rule.

These days you have to spell everything out to rookies.

I grab my phone out of my bag. Since drills are done for the day, I have some time to return a missed phone call.

"Hey Momma," I say, slinging my duffle over my shoulder, and heading out of the locker room.

"Hi, honey. Thought I should check on you and see how things are coming along. How's Berkeley doing?"

"She's good."

"And her recital? I'm so sad I missed it, but Isla sent me the cutest picture of her in her tutu. She looks so grown up."

I'm momentarily stricken by the memory of walking in on Berkeley and Isla getting ready in the bathroom before we left, the feeling of Isla's hand in mine as I led her through the crowd, and the sounds of Berkeley giggling with Isla while she got Berkeley ready for bed.

With every passing day, Isla and Berkeley become closer, and the gap Isla will leave when she heads back to Denver will be hard for me to fill.

"She was the star of the show."

I hear my mother chuckle.

"She's the product of her father."

"I don't know about that," I say, not seeing myself with that sassy spunk that makes Berkeley almost seem fearless.

"You were just like her at that age. So feisty. Ready to take on the world."

My mother's words hit my ears but I don't digest them. I only remember the darker years as a teen when I learned who my father was and that he left when he found out my mother was pregnant.

He was a salesman from Florida who traveled back and forth between the two company hubs. He worked in Knoxville, Tennessee and Jacksonville, Florida from week to week.

What my mother didn't know was that he had a family in Florida too. A wife and three kids.

I have half siblings but I've never met them.

When he found out about her pregnancy, he stopped coming around. She got worried and called his office in Knoxville asking for him. When the receptionist figured out what was going on, she told my mother the truth and gave her the wife's phone number.

My mother never called.

She didn't want to blow up another woman's life and that of her children.

He never reached out to check if I was okay. Or if we needed anything. Or to find out what kind of man I'd become.

It haunts me to think that Mia didn't think I had the fortitude to be a father because I never had one myself. Is that why she didn't trust me to do the right thing if I found out she was pregnant?

Did she think I would abandon her anyway?

Like my father did?

"I'm not so sure about that," I tell her.

"I am. And someday, I think you'll find yourself again."

I let out a sigh and she takes that as I sign to continue.

"I have good news! Your aunt has Christmas break to New Year's off, so she and her husband are going to come home and spend some time with Mamaw. Which means I get to come back to Seattle and spend the holidays with you," she says.

"That's great, Momma. Berkeley will be happy to see you and having you for Christmas will make our holidays that much better."

"Don't do any major decorating. You know I'll end up rearranging it anyway. I'll take care of Christmas Eve dinner so tell Isla not to fuss over it. And then we're having Christmas brunch at the stadium, right?"

Even though the NHL ruled out Christmas Eve to Christmas Day games in the seventies to allow players time with their families, Mrs. Carlton likes to play Santa Claus and hires a catering company to come do a huge spread for all the families.

Phil Carlton dresses up as Santa Claus and gives out presents to all the kids.

They don't put pressure on the players to come but sometimes our schedules are too tight for some of the players to go home for the holidays. Or some of our players don't have a happy family situation to go back to. The Hawkeyes family fills in for guys who need that. And those of us that live in Seattle full-time have made it part of our tradition.

"Yeah, we'll go to the stadium."

"Then it's set. My flight gets in around midnight the day before Christmas Eve. Be a dear and make sure you've pulled all the Christmas decorations from the attic down for me so I can get started right away."

"I will. Send me your flight details and I'll come get you."

"Oh don't be silly. I'll take a rideshare and I already know the code to get into the house."

"What do you even need me for?" I tease.

"To get down the Christmas decorations, of course."

Right... figures.

"We'll see you in two weeks," I tell her.

"Make sure you invite Isla to the Christmas brunch."

"I'm sure she has other plans, Momma."

And I don't need to see her fit even further into my life than she already has.

She's leaving for Denver in eight weeks and I need her to do exactly that.

"Kaenan Altman, if you don't offer that girl a proper Christmas, I will tan your hide."

"Momma, that hasn't worked to scare me in almost thirty years."

Little does she know, Isla isn't going to want anything to do with me anymore and spending Christmas with her isn't exactly going to help my situation.

"That's because I haven't followed through since you became too big to bend over my knee. But I'm not dead yet and I'm a lot stronger than I seem."

"Now I see where Berkeley gets it from," I tease.

"That little girl is my heart and soul."

"I know." I nod, even though she can't see me.

"Have you... have you heard anything yet?" she asks hesitantly as if her question might conjure up custody papers out of thin air.

"Not yet."

"Maybe she changed her mind." I hear the hope in her voice. I doubt it.

"Maybe. We'll see you soon."

I don't want to talk about what-ifs. I just want to prepare for war. It's what I know how to do. It's what I do every day when I step onto that ice every game day.

"Give that girl a kiss for me."

I just about say, "Which one?" but catch myself. She wasn't asking me to kiss Isla, but my mind went there.

"I will."

Then she ends the call.

Invite Isla to Christmas brunch?

I'll take my mother's wrath.

It will be a lot less painful.

Isla

"How's it going with the sexy hockey player?" Vivi asks, sitting across from me at Serendipity's Coffee Shop.

She met me for an early lunch after I dropped off Berkeley and then I spent most of the day out of the house so I wouldn't bump into Kaenan.

"He's your client, V."

"And he does it for you. Now spill your guts because it's like the Sahara Desert down there since we got back from Vegas."

It has to be a violation of the code of conduct to ask your nanny employee about her "sexy" boss... whom she lives with.

Vivi likes to make her own rules.

I push the empty plate that used to display my delicious club sandwich with avocado, toasted on freshly baked bread cut into thick, hearty slices.

"He's unstable," I say.

"The best ones in bed usually are."

"I'm not laughing," I say, giving her a side-eye.

"It wasn't a joke."

She pulls her cup of chai spice latte up to her lips. Her eyes narrow just above the cup as if to challenge me to prove her wrong.

She glances to her left at my sketch pad that I left open when I saw her coming in.

It doesn't have a Newport Athletic summer line sketch on the page I left open, so I didn't concern myself with hiding it.

"You sketched his jersey, number 81, on your Newport Athletics sketch pad? For you, isn't that equivalent to writing Mrs. Isla Altman all over your diary?" she jabs while lifting the pad off the table before I can snatch it back.

Sometimes I hate that she knows me so well. It can be frustrating when you're trying to avoid feelings for someone who just told you that you're a mistake.

Those words cut deep.

"Vivi," I whisper to her, trying not to cause a scene.

She starts to flip through more and more pages.

Okay, maybe I've been avoiding my real work and doodling instead.

Oh well. It happens.

"Oh. My. God...Isla."

Her eyes widen, and her mouth drops.

Great, here we go.

More poking fun at me for reimagining the Hawkeyes jersey into a summer dress style and tighter-fitting shirts that show off a woman's figure.

"I get it, okay? But I've had sketcher's block... or whatever you get when you can't design anything."

"No, the Newport Athletic stuff for summer might be your best work yet... but this? These cute jackets and shirts for the Hawkeyes merchandise... it's—"

"Those are amazing!" a higher-pitched voice than Vivi's calls out from behind Vivi. "Who drew these?"

I try to reach for the sketch pad again because I usually guard that sketchbook with my life. The contents in that book for our summer lineup and beyond are literally a trade secret.

Vivi pulls it away again, and then my eyes dart up to the newcomer looking over Vivi's shoulder at one of my sketches. I have no clue which one she's staring at.

"Penelope!" I say, grateful that it's at least her.

"Hi, Isla!" she beams back. "Is this yours?" she asks, looking at God only knows what.

Vivi smirks at me and turns the sketchbook around to show the cute windbreaker I designed with the Hawkeyes coloring, logo, and overall branding.

"Uh, yeah... but it's nothing. It was just a distraction from my other work."

"A distraction?" Tessa says, coming up behind Penelope. "That's the kind of thing you create when you just want a distraction? Can we trade superpowers?" she asks.

"I don't know—what's yours?"

"Making grown hockey players cry," Penelope cuts in.

Vivi throws back her head and laughs, then looks at me.

"I think you should take her up on that offer. That could come in handy right about now."

I roll my eyes at her.

"But seriously, have you ever thought about starting a fashion line? I know so many women who would love these." Penelope says.

Vivi hands her the sketch pad.

"V, you know that has sensitive Newport Athletic stuff in it."

"Newport Athletics?" Penelope asks.

She and Tessa squeeze together, flipping through page after page of my sketches. I even designed a dog sweater, which I hope to God they don't see, or I'll die of embarrassment.

"Do they know that you own and design Newport Athletics gear?" Vivi leans forward to ask me, but it's loud enough that Penelope and Tessa both pick up on it.

"You own Newport Athletics?" Tessa asks.

Penelope's eyebrows dart up to her hairline in surprise.

"Yes. I do." I say, giving Vivi a small scowl for outing me.

It's not as if I'm not proud of my company or proud to be a part of it. It's just that now they know what I do, and they are holding highly sensitive sketches in their hands. The kind of sketches I wouldn't want our competitors to see before we release our pre-order.

"Isla..." Tessa starts, her eyebrow lifting and giving me a similar reaction to Penelope's. "What are you planning on doing with these?"

"Nothing. They're just doodles, guys, really," I say, trying to look each of them in the eye to see if any of the three women standing in front of me will believe me.

"You know, my dad is the GM for the Hawkeyes, and he has an "in" with the person who makes the decision on licensing merchandise. You could submit an inquiry about getting the licensing for this. And I bet you'd have a good shot, considering you're the designer for a huge athleticwear company."

"Licensing? I don't know about that—"

"What could it hurt?" Vivi cuts me off. "You obviously have some interest in doing something like this. Why not open some more doors?"

She's right. I do have interest.

I've had more fun designing the Hawkeyes gear than I have for Newport Athletics in the past few months.

"I'll think about it. How about that?" I tell Penelope.

"Good, I'll get the mailing address."

Tessa and Penelope get their lunch to go and head back out to the stadium.

I didn't think I would run into them again here, but I'm glad I did. Hearing their excitement over the designs I only intended to keep for myself has me thinking about distribution.

Maybe it's time for a side project.

That no one can make me marry to keep.

CHAPTER TWENTY-ONE

Isla

I tiptoe down the staircase early on Christmas Eve.

I don't want to wake anyone since I know that Sunny got in late last night.

I heard Kaenan and Sunny on the phone arguing downstairs about how he wasn't letting her take a rideshare in the middle of the night. By the sound of it, he won.

He sent me a text since he and I barely speak anymore. Not since the morning he told me that I was a mistake.

Two weeks of bare-bones text messages if necessary, and even those are far and few between.

The only time we would need to speak would be about a change to the calendar, which hasn't come up. From what I can see, Kaenan is a creature of habit who sticks to his schedule. Very regimented.

Berkeley, my morning runs, and sketching are the only daily requirements of my life at the moment, so I never need to change anything either.

> **Kaenan:** Picking up Sunny after midnight tonight. Can you listen for Berkeley while I'm gone?

> **Isla:** Sure.

He hasn't attempted to give me more information on why he reacted the way he did, and I don't care anyway.

I'm tired of men using me when they want, and then tossing me aside when they don't.

I make it down the stairs without making much of a sound.

But then I realize that the banister is covered in Christmas lights.

There's noise coming from the living room and the light melody of "Grandma Got Ran Over By A Reindeer" playing in the living room. From the hallway, I can already see a nine-foot tree centered between the two rooms. And then my eyes catch on a person on a step stool.

Sunny.

I chuckle at the sheer volume of decorations already spread across the house.

There are snow globes on every flat surface, nutcrackers of varied sizes and themes, and tinsel on anything and everything that will allow for it.

Something catches my eye over the electric fireplace.

Four stockings hang with handwriting on the felt with a black marker.

One is for Berkeley.

One is for Kaenan.

One is for Meemee

And one is for...Lala.

My heart squeezes a little that Sunny thought to include me.

"Good morning. You're up early," Sunny says, snapping me out of my stare at the four stockings lined up together and the thought that next year, they won't hang mine.

That thought makes me a little sad.

I turn to her as she takes in my running gear.

"I'm up early?" I chuckle. "When did you find time to do this? It's like Santa's workshop exploded in here."

There are Christmas pillows and blankets on every couch and chair in the living room. Even Christmas kitchen hand towels hang on the oven handle and a Santa Clause cookie jar on the island.

This woman thought of everything.

"Oh, I've had hours. I started as soon as I got here."

"You didn't go to bed?"

"Nope. It's the Christmas magic. Berkeley needs to wake up and find the entire house converted into a Christmas Wonderland." She beams, taking a look at her craftsmanship.

"Where did you get all of this stuff?" I ask her, taking in several boxes sitting around the tree.

"An elf never reveals her secrets."

She gives me an eyebrow wiggle.

"She shipped everything to my house the day I closed on this place," says a deep voice behind me that almost makes me jump.

I glance over my shoulder to find Kaenan, in a black Hawkeyes T-shirt and the same basketball shorts he wore in Vegas when I knocked on the door to his suite. He's leaning a shoulder against the hallway opening, his hands tucked in his pockets and smirking at Sunny.

"There you go again. Spilling trade secrets. You know... Santa's going to put you on the naughty list," Sunny warns, hanging an ornament on a branch in front of her.

"I don't mind the naughty list," he says.

I dart a look back at him, a flutter in my belly when I'm met with his eyes already on me.

I divert my attention back to Sunny as quickly as I can.

"I stand by my comment that shipping thirteen boxes of Christmas decorations from Tennessee to Washington is wildly excessive," he continues.

He pushes off the wall and then walks past me, heading for the kitchen.

I keep my eyes fixed on Sunny, not wanting to chance any more eye contact with Kaenan. I think this morning was plenty for the rest of the day.

I hear him in the kitchen starting up the coffee maker.

"You were going to need Christmas decorations for Berkeley's first Christmas with us. You can't expect me not to bring the Christmas magic to her like I used to do for you when you were her age," she says, adjusting the garland that wraps around the tree.

When neither of them says anything, I see this as my chance to get out of here.

I'm not interested in being in any proximity to Kaenan for any longer than mandatory. More importantly, I need to get my run for the day.

"Well, it looks amazing, Sunny. I'll let you get back to it. I need to get to my run."

"I heard it's calling for snow," Sunny says. "Be careful out there this morning. It could be icy."

"I will, thanks," I say, turning to head back down the hallway.

"Hey, Isla?" Sunny asks.

I make a half turn to see her still adjusting the tree, not looking in my direction.

"Yes?"

"Did my son invite you to Christmas brunch?"

I shoot a quick glance over at Kaenan, even though I told myself I wouldn't. He stares at the back of Sunny with a coffee cup suspended in his hand and his mouth hanging open as if he just got caught.

Then he narrows a glare at me.

Is there something going on between these two that I should know about?

Like a power struggle, for starters?

"Christmas brunch?" I ask. "I don't know anything about it."

"It's brunch at the stadium on Christmas morning. We'd love for you to come if you don't have plans," she says, turning to me with a smile.

Do I have plans?

Usually, yes.

The clubs my father and I are involved in have parties from the day after Thanksgiving to Christmas morning. There is never a night that isn't spoken for.

Vivi usually goes to Vale with a couple of friends for Christmas or heads to her mother's house in California. Every year, she turns down my father's request, citing that she'd rather have a root canal than shmooze within my father's circle for the holidays.

I'm sure Vivi would let me tag along if I wanted, but Kaenan and I never discussed Christmas and whether he'd need me or not.

"I don't have plans, but—"

"Great, you'll be our guest," She says, turning back to her tree as if the issue has come to a resolution.

I don't want to argue with Sunny and I need to get my run in. Not to mention that I have a feeling the conversation that Sunny and Kaenan are about to have is not one I'd like to be involved in.

"Umm, okay. Thank you for the invitation."

I think.

I turn to leave as quickly as I can, hoping for no more surprises.

I'm starting to wonder if heading back to Denver early and agreeing to marry Collin would be better than spending Christmas with the Grinch.

But I'll do it...

... for Sunny and Berkeley.

Kaenan

"Momma, this is over the top."

"This is Berkeley's first Christmas here in Seattle with her daddy. I just want it to be magical for her."

"It will be. You always made Christmas special," I say.

"Grandparents are allowed to spoil their grandkids rotten, so here I am."

"She'll love it."

I sink my free hand into my basketball shorts and hand her the coffee I doctored up the way she likes it.

"Well, aren't you sweet?"

"Depends who you ask," I say, staring at the same angel tree topper that she bought on the first Christmas in our first house.

"Are you referring to someone specific?" She asks, watching me carefully.

I shake my head.

I scan the Christmas tree, fully decorated and reminding me of my childhood. I'm glad she went through the trouble even though she shouldn't have. At least I made her use my card to pay for the highway robbery shipping cost to send everything over.

My mother has always been savvy with her money, and she sacrificed a lot to make sure I had the hockey gear I needed for practice. Those summer camps at our local ice rink weren't cheap either, but she never gave up on my dreams.

Now, with the kind of money I make, I make sure she has everything she needs and more. Though it can be hard to make her take it.

I had to call her bank myself to get the payoff amount for her house. She didn't like that surprise at first.

"When Berkeley wakes up, I'd like to take her to the grocery store to pick up the turkey and all the fixings for tonight," she offers and then starts climbing down the step stool.

"I'm sure she'd like that."

"That will give you plenty of time to convince Isla that inviting her to Christmas brunch was your idea."

"Momma..." I say, shifting my weight in annoyance.

"Don't Momma me. You're going to do this." She turns and stares at me. "She's the woman who cares for your child most of the week. You can show some southern hospitality."

"She doesn't want to come."

"That's because you glared at her when I asked her the question."

"How would you know? You were staring at the tree," I say.

I know full well that she doesn't have eyes in the back of her head.

I checked once, when I was three.

I couldn't figure out how she was always on to me.

"Mommas have spider senses," she says, putting her arms straight out from her sides and then makes a wave motion from fingertip to fingertip. "We can sense things that most cannot. Things that you're not ready for."

"Sense what?" I ask.

I hate when she's cryptic.

"You'll see when you're ready for it."

Then she smiles and takes a sip of her coffee with cream and spins back around to look at the tree.

I already know that Isla won't come if I ask her.

The silent treatment she gives me is for both of our benefits. Getting closer to her again will cost me... I just know it. But that still doesn't change the fact that for the last two weeks, she hasn't touched the breakfast that I leave out for her.

She's still pissed at me so there's no way she'll agree to come.

But I can handle rejection.

I should be a damn pro at it by now.

It's been an hour and a half since Berkeley and my mother left to go grocery shopping together, and Isla isn't back yet.

I stare out the back window to see the snow starting to stick on the ground floor, no longer melting when it hits the ground.

I check my watch.

I shouldn't know her run time by heart, but I do.

I've been timing her runs for the last two weeks but not telling her about it.

She's improving every day.

Based on when she left, she should be back by now.

I decide to wait a few more minutes before running for the car, even though my feet itch to take off towards the direction

I know she left in. I got dressed after Berkeley got up and I'm glad to be ready to fly out the door if she doesn't walk through that front door any second now.

I watch the clock on my cell phone, and when five more minutes have elapsed and she still hasn't walked through the door, I look outside the front window. Her car is still here but her running shoes are gone. The weather has now shifted, with large fatty snowflakes falling and covering every inch of grass and asphalt. The neighbors roofs are solid white and something just doesn't feel right.

Where could she be?

She's never late.

It's just not like her.

I try her phone, and even though she hates me enough right now, she probably won't answer. Then I hear it ring upstairs in her bedroom.

Goddamn it!

I throw on a jacket and my shoes, snatch Isla's keys that she hangs on the key ring, and haul ass out to Isla's Range Rover since my SUV is at the grocery store with the girls and my sports car in the garage is only front-wheel drive and handles like shit in the snow. I start the vehicle and then throw it in reverse.

I know her route... mostly, unless she's changed it. It's at least a good place to start.

Driving down the street, I know I should have started running with her in the morning. I should never have let her be out here alone in the first place.

I check the route inside the gated area first, but there's no sign of her. I don't like how this is going.

I could stop and ask the guard if he's seen her, but I'm too wired to stop. I'll come back if I don't find her myself.

I take a left at the stop sign and pull out onto the city roads, knowing that this next stretch is about four miles from where she turns around.

I only make it one and a half miles when I see a woman sitting on a park bench along the sidewalk that Isla uses. Snowflakes fall on her blonde ponytail and jacket while she seems to be gripping around her knee.

Then I see it.

Blood.

Not a ton of it but it looks like she's sustained a pretty deep gash to her knee.

Shit.

I pull over to the shoulder and throw my hazards on.

"Isla," I call out, the second I whip open my driver-side door.

Her eyes dart up from her knee to me.

I jump out of the SUV, pushing the door shut behind me, running around the front of the car.

The door slams loudly behind me.

"What are you doing here?" she asks, watching me haul ass up the sidewalk toward her.

"You didn't come home, and the weather's getting worse."

"I know," she says, staring around at the snow starting to build up around us.

Visibility is getting worse, and she looks wet and cold.

"What happened to your knee?" I ask, taking the last few rushed steps to stand in front of her.

"I slipped on some ice that I didn't see. I have an old knee injury from running but it's been fine without my knee brace... until I slipped."

I kneel down in front of her, my jeans dampening as the snow melts under my knee.

The cold doesn't bother me but even if it did, it wouldn't stop me from analyzing her injury. I've seen enough knee injuries in my career to get an idea of how bad it is.

When I reach for her knee, she pulls her hands away to let me take a look. She lets me touch her, gently laying my hands on either side.

"Can you put weight on it?" I ask, trying to determine if we're going back to my house or the ER.

"I can but it hurts and I don't think I could make it back if I had to walk the whole way."

I need to get her home immediately and then get the gash cleaned up.

"Come on, then," I say, sliding my hand around her back and one under the knees, hauling her up against my chest in a cradle hold.

The same way I carried her into the house from the hot tub.

Her running pants are damp, her hair is wet and matted down, and her nose is the color of Rudolf's red nose, but she's still as beautiful as ever.

The smell of mangoes hits me when I hold her close. Probably from her shampoo—I saw the tropical hair product the last time she went grocery shopping.

"You don't have to carry me."

"You shouldn't walk on it until I can take a better look at it out of this weather."

I carry her to the passenger door while she reaches for the door handle and opens it. Then I set her down inside, happy to have found her in this condition instead of something worse.

Once she's safely inside, I shut the door and run around to my side. I open the driver's door and jump inside. I flip a bitch in the middle of the road and then turn off my hazards once we're headed back to the house.

"You didn't bring your phone again. What was your plan if I didn't come by?" I ask.

"I saw your mom and Berkeley wave to me when they left for the grocery store. I figured I'd wave them down once they were on their way back."

"If you'd had your phone, you could have called me," I say, turning right and heading for the gate to the neighborhood.

"You're the last person I would have called," she says flatly, her head turned towards me.

I glance over at her while I wait for the gate to finish opening for us but after a few seconds of her glaring at me, she glances away.

She's still pissed at me but the idea that I'm her last call makes me grip the steering wheel tighter.

This should be what I want.

To keep her at arms' length.

But right now, all I want to do is keep her close and keep her safe. I want to be her first call, not her last. When she's in trouble, I want her to know that I'll show up for her. No matter where, no matter when.

We get through the gate and hang another right down the street.

I don't say anything back in response. I know why I'm her last call, and I earned that spot even if I don't like it.

We finally arrive back to the house and I park in the driveway instead of the curb where Isla usually parks. The SUV still isn't back so the house is empty.

I jump out of her car, shutting the driver door behind me and make it around the front quickly as Isla opens her own door and tries to exit on her own.

"Hold on, I'm coming to get you," I tell her, not wanting her to put any more pressure on it until I've had a look at it.

"I can walk—"she says, stepping down and then just about flops to the ground when she grunts in pain.

I grab her before she falls, pulling her into a cradle hold again.

"Come on. Let's get you up to the bathroom. I have bandages in there and better lighting. We'll take a look at it to make sure everything's okay before you take up tap dancing."

She doesn't say a word but there's a small smile across her lips that she attempts to hide.

We head up the walkway and through the front door. I carry her up the entire flight of stairs without trouble.

We pass by Berkeley's bathroom when Isla's eyebrows furrow.

"I thought we were going to the upstairs bathroom where the bandages are."

"We are. They're in my bathroom," I tell her.

I feel her stiffen a little in my hold but she doesn't say anything.

We make it down the hall. I open the door to my bedroom, carrying her past my four-poster king-sized bed, a similar cherry wood to the bed in Isla's room. Penelope and Tessa picked out everything in this house while I was in Montana. Not all of it is to my taste but they did a great job with having to source everything already in-stock and deliverable before we brought Berkeley back.

I carry her through the door of the master suite and set her on the white marble countertop of my double vanity. A vanity that only has one user.

She peers around the bathroom, taking in the large walk-in tiled shower and soaking tub that I only use if I'm filling it with ice. If I need heat for my muscles, I use the hot tub downstairs. There's a door that leads to a separate bathroom and a door that leads to a large walk-in closet that's filled to about ten percent with my limited wardrobe.

"This is nice," she says, but the compliment doesn't reach her eyes.

Again, she's not impressed.

What kind of life did she lead before she became my nanny? I mean, this house isn't the Taj Mahal but for what I paid, a little sparkle in Isla's eye wouldn't hurt.

I turn to the built-in linen closet where I keep the towels and first aid kit for upstairs.

"Thanks. It's more than I need for just me but it came with the house already."

I open the cabinet door and pull out the bin that I keep the hydrogen peroxide and cotton pads to clean her wound.

"I'm sure someday it won't feel like too much room," she says.

When I turn to her, she already has her eyes cast down at her injured knee.

Did she mean what I think she meant?

That this bathroom will fill up with a woman in it?

"I don't have plans to fill this house with anything but what's in it right now," I tell her, before considering that she's included in that at the moment.

She nods but doesn't seem to catch that small detail. It's just as well. This situation has gotten more complicated than I could ever have predicted.

I pick the container up off the shelf and head back towards her, setting it down next to her on the countertop.

I pull the dark brown peroxide bottle out of the bin and grab a flat cotton pad. Unscrewing the bottle, I tip the peroxide bottle against the pad and feel the cool liquid absorb into the pad and across my fingertips.

She watches my movements.

I set the bottle back down and Isla grabs the lid, screwing it back on the top while I set one hand on the side of her knee.

I bend down to get closer to her knee and swipe the cleansing liquid over the bloody gash.

She flinches when the pad touches her knee, but it's not enough movement that I stop my action.

I continue to clean as I analyze her injury.

"You should probably sit on the couch for the rest of the day and ice your knee. Wearing your brace, after you get the swelling down, is probably a good idea. I'd make an appointment with your doctor, too, just to make sure."

I'm not a physician, but I've seen enough injuries like this. I just don't know her history or how bad her last injury was.

"My doctor is in Denver."

Oh, right...

"Come into the stadium and I'll ask the physical therapist to take a look at it. He's one of the best in his field, and he knows his shit. He won't mind doing Berkeley's nanny a favor." I smirk, thinking about how he keeps little kid gummy packets in his desk draw for her when I've had to bring her in for a session. He has a son about her age so we talk about them the majority of my therapy appointment.

"Everyone loves Berkeley, huh?" she asks with a smile. "Seems like people fall in love with her everywhere she goes."

I nod. Berkeley does have that effect on people. Isla has that too.

She won over Berkeley in five seconds and my mother in five minutes.

All I had to do was see her on the other side of an elevator door to know that I had to get to know her.

"Yeah, they do," I say, pushing back now that I have her wound cleaned.

I walk across the bathroom and open the door to the toilet. I only have a trash can in there. It's not something I use often so it's not an issue. I could use a minute anyway to dislodge the memory of the first night we met.

"Where are the bandages?" she asks.

Her voice muffled a little from the small room I just walked into.

"In the top cabinet on the left," I tell her. "But I can get it."

I hear her slowly slide off the countertop and head for the cabinet as I drop the cotton in the waste basket next to the toilet. I can hear her limping across the floor, but probably more to take it easy than because she can't put weight on it.

I hear her open the cabinet and rifle through the cabinet... and then nothing.

Did she find the bandages that quickly?

I head back out of the enclosed bathroom and the minute I see her standing in front of my cabinet staring at something in her hands... I know what it is immediately.

Fuck.

"Isla..."

She turns to me, her finger rubbing over the soft material of her nude underwear I kept from Vegas.

"What is this?" she asks, still staring at her panties in her hand.

Is she not making the connection?

Or is that a rhetorical question?

"Listen, I—"

"I searched everywhere for these. Where did you find them?"

Shit, she's going to make me admit to it... or make me lie about it.

Either way, I kept a woman's underwear after the best fucking sex of my life. I can't see into the future, but I'm going to guess that this isn't going to turn out well for me.

I take a step across the bathroom floor towards her.

As I get closer, she spins towards me, almost protectively facing me head on and keeping her hands out front, clutching the one thing that's kept me barely sated since that night in Vegas.

"I didn't find them," I say. I've only lied to Isla once in the time we've known each other. I told her she was a mistake. I won't lie to her again. Not after what it felt like this morning when I thought she could be in real danger.

"If you didn't find them, then how are they here? These are definitely mine. I cut the tag out," she says, opening up the underwear and checking inside.

"I slid them into my pocket right after I took them off of you."

Her eyes dart up to mine while her forehead creases and her eyebrows knit together.

"You stole these?" she asks, her lips parting in disbelief as her eyes search mine for the answer.

"I know it makes me a hypocrite for taking something of yours to remember you by, but can you blame me? I needed something of you to keep."

I take a step closer and she doesn't move.

I don't know if she's not retreating because she's in shock or if it's because she wants my closeness like I want hers.

Fuck, I want her close.

I can't deny that no matter how much I try.

Not knowing where she was this morning or if she was okay felt like a punishment that I deserved. I didn't earn the right to know.

"Can I blame you?" she repeats my question as her eyebrows furrow even deeper, if that's possible.

She peers up at me through the slits of her eyes.

"You made me feel crazy. You made me feel like I had done the most unforgivable offense..."

"Shit, Isla, I know. I'm sorry," I say, reaching out my hands for her arms but she takes a step back to show she doesn't want to be touched.

"Don't say you're sorry, Kaenan, because I don't believe you. I'm tired of being the villain in your story. The kleptomaniac who stole your daughter's stuffed giraffe. The nanny who you screwed in the hot tub and then called your dirty mistake. I'm sure the guys in the locker room loved that story."

That's how she sees our history.

This is how she boils down our time together, and I can't blame her because I'm responsible for so much of it.

"You're not my dirty mistake. And I don't tell them shit about us."

She stops retreating back towards the bathroom door and glares up at me.

I should say more...

I should say so much fucking more...

But I can't open my mouth and tell her things that I can't promise.

"There is no us, Kaenan. There's you... and then there's me."

Her hands fall down to her sides, her underwear loosely still held between her fingers.

My vision casts down to her knee again and I remember that I haven't finished my job. Now with the gash cleaned up and her walking on it, new bright red shows. It needs a bandage to keep it covered.

"Can I finish before you walk out? You still need a bandage so that it will heal."

She looks down and sees the new spot of blood on her knee.

She lets out a sigh and hesitates for a second and then walks over to the counter and climbs back up.

I want to wrap my hands around her waist and set her down carefully so that she doesn't re-injure it but she doesn't ask for my help and I don't want to get slapped.

Not because I'm worried it would hurt. I get hit a hundred times harder than Isla could slap, in every game.

I just don't want her to feel threatened enough to feel like she has to do it.

I turn to the cabinet and find the bandage container that sat right in front of where Isla's panties used to sit in between washes through the laundry, after... use.

How I forgot about them today, I don't know.

I bring the container over and rifle through the bandages. Isla has her eyes cast down on her knee, not bothering to make sure I'm selecting the right bandage. She doesn't want anything to do with me at this point.

I pull out a large bandage that will cover her entire knee and then pull off the multiple backings to it.

Pulling the bandage against both sets of fingers, I align it perfectly, making sure the gash is in the center. Then slowly, I let down the first side of the bandage, taking my index finger and running it along the adhesive cloth to make sure it's laying perfectly flat.

"What did you do with the underwear?" she asks softly.

I glance up to find her eyes watching my fingers as they trail over the edge of the bandage.

I lay the top side of the material down this time and repeat the process, sliding my fingers slowly and softly over it and stretching out until my fingertips slide over her skin.

"When I left Vegas, I couldn't stop thinking about you. I was mad that you left without so much as a note, and the giraffe, but mostly just for leaving."

I watch as small goosebumps raise up her thigh when my fingers run a little high, securing the same part of the bandage for a third and unnecessary time.

"Some mornings I'd wake up hard as steel thinking about the way you came for me in that suite. And how good you felt wrapped around my cock."

I glance up to see her chest rise and fall.

Next, I lay the left side of the material down against the skin of the inner part of her knee. My fingers slide over her skin.

"So I'd come into my bathroom, grab your panties from the cabinet, walk into the shower, wrap them around my cock, and slide them over and over until I came."

I look up again before I finish the bottom side and have no other reason to touch her.

Her chest is red and splotchy. The way it got in Vegas when she was nervous. It's so damn cute and I revel in the fact that she can't hide her emotion from me.

"And now that I'm here?" she asks.

I bite down on my lip to think of whether I should admit how many times I've jacked off to her while she was asleep on the other side of the wall.

"When you and I fight, or I can't get you out of my head, I walk into the bathroom and grab your panties, and then head for my shower to get some relief," I say, laying the bottom side of the bandage down and then smoothing my finger across it for the last time.

"Even still?" she asks.

My vision cuts from the bandage, and I peer up at her.

"If I didn't, I don't think I could stop myself from knocking on your bedroom door and asking to sleep between your thighs."

I know I shouldn't, but I can't stop myself.

She might slap me for this, but I'll take the risk.

I wrap my hand around the back of her neck and lean in, pulling her mouth tight against mine.

I kiss her harder when she doesn't pull away the first time, my hands sliding under her ass and cupping each cheek while I pull her closer against me. I try to be careful not to bump her knee as I wrap her legs around my hips.

Her ass is in my hands, her lips are opening for my tongue, and her little moans tell me that she wants this too.

I hear the front door sensor chirp downstairs in the kitchen and then the windows upstairs shake a little at the front door closing hard.

Then I hear the gleeful squeal of my daughter.

They're home.

Isla hears it too because her hands slide down against my chest and push me back.

"No," she says.

"No, what?"

"No... that was the last time."

"The last time for what?" I ask.

"Kaenan... Isla... we're home!" My mother hollers in the entryway.

Isla gives me a bigger shove and I take a step back. Not because she is strong enough to make me move but because she obviously wants me to take a step back.

"Move... please," she says.

"What just happened? Where's the change from what we just did a minute ago?" I ask.

"No change. Just you and me making another mistake."

She slowly slides off the counter, her panties still in her hand.

I grip around her hip to try to help ease her down.

"That kiss wasn't a mistake," I tell her, but my comment doesn't even earn me a look.

The minute her feet touch the tile of my bathroom floor, she turns and walks towards my bedroom and out of the bathroom. She still favors her injured leg, but otherwise, her knee looks better than when I picked her up.

"You're not the only one that gets to decide."

She stops in the bathroom door jam and glances to her left at the vanity countertop and then at her underwear in her left hand. She steps toward the marble and sets it back down on the countertop, then steps away.

"Here, keep them... if it stops you from knocking on my door."

And then she walks out, not stopping until I hear her open the baby gate at the top of the stairs and then hobble down the staircase.

I give us both a minute to cool off. Then I head downstairs to find my mother unpacking the groceries in the kitchen. And Berkeley and Isla snuggled up on the couch together watching Beauty and the Beast for the hundredth time, Isla's knee propped up on a pillow, topped with an ice pack, and Berkeley with a bowl of goldfish.

I bend over the couch and kiss Berkeley's head, but Isla ignores it.

Back to life as usual.

Avoiding each other whenever possible.

Living ghosts in the same house.

Only there's one thing that will be changing going forward.

Isla doesn't run alone.

CHAPTER
TWENTY-TWO

Isla

I slap my phone to tell my alarm to shut up.

Waking up this early on Christmas morning?

That's why it's called dedication. You run in the rain, in the snow, with a bum knee, and even on Christmas morning.

Since Santa Claus didn't visit my chimney, leaving me presents last night, I'll leave the family to enjoy their Christmas morning without intruding. I'll just jump in my car and take a nice drive today and think of the things I'm grateful for.

Getting out of my warm bed is a little tougher than I thought it would be, but once the warm duvet cover is off my body and I stand, my muscles start to itch for that runner's high.

It's freezing out this morning, but with the knee brace I'll have to wear when I run, I opt for shorts. By the time I hit mile one, I'll be more than warm and can layer up top to make up some of the difference.

I pull on the rest of my running gear and quietly open my door and head downstairs.

Sunny must have left the kitchen light on after bringing down all of Berkeley's gifts last night. Usually, it's pretty dark down here in the morning, and I try not to leave any lights on when I leave.

I go to unlock the front door, but it's unlocked. Maybe Kaenan forgot to lock it last night? Or maybe Sunny was going in and out early this morning, bringing in more things from the car?

I shake it off.

Whatever the reason, it doesn't matter. I need to get my head in the game for today.

I close the door behind me and promptly hit the lock button on the keypad. Then, turning, I jog down the stairs and follow the path.

Thankfully, it's not snowing this morning, but it's freezing, and there could still be ice.

I watch my step as I walk toward the sidewalk, when all of a sudden, I notice Kaenan standing out on the sidewalk out by my car.

"Merry Christmas," he says.

A puff of steam escapes from his mouth into the cold air.

I stare at the cart thing in his hands with one of Berkeley's favorite blankets covering the entire thing.

"What are you doing out here?" I ask, surveying what he has out in front of him.

It looks like a... jogging stroller.

"You're not running alone anymore. Berk and I are going to run with you."

What?

"Berkeley's in there?" I ask, stepping closer and then bending down, pushing a little bit of the fabric to find a sleeping Berkeley with piled high blankets on top.

"Yep," he says, messing with something on his wristwatch.

"You don't have to do this," I assure him.

"You won't carry your phone, and I could use the cardio anyway."

"Kaenan—"

"Let's go. I already input your route on the app on my watch. It will tell us where you can improve in your route."

"You downloaded a running app... for me?"

"Don't think too hard about it, Isla. Let's just run."

I hate to say that it's comforting to know that he's out here with me. Especially since this will be the first time I'll be running on my knee since yesterday's incident. He just went through so much trouble, and after yesterday, I thought we'd go back to strangers, both just doing our part.

I still haven't decided whether I overreacted to that kiss.

Back on that sidewalk bench yesterday, seeing my car pull up and Kaenan jump out of it, had my heart racing the second I saw the look of concern on his face.

He scooped me up and carried me off, taking time to clean the cut and add a bandage to it.

He came searching for me when he knew I was supposed to be home, like the protector he is. What he said to me when I first moved in came back to me.

"...since you live here now, you're under my care."

Kaenan finding me like that was the first time anyone has truly shown up for me, not because I asked for it, but because they intuitively knew I needed it. Like he could sense that I was in trouble and came to find me without being prompted to do so.

"Are you sure you can run five miles there and five miles back?" I ask.

"I'm a professional athlete. Just lead the way," he says, his hand open and motioning for me to start running in front of him.

"Okay, here we go," I say, pulling on my headphones and selecting my favorite running playlist.

Two hours later, I get back to the house two minutes ahead of Kaenan, but I wait for him at the garage.

He did really well, but by mile eight, he started to get a little winded. In all fairness, he was pushing a stroller as well. Just like a true athlete, he kept pushing through.

Berkeley had woken by then and was having a blast watching all the Christmas decorations as we ran by them.

As soon as Kaenan arrives, I pull Berkeley out of the stroller. He's completely gassed out.

I can't help but smile at him, though. Seeing him pushing a baby stroller with red cheeks and trying to catch his breath, I remember exactly why he just put himself through this. Not for any other reason than to protect me.

He didn't do this because he needs the cardio like he claimed. Between drills and the amount of time he spends on the treadmill every week, he gets plenty of cardio.

And no one wakes their two-year-old daughter and creates an entire bedding system for her so that they can run at the butt crack of dawn when they could run later while the nanny has the child.

He did this for me.

It's that simple.

Neither Collin nor my father have ever done anything like this for me.

"Where did you find the stroller?" I ask.

"Went down to the store and bought it last night while you were icing your knee. Had to arm wrestle a forty-year-old mother for it, but it was worth it," he says, holding his watch up close to his face.

"No, you didn't," I say, calling his bluff, or at least I hope I am.

"No, I didn't. Who would buy themselves a jogging stroller on Christmas Eve? That's a terrible gift," he says, reading something on his watch.

"I think it's a pretty great gift. Thank you," I say, with Berkeley on my hip.

He looks up from his watch and our eyes connecting.

"You're welcome," he says and then looks back down. "You shaved off one minute and forty-five seconds from the day before yesterday. I'm not counting yesterday since you were missing."

"That's good considering I haven't run with my brace in a while."

I should have run worse today with my knee still being sore. But maybe I had a little more motivation to push harder in order to impress Kaenan.

I hear the garage door open, and Sunny is standing inside.

"Hey, you three. We need to open presents so we can get ready to leave for brunch."

Berkeley and I head inside while Kaenan parks the stroller.

Twenty minutes later, Sunny hands me a cup of coffee, and I sit on the couch while Kaenan helps Berkeley rip through the gifts. She doesn't seem to have the concept completely down yet and she'd rather play with the gift she just opened than open a new one.

Between the gifts that Kaenan, Sunny, and I got for her, I have no idea where we'll put all the new ones.

I'll have to start a donation box tomorrow to make room and give to other kids.

We get through all of Berkeley's gifts and then it's time for us to exchange gifts.

I give Sunny a digital picture frame so Kaenan and I can send pictures of Berkeley to her after she goes back to Tennessee. That way, she misses fewer moments until she comes back.

Sunny hands me a small box, and I open it.

It's a tiny diamond hummingbird necklace with small jewels to make up the hummingbird's colorful chest.

"A hummingbird necklace? It's beautiful."

In my peripheral, I see Kaenan shoot Sunny a look.

"In the Altman family, we have a tradition that started back with my great-great Mamaw. All women who enter the Altman family... at the appropriate age," she adds, looking down at Berkeley, who isn't paying attention, "get a hummingbird necklace. It's meant to connect us women through the generations but also to remind the women in our family that we are strong, fierce, and powerful, even when we think we are too weak and can't do it on our own. You are more capable than you think, and all you have to do is flap those wings, little hummingbird, and you'll do great things."

"Momma..." Kaenan seems to almost warn.

"I'm not an Altman, though. Will great-great Mamaw be upset?" I ask, not wanting to give the necklace back but not wanting to overstep.

"Blood or a last name doesn't make you family, darlin'. You came into this family when we needed you most, and as the most senior of this family, currently in this room, I dub you an honorary member."

She gives a little wink.

I see her eyes flash to Kaenan quickly and then back to me.

"It's perfect," I say, staring down at the diamond-encrusted pendant and running my thumb over the design.

I feel Kaenan's eyes on me, but I don't look back at him.

"Kaenan, get up and help her put that on," Sunny demands.

Kaenan stands at her request and walks behind the sofa where I'm sitting.

I pull out the pendant and chain, handing it back to him.

Our fingertips touch as he takes the necklace, lifting the pendant over my head and around my neck.

He engages the clasp, his fingers brushing over the back of my neck. Goosebumps break out where his fingertips connect with my skin. He sets the chain down against my chest softly.

He dips down near my ear.

"It looks good on you."

His approval of me wearing a symbol shared by the women of his family makes me proud to be considered an honorary member.

After Kaenan and I each get showered and ready for brunch, we all head out to the stadium. I'm excited to see it since I've never been there before.

We pull into the players' parking lot.

"There's a lot of vehicles here," I say.

"Players and their families look forward to the Hawkeyes' tradition every year. We have brunch out on tables set up on the ice and the kids get to skate to their heart's content," Sunny beams.

Sunny carries a bag of gifts she bought to hand out to the kids as well, while Kaenan pulls Berkeley out of her car seat and carries her against his chest.

He waits for me to exit the car and then gives me his arm to hold onto since the parking lot is icy and I'm wearing wedge heels.

We head for the door when a man in a Hawkeyes jersey beams at us from the sidewalk of the stadium.

A fan?

Kaenan steps up to him a bit cautiously and hands Berkeley to me to hold. He takes longer steps in front of us as if to block us but there seems to be no threat that I can see.

"Kaenan Altman, can I get your autograph? I'm a big fan," the man says.

"Yeah, sure man," Kaenan says, but then the man pulls out an envelope that he had tucked behind him and hands it to Kaenan.

"Mr. Altman, you've been served."

Served?

What?

By who?

The man hands the envelope to Kaenan and turns to leave.

"In front of my family?" I hear Kaenan mutter to the guy.

"Sorry, Mr. Altman. I truly am a fan. Good luck this season," the man says and hightails it in the opposite direction.

"On Christmas morning?!" Sunny yells after him. "Your momma would be ashamed."

But the guy doesn't slow down or glance back over his shoulder. He's gone, and I have no idea what just happened.

"What the hell was that?" A voice from behind us says.

I peek over my shoulder with Berkeley still in my arms.

I recognize the pair.

Brent from the elevator in Vegas and Tessa from the coffee shop.

Oh, right... She said that her brother's name was Brent and that they lived down the street.

Kaenan walks over to him, almost like he doesn't want Berkeley to hear, not that I think she would understand what's going on. Though kids pick up more than they let on.

"I just got served," Kaenan tells him.

"Shit... I just saw it. That's pretty fucked up to do it on Christmas morning. Heartless," Brent says.

Tessa walks over to me, giving them space, and holds out her hands for Berkeley.

"Hi, pretty girl," she says to Berkeley. "You okay?" she whispers to me.

"Yes. I'm just not sure what happened."

I watch Brent and Kaenan's exchange.

"Listen... you don't have to come in. I'll explain it to Sam and Phil. They'll understand. We knew this was coming," Brent says to Kaenan. "Just go home and take care of your family."

What was coming?

Kaenan nods.

"He did it right in front of Berkeley," Kaenan says.

Brent lays a hand on Kaenan's shoulder. "You're going to win this. The whole Hawkeyes family will show up to that court if that's what it takes. Berkeley couldn't have a better support system, and you've done the work to show the courts that you have it all worked out," Brent says.

Support system for Berkeley?

What does she have to do with this?

"It's going to be fine. We'll call the lawyer in the morning. He's been waiting for this," Sunny says, rubbing Kaenan's back.

Kaenan twists the envelope into a roll in his hand and grips it tight. It's a thick envelope, but Kaenan's hands don't seem fazed besides the white of his fingertips.

"We can stay if you want," Sunny says.

"No, let's go home. The lawyer told me to call day or night when I get it. He'll want me to come in tomorrow."

Got what?

Sunny nods, and then Kaenan walks past her, taking Berkeley into his arms and kissing her on top of the head.

"We'll see you later," Tessa says, and then she and Brent watch us leave for a moment before heading inside to the stadium.

Kaenan juts out his arm for me again, and I latch on tighter than I did before.

"What just happened?"

"I'll tell you when we get home."

CHAPTER
TWENTY-THREE

Kaenan

I wait for my mother to take Berkeley upstairs for her nap and then I take a seat near Isla, a couch cushion worth of space between us.

"Berkeley's grandmother is taking me to court for full custody of Berkeley."

"What? How can she do that?" Isla asks.

"She had temporary custody of Berkeley when Mia was in the hospital and then the courts extended it an additional two weeks until Mia's funeral. Now, she's trying to get full custody of Berkeley, on the grounds that Mia didn't tell me about Berkeley because she didn't trust me as a father, that I have a criminal record, and that I travel too much for work to provide a safe and supportive environment for her."

Seeing the paperwork from the lawyer confirmed that Mia's mother is citing that Mia told her that I'm unfit to be a father—and that hits me hard.

The anger I have towards Mia continues to grow.

The last thing I want to do is air this out for Isla. I don't want her to see that I'm flawed enough that the courts might actually give my daughter to her ex-junky grandmother.

What does that say about me?

"You've created a great life for her. She's a happy two-year-old little girl growing up with her biological father. Can't the courts see that?"

"That's what I will have to prove, which is why I had to hire a nanny when my mother had to head back to Tennessee. You came in because no other nanny services would take me, so I needed to establish you in the home to create a history of Berkeley thriving with you."

"That's why Sunny begged me to stay when she gave me the tour."

I swallow hard at the feeling of having to convince Isla to stay so that I won't lose my daughter. It should never have come to that.

"Yes."

"Why didn't you tell me any of this?" she asks.

"I was taken off guard when it was you on my front doorstep. And then maybe I hoped this was all a precaution and it wouldn't end up happening."

"This is why you've been worried about me being a distraction."

I nod.

"This is all I am capable of right now. Berkeley is my world and I can't lose her," I say.

The thought of watching the courts pull her out of my arms and hand her to someone else makes my stomach turn and my fists clench.

"You won't. We'll do everything we have to in order to win the case. Berkeley isn't going anywhere," she says, inching closer and sets her hand on my thigh.

I look down at her hand.

I want to take it into mine and lead her upstairs.

But now, more than ever, I need to focus on winning this case.

The more I want her, the more I could slip up somehow.

"I only have room to take this on. I can't pursue anything with you," I say, staring at the hummingbird pendant around her neck and wishing things were different.

In eight weeks, Isla will be gone and with the date for the hearing around the same time, she'll be gone before the dust settles.

I'm going to lose her, but I don't have a choice.

"I understand now," Isla says, pulling her hand off my thigh and I fucking hate that I have to let her go.

I want to tell her that if Vegas had happened a year before, I would have had the capacity for this.

"Thank you," I say, instead of all the things I want to.

"Let me know what I can do to help," she says, and then stands up from the couch.

I don't like that she's leaving so quickly after our talk but I have to let her do what she needs to do for herself.

"I'm going to lie down for a little while and ice my knee. It's starting to swell again."

"Yeah, you should," I confirm. Her knee is no doubt inflamed from our run this morning.

She leaves the room and heads to the kitchen. I hear the sound of her retrieving an ice pack, followed by the heavy steps of her ascent up the stairs. When her door shuts, I close my eyes and take a deep breath.

I can't lose this custody battle.

It's the last thing I think before I fall asleep on the couch.

CHAPTER
TWENTY-FOUR

Isla

It's been almost five weeks since Christmas Day, when Kaenan was served legal papers, and he told me he couldn't pursue anything with me.

Since then, things have been awkward between us. Though he and Berkeley still join me for morning runs, and we remain civil, there's an undeniable strain. It's different from the initial tension when I first moved in; now, there's a sense of resignation in his gaze that weighs heavily on me. Every part of me desperately wants to wrap my arms around him, to assure him everything will be alright, but those promises are beyond my reach.

And any touch, however comforting for both of us, only makes the inevitable of letting go even more painful. Maintaining our distance seems like the safest path. Physical contact only seems to get us in trouble.

At least now, I understand the depth of his struggle and why he has to maintain his distance.

"Who wants to bet on how many minutes Lake spends in the penalty box this game?" Tessa asks of her new boyfriend since the last game when he beat up her ex-boyfriend out on the ice.

The same man who pressed charges against Kaenan.

Maybe I enjoyed that fight more than I should have. Seeing Lake serve him up felt like Lake was getting even for all of us, though they did kick him out of the game and he almost got suspended.

For the past month, Tessa, Penelope, and Briggs's girlfriend, Autumn, have invited me to the games up at Penelope's apartment and lunch dates at Serendipity's Coffee Shop.

Autumn is the last of the group I met when Berkeley and I went to our first game. Her hazel green eyes and shoulder-length light brown hair flow over her Conley jersey. Her smile is warm, and she just has that "best friend since grade school" feel about her that makes it feel like I've known her for years.

It's been nice to have friends in the hockey world who can help me navigate through what to expect and how the sport and franchise rules work. More importantly than that, these strong, independent women have been role models for me that I've never had before.

Tessa's fierce and loyal spirit.

Penelope's outgoing and bubbly soul.

Autumn's vivacious goals and career aspirations.

I've never had women like this in my life, besides Vivi, who want more for themselves than a rich husband who is almost never home, designer pedigree dogs, and social-media-ready snaps of a life that now feels empty of anything truly tangible.

It's the life I'm heading for in three weeks, and the only thing keeping me going is that I can make my business my life. I'll dive nose first into work to keep myself busy and my mind off the home life I cannot control.

It's what Collin does.

Maybe, if I don't think about the world I'm leaving behind in Seattle or think of it all as one beautiful dream, I can live in the world my father designed for me and play within his rules like I have my whole life.

I clutch the hummingbird pendant when these thoughts get too overwhelming for me, and I remember Sunny's words to me.

"No betting for me. You wiped me out at the last game," Penelope says, handing Berkeley a blue building block while they sit together on the carpeted floor in front of the TV.

"And I'm too smart to bet on you after my losing streak. But Briggs wants two minutes on Brent against Cincinnati's right-wing. I guess they have bad blood," Autumn says, locking in Briggs's bet like the good girlfriend she is.

"Easy money. I'll take that bet. The big sponsor is in the house tonight to watch the game. Sam told me this morning. Everyone will have to be on their best behavior," Tessa gives an evil smirk.

"Damn... you're good." Penelope laughs, handing Berkeley another block that she bought so Berkeley would have toys when we come up to visit, which now has become a more regular thing.

We watch the game and though I'm starting to understand more plays, and the calls from the ref, all the hockey lingo is still taking some time. I follow the puck from one side to the other, but my peripheral always knows where Kaenan, number 81, is on the ice.

I can't help it. It's automatic now.

I want to know where he is on the ice at all times.

I watch carefully as the opposing team player number seventy-one shoulder checks Kaenan as Kaenan defends Reeve at the goal.

Kaenan goes down first, then number seventy-one falls too, just to Kaenan's left.

Kaenan slides into the sideboards, and the guy who checked him slams into Kaenan.

Autumn, sitting to the right of me, grabs my wrist instinctively, and we all cringe at the hit.

We can hear the stadium gasp like everyone knows how bad that hit is, and people near the sideboards all stand to see if Kaenan is okay.

He didn't get knocked out even though his helmet bounced off the boards.

He instantly grips his shoulder, the shoulder I massaged in the hot tub. That same shoulder took the initial hit into the sideboards.

Oh, no... he will be so sore when he gets home tonight.

The paramedics start skating out to him, but Lake and Brent get to him first and help him up.

He skates off the ice on his own skates without assistance, though neither Lake nor Brent leave his side until they skate him over to the box.

Kaenan steps off the ice, his hand gripping his shoulder, and the Hawkeyes' physical therapist and a paramedic are already asking him questions as they walk back to the locker room.

Within seconds, Kaenan is off the ice, and his alternate is already in the game.

My instinct to call him right now is wrong. He doesn't check his phone during the game, so he won't get it until after the game is over. I know he'll call once he's on the way from the team bus to the Hawkeyes jet to check on Berkeley to see how everything is going at home, like he always does.

I'm relieved he's coming home tonight.

This is the longest he's been gone, and it's sweet how much Berkeley's been asking for him. But I'm also relieved because he'll need a couple of days to recoup after that hit unless it's even worse than I know.

I hate when he walks back to the locker room during a game. I can't see him or know what's going on, so I'll have to wait.

A couple of hours later, relief finally comes when he texts me.

Kaenan: Headed to the jet. Hoping to get home to put Berk to bed.

He's coming home.

Kaenan

I'm finally headed home, and the anticipation of wrapping my arms around Berkeley and seeing Isla's smiling face is the therapy I need the most right now. Along with several ice packs and a hot tub session with Isla.

But these days, I only get to use ice packs.

I've kept my distance as best I can. It's hard not to reach out to touch her in the morning while I make breakfast for us three, or when she jumps up and down when she has a new personal best on our early morning runs. But the hardest is when I see her with Berkeley in her lap, braiding her hair, or the happy squeals of my daughter in the bathtub while Isla sings nursery rhymes to her. Or when Berkeley got a bad cold and was too uncomfortable to sleep, so Isla stayed up all night rocking her until she finally passed out.

Isla fits with us, and the longer she's in our lives, the more I can't ignore the aching feelings that if she leaves in three more weeks, Berkeley and I will have a huge gap in our family that will be hard to fill.

I don't tell Isla any of this because I can't keep her tied to me. I selfishly want to ask her not to return to Denver, but I'm still not capable of giving her any part of myself in return.

After climbing off the Hawkeyes jet all of twenty minutes ago, I'm back in my SUV hauling ass down the road and heading straight for home.

I haven't been gone this long since I brought Berkeley home. Five days is too long. Especially not knowing if these three weeks are the last that I have with her. But with charity events and sponsor deals, work beckoned, and I have no choice but to answer. I still have to show financial stability to help with my case, so I can't just quit hockey, and having it on my record that I'm difficult or not a team player won't win me any favors with the court either.

I told Isla I would try to make it home to put Berkeley down for bed this evening. But a flock of migrating geese covered a portion of the runway, and until they could clear it, it wasn't safe for takeoff. We left Cincinnati later than I expected.

I watch the time tick down on the display of my vehicle's touch screen— she should already have gotten to bed at least twenty minutes ago— and that's if she went down without a fight.

With every passing day, the date for the custody hearing inches closer, and with it, the uncertainty of how many more bedtimes I get with my daughter. I want to make sure I'm there for every last one of them... just in case it's one of my last.

My lawyer says I've done everything I can do to give Berkeley a solid home life. Now, it's just up to the judge. He says we should be ready for any curveballs that her council will throw at us, but I have no idea what curveball she might have up her sleeve. What holes could the court find that would give her custody over Berkeley's own father?

Trisha Logan's statement that Mia confided in her doubts about my ability to be a good father, forces me to confront my own fears.

He told me to be ready because they usually try to toss one more thing at you at the last minute so you can't prepare.

The past five weeks have been packed with away games, and Phil Carlton sent a few of us players out to meet with a big sponsor willing to pay big dollars to put their company name on the side of the stadium.

This could mean state-of-the-art facility upgrades, more support staff, and possible pay increases in our new contracts.

As one of the players with a kid, Phil has been asking me to accompany him on most of the meetings with the owner and CEO of this mega company whose family image is important to them. Taking a risk on a hockey franchise would pay off for them in dividends, but if bad press follows the team, it could mean trouble for their billion-dollar company.

This last game we played in Cincinnati kicked my ass. My shoulder is killing me from getting tripped up by an opposing player and sailing into the sideboards.

On the Hawkeyes jet back home, everyone was icing something. It was a hard game, and we fought for every damn goal and barely brought the win home. Every win we pull off puts us closer to Stanley Cup victory, something very few of us can say we've accomplished in our careers. But this team is the closest I've ever felt to the possibility of pulling it off.

I check my watch just before I head into the house.

I know it's not likely that she's still awake, but just seeing my daughter safely tucked in her bed will go a long way in mending my injuries. The mental ones, at least.

When I walk into the entry, the house is quiet but the glow of the living room with the flickering lights from the electric fireplace invites me in.

The house has that smell.

A smell unique on its own.

It smells like the cinnamon wall plug that we have throughout the house. There's the faint smell of mangoes and vanilla, an add-in from the beautiful nanny who lives here too.

In three weeks' time, that smell will fade away as Isla packs up and leaves for whatever life waits for her back in Denver.

I enter the living room to find Isla sitting on the couch with a blanket and a book. The fireplace crackles and offers a warm glow over her already beautiful face.

"Hi," she says, her gaze briefly meeting mine.

She puts a bookmark in her book and lays it down on the couch next to her.

"Is she asleep?" I ask.

She nods. "Poor little trooper couldn't keep her eyes open after all the fun at Penelope's."

I appreciate how Isla bonded with the other players' girlfriends. It reinforces my feeling that she fits into this life. "What's waiting for you in Denver?" I ask, needing to understand her choice.

She hesitates, her eyes flickering away to the fireplace. "A life different from this one. One that's been meticulously planned out."

I can sense the unsaid words hanging between us. "And what does that life entail?"

She looks down, playing with the blanket nervously. I sense her discomfort, but I can't back down now. I've opened up to her more than I have with anyone else, and I need something, anything, in return.

"I don't have full control over my business there; my father does. He's expecting me to return and fulfill my commitments. If I don't..." She trails off, a hint of resignation in her voice.

"He can force you out of your own business?" I ask, my voice edged with disbelief.

How can a father do that to his own daughter? The thought of ever forcing Berkeley into a corner like that is unimaginable to me.

"My father always ensures he has the upper hand." Her voice is tinged with a bitterness that tells a story of its own.

I get the feeling that there's more to it than just the business but as I'm about to delve deeper, the baby monitor interrupts, bringing our conversation to an abrupt halt. Unanswered questions hang in the air, adding to the complexity of our situation.

Berkeley's waking up, so this is my chance to lie down with her and say good night.

Isla pulls the blanket off her legs to stand.

"I've got it. You just relax," I tell her.

I drop my duffel bag on the floor near the entry of the great room and head toward the stairs.

I climb the staircase quickly even though my body is sore.

I creak open the door as quietly as I can to find Berkeley's eyes fluttering open and then shut.

She's rubbing her eyes and is too tired to sit up.

I walk into her room, leaving the door open.

"Hi, baby," I whisper, and walk slowly to her bed. I lay my long legs on the outside of her bed and lie next to her. "Daddy's home."

Within seconds, she falls back to sleep and so do I.

CHAPTER TWENTY-FIVE

Isla

I watch from the baby monitor as Kaenan lies with Berkeley, his strong arm wrapped around his little mini. The resemblance to the Beauty and the Beast graphic on the wall is striking, tugging at my heart.

Belle and her Beast.

I try to focus back on the book, but I can't help that my vision slides off the page more often than I'd care to admit, to watch them together. If Mia could see the father that Kaenan could be, she would never have denied him. He missed out on so much, and that's sad to me.

Kaenan has so much to offer someone.

I try to focus back on my book when I hear groans from Berkeley's room. Kaenan's shoulder is bothering him, and he's groaning in his sleep. He needs to ice his shoulder to take down the swelling, or it will only get worse.

I throw off the blanket and set the book on the small end table next to the lamp. The baby monitor has a belt clip, so I attach it to my hip because I don't like being without it.

As I head up to Berkeley's room, I realize too late that I should have brought ice packs with me.

I push the bedroom door open a little more and walk in, softly whispering Kaenan's name so I don't wake Berkeley.

"Kaenan..." I whisper.

"Huh?" he mumbles incoherently.

"You can't sleep here. You need to ice your shoulder."

His eyes flutter open, and he looks over his shoulder back at me.

"Yeah... right." He grimaces as he sits up out of her bed and then stands. "I want to take a shower first."

I know the players usually take a shower after a game, but maybe he didn't after his injury?

Either way, the man can take a second shower if he wants.

"You can go do that, and I'll get you ice packs."

He nods, and we head out of the bedroom.

He takes a right down the hall, and I take a left toward the staircase.

"Isla," he says.

I turn to see him standing in the hall, trying to pull up on his shirt.

"I need help. My shoulder can't lift my shirt that far over my head."

Right... his injury.

"Of course."

I follow him into the bedroom and then into the bathroom. The last time we were in here together, he told me what he does with my panties and then kissed me.

And I kissed him back.

He turns to face me as I walk up to him. My fingers slowly reach for the hem of his turquoise Hawkeyes T-shirt. The shirt fits tight against his body, leaving nothing to the imagination of the man who lives in my fantasies. I lift up on the fabric, helping to pull it up and over his head to reveal the chiseled abs underneath.

Once his head is free, he pulls his arms back down and pulls the shirt off the rest of the way. I attempt not to gawk at the perfect body in front of me, but everything about him is perfect.

"Have a good shower," I tell him.

I turn to walk out of the bathroom, but his fingers wrap around my wrist, and he pulls me back to him.

"Did you need something else?"

"Yeah... I need this."

He bends down, gripping around my jaw, and pulls my lips tight to his. His full lips are pillow soft, something that I think about more than I should.

He spins me around and backs me up to the wall next to the shower. Then he pushes up against me. His mouth pulling and sucking. His tongue dips in to taste me.

He sucks in my bottom lip and nibbles on it.

I whimper at how much I need this.

How much his touch is the only thing my body craves, and I feel as though I might go crazy without it.

I know he said he can't offer me anything right now, but I can't leave for Denver without being with the one man who wants me the way I've always dreamed someone would.

Collin will never hold me like this, or kiss me like this, or fuck me like this.

I slide my hands between us and bury my hand beneath his waistband. I know I'm the one taking this to the next level, but he started it, and I don't want to stop until we both finish. His cock is already hard and waiting for my touch.

He pushes his sweats down and tosses them off to the side. He's completely naked in front of me, and all I want to do is lose myself in him tonight.

The moment I wrap my hand around his cock, he lets out a hiss against my mouth.

My thumb runs gently over his tip. I want to remember every detail of him. I want to remember how the deep vein that runs along his erection feels against my thumb. I want to remember his girth and length of him, but most of all, I want to remember how desperate he sounds when I touch him.

His kisses become more urgent.

He grips the hem of my shirt, and I nod into his kiss, giving him permission. He pulls my top off and looks down as he cups my breasts.

"I fucked up, baby. I fucked up so bad," he says against my mouth.

"How?" I ask, my hand gripping him still.

His jaw clenches as my hand pumps him gently.

"I know I said I can't have both, but I have to try. My self-control is shot to hell. I need you, Isla. I can't watch you leave in three weeks. I can't watch you belong to someone else," he says, bending his forehead down against mine as we watch the tip of his head glisten with a drop of precum.

"Tell me you need me too," he says. "Tell me you need me right now."

I nod against his forehead. "I need you... now."

Kaenan reaches into the shower and turns on the water.

He reaches down for his sweats, where his wallet is, and pulls out the condom he has in it.

Then his thumbs hook into the waistband of my pajama shorts, pulling them down until they fall the rest of the way.

He opens the shower and then wraps his arm around my middle, bringing me with him inside.

He closes the shower door and locks it into place.

"Now turn around," he instructs.

We turn together to face the opening of the shower.

He reaches up and adjusts the shower head to angle toward the glass door we just walked through. The rubber railing that the door slides through keeps all of the water sealed inside.

He takes another step, pushing me gently against the glass door. My palms flatten up by my head, and my breasts press against the cold glass, causing goosebumps to cascade down my arms and legs.

Kaenan reaches up and secures his hands around my wrists, the coolness of the condom foil package pressing between my right wrist and the inside of his palm.

He holds me in place with his body pressed against me from behind.

He adjusts his cock to angle down, and it nestles between my cheeks.

"Look at you, baby," he says against my hair.

The mirror of his vanity is directly across from us. The reflection of my breasts, flat against the glass, with the dark circles of my areolas, has even turned me on. But when my eyes connect with Kaenan's reflection as he watches from behind me, it's a level of erotica that I've never experienced before.

"Now I'm going to fuck you while we both watch."

He pulls his right hand back with the foil wrapper in it.

I watch from the mirror as he puts the package between his teeth and rips it open.

His eyes don't leave mine, and he rolls the condom on.

"Spread your legs for me and stick your ass out."

I do as he instructs.

He squats slightly to get under me and aligns himself with my opening.

Just feeling his head at my opening has me whimpering.

He presses his tip into me and then rocks back and forth as he enters me a little more with each thrust.

Our eyes lock in the mirror while his cock demands that I stretch to accommodate his size. It feels tighter than usual, but maybe it's the position.

I have nothing to hold on to, and I'm at his mercy like this, but I like it.

We both watch as my breasts slip and slide over the glass with every advance he makes into me.

"I've fantasized about fucking you against my shower for so long."

He changes position with his hips and hits a spot that has my eyes rolling to the back of my head.

"That's the spot, isn't it?" he asks.

It's not really a question. He saw my response.

He changes his hip rotation and hits it again.

"Kaenan," I whimper.

"Yeah, baby, that's my name. Say it again," he says, hitting the same spot for the third time.

"Oh God!" I say, my head falling forward as I try to keep my feet from giving out from under me.

"That's not my name," he says. "What's my name?"

He thrusts one last time until finally my body tremors so hard that something breaks loose, and I free-fall into an orgasm that has my center spasming over his cock.

"Kaenan!" I cry out.

"You're gripping me so good," he says against my neck.

I can hear how close he is in his voice as he groans at the feeling of my orgasm.

He keeps up his rhythm until finally, he can't take it anymore either.

He bucks one more time and then groans against my neck as he comes.

We take a couple of minutes to come down and Kaenan pulls out slowly. He opens the shower door and grabs us two towels. I step out on the shower rug, and he pulls a big, fluffy white towel around me.

He gives me a second one for my hair, and I rub it around my hair for a moment until it dries.

He wraps a matching towel around his waist and then pulls me out of the bathroom and toward his king-sized bed.

"I'm thinking we should do that every morning after our run," he says.

I smile at the idea that he's making plans, but I feel like this has happened before.

He pulls the sheet back on his side, and I slide in far enough for him to have room too.

When he slides into bed, he's careful to lay his shoulder down gently.

"Come here," he says, patting his chest for me to lay on it.

I do as he asks, relishing that he wants me close still.

We've been here before... twice—and it never worked out. I need to be sure it will this time.

"What do you mean in the mornings after our run?"

"If we start our morning twenty minutes early, we could fit in a shower and morning sex before I have to go in for practice."

"For the next three weeks?"

I listened to what he said in the heat of moment, but I need to hear it now that he's been satiated.

His eyes search mine for a second before he speaks.

"Don't leave in three weeks. Stay here... stay with me."

I never expected to start this nanny job with Kaenan and have it lead us here. I never could have predicted this with how things started.

Staring into Kaenan's eyes, a mixture of hope and uncertainty swirls within me. "I want to say yes, but you've hurt me before.

Saying yes means I have to let go of something incredibly important to me—my business, my independence," I say, brushing my hand over his chest. "How do I know you won't change your mind again?" I ask, seeking an answer I can use.

Kaenan exhales deeply, his eyes reflecting an honest remorse for the emotional whiplash he's caused. "I know I've made mistakes when it comes to you, but I'm asking for a chance to prove to you that I'm a reason to stay. I won't let you down again."

His words stir something in me. They're what I needed to hear. "You're already a reason for me to stay, Kaenan."

"But what about your father? Will he really take away your business? And is it even fair for me to ask you to choose?" His voice is tinged with concern.

I nod, feeling the weight of my decision. "Yes, he might. And it's not about choosing between two competing options. My business is something I built from the ground up. It's the one thing in my life that's truly mine. Everything else has been given to me. If I walk away from it, that door closes forever."

As I speak, a thought nags at the back of my mind—the unspoken expectation of my father, the plan for me to marry Collin. I've never mentioned Collin to Kaenan. How would he react knowing that marriage to Collin was always a part of my father's design and that I've intentionally kept that information from him?

But then again, what does Collin matter now if I'm considering not going home?

"So, where do we go from here?" he asks gently.

"I want to go slow and see if this is real. If you and I can make it work for the next three weeks while we try to win this case."

"And if we make it work…?" he asks, anticipation in his eyes.

"Then I'll stay here with you, and I won't go back to Denver. I'll start a new chapter with you and Berkeley."

The thought of closing the door and starting a life that's my own is both exhilarating and painful.

My father, despite his flaws, is the only parent I've truly known. He's been overbearing, yes, but also a constant presence in my life. He might not have always shown his love in the best ways, but I know he cares. No matter what unfolds with Kaenan, it's time for me to set some boundaries with my father.

"We can still fuck, though, right?" he asks with a grin.

His fingers glide gently down my back before wrapping around my waist, where he gives a light, playful squeeze. Knowing it's one of my ticklish spots, his action elicits an involuntary squeal from me as I squirm in his arms. He flashes me a devilish smile, clearly satisfied with the reaction he's provoked.

Seeing this playful side of him towards me, that I haven't seen since Vegas further convinces me that this time might work.

I give his chest a light slap to get him to stop and he does. I can't answer the question if I'm being tickled.

"Actually…"

He groans and pulls me tighter against him. He knows he's not going to like my answer, but he still wants me close.

"Sexual chemistry isn't our problem. But it's been the leading cause of our issues in the past."

"The sex wasn't the issue," he argues.

"I know, but you understand what I'm getting at?"

"Yeah… alright… no sex," he agrees even though he's practically frowning when he says it. "We're dating, right?"

"Yeah, I guess we are."

The thought of dating Kaenan causes my belly to flutter unexpectedly. I didn't realize how much that title for dating solidifies things.

"So no sex, but can I kiss you?"

I smile at him. "That would be nice."

"Will you sleep in my bed?" he asks.

"Let's wait... maybe too many changes for Berkeley isn't good right before the trial."

He nods. "Okay, you're right."

I hate telling him no when he asks me to sleep next to him, but the no-sex rule will be hard enough without sleeping together. We need to stay in our own beds for now. Even though I want to kick my butt for making these stupid rules.

Three weeks, no sex, and by the end of it, I have to make a decision.

Do I go back to Denver and live the life I was designed for while still keeping my company?

Or do I stay in Seattle and give up the company but get everything that makes me happy? Like Berkeley, Vivi, my new Hawkeyes friends, Sunny, and of course, Kaenan.

I already know which one I want...

But goodbyes are hard.

CHAPTER
TWENTY-SIX

Isla

It's the day before the custody hearing, and Sunny is back in town. Since Kaenan's grandmother is now healed from her surgery and seems to be doing well at the memory care center, Sunny and her sister have agreed to take turns checking in on Mamaw so that Sunny can be here with us more weeks in a row.

I find Kaenan in the kitchen.

He hangs up his cell phone and sets it on the island. His hands are planted against the granite, and he's leaning in.

"What was that?" I ask.

"The lawyer said he got an offer from Trisha Logan's attorney," he says flatly, staring at nothing like he's trying to piece it together.

"An offer?" I ask.

He shakes his head, looks at me, and walks to where I stand. He reaches out and rubs my arm for a second, then bends down and gently kisses my lips.

He's done a complete one-eighty over the last three weeks. He's become increasingly attentive and affectionate, often stealing moments for gentle touches or a kiss.

We've also been spending more quality time together with Berkeley as a family of three. Our days have been filled with visits to the park, attending her ballet classes, and jointly taking her to school.

"He wants me to come in and talk about it in his office. Can you and Momma pick up Berkeley at school and take her to ballet? I think I'll miss it." I see the disappointment in his eyes to miss anything of hers, but this sounds important.

"Of course, we can," I assure him.

Kaenan has been lucky to have mostly home games for the last three weeks, so Berkeley and I have attended every one. We have passes to the owner's box with Tessa, Penelope, and Autumn. But we've had a couple of away games too. It's always hard for Kaenan to leave us, but the closer we get to the hearing, the sadder he looks when he leaves.

It guts me to see him like that.

He always comes home as fast as he can to be with us, and the reunions are getting harder and harder not to have the physical connection we both want.

Tomorrow is the hearing and, subsequently, day ninety on the calendar.

I've informed my father that I need a few more days but will return home soon with my decision. I haven't mentioned packing my things, but he'll find out soon enough.

"Are you leaving for his office now?" I ask.

"We have until the end of the day to answer them, or the offer is off the table."

"Did he say what it was?"

"No, but something in his voice... It doesn't sound good. I need to go and find out before tomorrow's hearing."

"Right, yes, you should do that then," I agree.

He bends down and kisses me again.

"I'll call you after I get out of the meeting, okay?"

I nod, and he turns back, swiping his phone off the counter and heading for the front door.

I hate the waiting game.

I can only hope that whatever shared custody she's offering ends up being reasonable.

Maybe she only wants a couple of days a month of visitation in Seattle. Or she wants Berkeley to visit every third Christmas. Something like that could be manageable, and we could walk away with everyone getting something.

Everyone gets something they want.

I wish my decision had the same potential.

Kacnan

Marc leads me back to the same room, where Corrin and Sherry are already waiting.

"Thanks for coming in to discuss this letter we received from the plaintiff's legal counsel this afternoon."

I survey the room to find Sherry and Corrin both staring at me as if I'm a bomb about ready to detonate.

"Before I read the letter, I want to preface this by saying that this letter, although not as common, has been seen by offices plenty of times before. Most commonly, custody hearings are between two parents, so this type of offer is less seen between parents and grandparents of a child."

"But not nonexistent, unfortunately," Corrin interjects, snarling as if this type of offer physically upsets her.

Sherry and Marc both nod in agreement.

Goddamn, will someone just spit it out already?

Marc leans in and then pushes a copy of the letter from Trisha's lawyer to my lawyer.

I read the top and then skim down to the number.

"Now this isn't—" Marc attempts.

"Holy fuck, she's demanding one million dollars to not go through with this hearing?" I say, about ready to get up and punch a hole through the drywall.

Instead, I grip the letter so hard that I crumple it in my hands.

"Kaenan—" Marc starts.

"That's extortion!" I yell, glaring at the paper. "Can we take this to the judge?"

"Offers made out of court aren't allowed to be presented to the judge," Corrin says.

"But a million dollars? Has she lost her mind?" I ask, feeling a surge of anger pulse through me.

"Her legal council is basing this off of child support payments until Berkeley turns eighteen, plus the years of back child support from when Mia didn't tell you about Berkeley. Since you're a high earner, and she's going for full custody, this is what they're basing it off," Corrin says, reading her notes that she must have taken already.

"Back child support? I didn't even know she existed until I got the call from Mia's lawyer," I say, my eyes searching between all three of the people in the room hoping someone can make sense of this.

"Those numbers are open to negotiation, should you choose to go down that path," Marc says, folding his hands together on the conference table with a measured tone.

"You're suggesting I should consider this offer?" I ask, disbelief sharpening my voice.

My eyes are on Marc, but I see in the peripheral, Corrin is slowly shaking her head.

I know I'm the one who has to make the decision, but do they think I should take this because it's the only way to keep Berkeley.

"We can't make the decision for you. I think we have a solid case here, but we can't predict a judge's ruling," Marc says. "You're the one who has to make the call."

"This is why she didn't ask for a paternity test," I say, looking down at the letter in front of me.

Marc had said in passing that it's common for a question to be drawn about the legitimacy of the father's claim just by suggesting a DNA test—and that it was unusual that Trisha hadn't tried that angle.

"I had a hunch this might happen, but I was hopeful she wouldn't try to go this route," Marc says.

"How many people end up taking the deal?" I ask.

"About half, but the amount isn't usually this high. And their custody claim is a little more complex," Marc says.

"And some people just want a sure thing," Corrin adds.

Marc nods in agreement with her.

I want a sure thing too, and I would pay a million dollars without batting an eye to keep Berkeley. But paying someone who's trying to exploit her own grandchild for a nice payday is sick.

While the option to throw money at this problem and make it disappear is tempting, I can't let her get away with using my daughter.

I'm the better option for Berkeley, and I have to trust that the judge will recognize that and see through a woman who's willing to sell her granddaughter for a score.

"No deal. Tell her, I'll see her in court."

Corrin smiles a little as she writes down the note, and Marc nods like he agrees with my decision.

"We'll inform them that we'll meet in court tomorrow," he says, coming around the table to shake my hand.

Then he walks me out the door, giving me instructions on where he and Corrin will be in the morning and where to meet them.

I get in my SUV, and the first person I want to call has changed from who it used to be.

Now, I just want to hear Isla's voice soothing my raging nerves and tell me that we'll get through this together, like she has for the last three weeks.

"Hey."

"Hi, how did it go?" she asks.

The pitch in her voice sounds a lot like hope. I wish I was giving her something good.

"She wants a million dollars to go to hell."

"She actually sent you an offer to pay her a million dollars to drop the hearing?"

"I've informed my lawyer that we'll face this in court tomorrow."

I hear her sigh. She was hoping I was coming home with a resolution that didn't require courtroom time, but this is what Mia did. If anyone should be held responsible for this whole shit situation, it's her.

She's the one person I'll never get a resolution from. I'll never get to ask her why she did it and why she left me in the position to fight Trisha for our child. If she wanted her mother to have Berkeley, why put me through any of this anyway?

If I lose Berkeley, I'll never forgive Mia for this.

Healing and moving on doesn't exist... not completely. You never truly heal and you sure as hell never move on. You just learn to live with the pain people put you through.

But for the first time in my life, I want to leave it all in the past. Isla makes me finally feel good enough. Like I might actually be the guy who gets it all.

CHAPTER TWENTY-SEVEN

Kaenan

Today is the day of the custody hearing.

The courtroom is packed with my Hawkeyes family, with Isla and my mother sitting on the bench directly behind me.

Mia's lawyer is here too and she acts as a witness to Mia's wishes.

We've done everything we can at this point.

I glance over at Trisha Logan and Mia's sister. It's weird to see Mia's twin who looks so much like her. Mia's twin appears rougher like life has been hard on her. I guess that happens when you spend your life fucking other people over... you don't age well.

They both look stone-cold and don't make any attempt to make eye contact with me.

Marc had me line up three character witnesses to read a statement regarding my character as a father and then Mia's lawyer would follow at the end with her own assessment of my character and whether I'm still the best option based on Mia's wishes for Berkeley.

Sam Roberts goes first, and what he has to say about my character means a lot. As he finishes and Ryker Haynes takes the podium to read his letter, Mia's lawyer hands Marc a letter.

I try to focus on Ryker's words but I see my name written on the letter that Marc is beginning to open.

Marc reads it quickly and then smirks. He hands the letter to Corrin and after she reads it, she smiles and passes it back to the lawyer.

Corrin and Mia's lawyer cover their mouths as they talk but they both seem to be nodding at something.

When Ryker finishes, I give him a nod of gratitude. Sam and Ryker did me a solid and their letters mean more to me than they will ever know. Now it's Isla's turn next, and as the nanny who's spent the most time observing me as a father, Marc wanted to save her for last as the most important character witness.

But as Isla stands, Corrin gently motions her back down, and Marc nods to confirm that she isn't going up to the podium. Mia's lawyer stands instead and heads for the podium.

Isla, my mother, and I glance back and forth in confusion, but there's no time to ask questions. Marc and Corrin know what they're doing, so I have to trust them.

My hands tighten against either side of my thighs in the slate gray slacks of my suit. I don't know what she's going to say, and that makes me uneasy.

"Your honor. You were supposed to hear from a wonderful woman who has been Berkeley's nanny for the last two and a half months and has done an amazing job with her," she says, unfolding the letter that Marc and Corrin read.

"However, it has come to my attention that we have a character witness letter from maybe the most important person that you should hear from today. This woman was someone that I had come to know as a beautiful soul before her life ended so young. She came to me to protect her wishes for her daughter and I would like to read the letter that she gave me to give to Kaenan the day he picked up Berkeley. However, the letter never made it to Kaenan." The lawyer looks over to Trisha and glares for a second. I never found the letter the lawyer told me was in Berkeley's bag but since I never planned to read it, I didn't concern myself with it. Did Trisha take the letter out of Berkeley's suitcase before giving it to me at the funeral? "Luckily, I was the one who typed up the letter and had a hard copy on my desktop. With your permission, I would like to read it to you now."

The judge nods for her to proceed.

Kaenan—

If you are reading this, it's because my condition finally became something my body could no longer fight. Which means you probably have, in your possession, one of the sweetest little girls the world has ever known.

Our Berkeley May Altman.

God... I can only imagine how furious you are with me right now, and I deserve it. I deserve your anger, but please know that I never meant to hurt you.

In those two short weeks we spent together, you were the first thing in my life that made me believe in love. Your big heart, protective spirit, and ability to love a girl whose childhood traumas made me almost too skittish to love. But you held on, and I will love you until my last breath for showing me that I was worthy of it, even just for that brief moment.

I know I broke your heart, but please know that I did it to protect you. The moment you offered to bring my mother and sister with us to Seattle was the moment I knew that if I loved you... if I truly loved you, I would protect you from the woman who raised me. Her soul is not gold like yours, and her intentions would have found a way to drain every dollar she could by exploiting you to feed her addictions.

When I found out I was pregnant, I lied to my mother and told her that I didn't know the father. My heart has been deteriorating for some time and I wanted Berkeley protected from being a target. If my mother knew that Berkeley's father was a professional athlete, I knew she would fight for custody in order to get the child support payments.

My greatest fear is that my mother will end up raising our beautiful girl, and she will grow up as I did. I went to great lengths to ensure my last will and testament clearly gives you all parental rights.

Fight for her and raise her up to be strong and fearless, just like you.

Forever and Always, Mia

I glance over my shoulder at Berkeley sitting on my mother's lap.

The emotions stirred by that letter hit me hard. How can so few words soothe so much pain?

In a single moment, an entire misconception of a failed relationship is resolved. Mia didn't think I would make a poor father, and she did want to come to Seattle with me. She made the decisions she did to protect me, and I'm just now understanding the depth of her actions.

I wish she had allowed me to help her too. I wish she had known that I was strong enough to face whatever Trisha threw at us.

I have to come to terms with how things worked out and forgive Mia, something I never thought I would be able to do.

After a short recess, the judge comes back and rules in my favor. I get to take Berkeley home, and Trisha goes home empty-handed.

We leave the courthouse with Berkeley in my arms and Isla's hand in mine. Marc and my mother stop to talk for a minute outside the courtroom doors. This is the time to get the answer I need from Isla.

I pull her with me, down the courthouse stairs and under a large oak tree in the courtyard.

"We got one winning verdict today," I say, facing her with her hand in mine.

"It's been a good day so far." She beams up at Berkeley.

"Someone else owes me an answer today as well. Something about staying in Seattle, maybe?" I ask, pushing her in the right direction.

"Oh right, I— "

"Isla?" I hear a male voice behind me and quick footsteps approaching us.

Isla's face drains of color and concern has me wondering who could affect her like this and how they knew where to find her.

I turn to see a sharply dressed man approaching.

She knows this guy?

"Collin, what are you doing here?" she stammers, releasing my hand and stepping towards him.

He's a lot smaller than me, but he looks like an Ivy Leaguer, and he's in decent shape.

"I came to find you. You're not answering my texts or calls anymore," he says to her, and I don't like the tone he's using towards my girlfriend.

I step up with Berkeley in my hands even though I'd prefer to hand her off to my mother but she's still up at the top of the stairs with Marc.

"You said you're coming home. What the hell is going on, Isla?"

"Hey! You'd better watch the tone you're using with her," I threaten taking another step towards him.

I wish my momma would see what's going on and come take Berkeley from me while I handle this asshole who thinks he can talk to Isla like that.

"Kaenan... can we just have a minute?" Isla asks, putting her hand on my chest as if to push me away.

She's pushing me away?

What is going on and who the hell is this guy that has her giving him the time of day out of nowhere?

Someone better explain what the hell is happening.

"What is going on, Isla, and who is this asshole?" I ask, staring down the man in front of me.

I've got a solid six inches of height on him and about a hundred pounds. If he doesn't learn to speak to my girlfriend with more respect, he'll get a first-hand lesson on what happens when someone fucks with something that's mine to protect.

"Kaenan Altman, left-defense for the Hawkeyes," the suit says, with a smirk.

"Okay... you know who I am... who the hell are you?"

"Kaenan, please! Give me five minutes," Isla begs.

He ignores her and this dick isn't getting 5 seconds with her, let alone five minutes.

"Collin Westfall..." he says proudly.

Isla's eyes turn back to him and she gives him a pleading look.

"Collin, let's go somewhere and talk." She attempts again but he's a cocky prick... I'll give it to him, and he has no intent to back down.

"... Isla's fiancé from Denver. I'm guessing she hasn't told you about me yet." He locks eyes with her and she shakes her head at him in response.

"Your fiancé?" I ask stunned, turning to look at her.

The hair on the back of my neck prickles at the thought of someone else claiming Isla with the title.

By now, my mother must have heard what was going on and scoops Berkeley out of my arms and backs away with her to distract her from what's going on.

"You've had a fiancé this whole time. That's why you had to go back to Denver?" I ask, facing her dead on, my hands on my hips.

"Kaenan, can we please talk about this somewhere else?" she asks, taking a step towards me and reaching out a hand to touch my arm.

I pull back before she can touch me. I need answers first.

"So you weren't going back to keep your business... you were going back to get married?" I ask, my blood beginning to boil in my veins. "Were you ever going to tell me that you're engaged to someone else?"

My jaw clenches at the idea of how goddamn happy I've been for the last three weeks thinking I was going to end up with her, when she was keeping this from me the entire time.

"We're not engaged. I told him it was over... but—"

Always with the fucking buts...

"I don't care, Isla. I don't want to hear your excuses," I say, walking towards my mother and pulling Berkeley gently back out of her arms.

"Kaenan, let her explain—"

"Don't start," I say under my breath, giving my mother a warning stare.

I won't disrespect my momma in public—I'm too southern for that but if my mother can't see what's transpiring in front of her own eyes, I can't help her.

I start making long steps towards the car, leaving Isla behind in the four-inch heels she's wearing that I couldn't wait to fuck her out of tonight.

Jesus, how could I have thought this was going to work out for me for once? I let my guard down. I let her in.

I'll never learn, will I?

"My father, Kaenan," I hear her heavy breathing behind me as she tries to keep up, the clicking of her heels becoming more erratic. "My father made a business deal with Collin's father. He told me I have to marry him if I want to keep my company... but none of it is real," she says, chasing after me, but nothing she says is going to make a difference.

She kept this from me on purpose after I asked her repeatedly why she had to go back to Denver. Never once did she say that she had a fiancé waiting for her.

"Kaenan, wait! You don't understand – it was never about Collin. I was going back to stand up to my father, to choose my own path. I chose you, Kaenan, only you," Isla pleads frantically behind me, breathless from the strain of keeping up, her voice cracking with emotion.

I turn around to face her now that we're in the pay-to-park parking lot where no one else has followed us, except Collin who stands at the end of the curb.

He digs his hands in his pockets waiting for this exchange to be over.

He seems so sure that he's going to end up with the girl in the end. He doesn't even seem threatened by Isla chasing after me.

Fucker.

"Chose me? How am I supposed to trust that, Isla, when you've kept such a significant part of your life hidden from me? What does it mean to be your choice now?" I ask, hearing the bitterness in my voice. "I asked you in Vegas if you were married—"

"I'm not." She interrupts, her chest rising and falling as she tries to catch her breath.

"You were engaged and then you spent the last three months planning to go back to him, while you fucked me in the meantime. I hope I could pass the time for you," I say sarcastically.

I'm not proud of what I'm saying, especially in front of Berkeley, but the pain of betrayal is overwhelming. Was I ever really a choice for her?

"Kaenan, wait... please, you don't understand the whole story," she says, attempting to take a step towards me.

Berkeley squirms in my arms and reaches out for Isla, calling out her name.

Isla reaches out in response but I pull Berkeley back. I'm not proud of my reaction but Berkeley doesn't need to be involved in this escalating tension. I know how this ends because it always ends the same way for me.

And I don't need Berkeley to witness any more of this.

"I just need the ending. And now I have it. You can pack up your stuff now and be gone in an hour. I'll ask my mother to be there to make sure you don't take off with any more stuffed giraffes," I say, though the second I say it, I know that was a step too far, whether she deserves it or not.

The fury, anger and hurt is starting to boil over even though I'd rather bottle it up and not let her see how she's affected me.

She swallows hard at my words and now I know I hit deep... deeper than I should have.

No matter what she's done, I was falling for her and seeing her watching me with tears starting to well in her eyes is too painful to watch anymore.

I glance down at the hummingbird necklace around her neck.

She hasn't taken it off since she got it for Christmas. Something about seeing it around her neck every day gave me hope that she and I were going to make it work.

I turn around and walk to the SUV.

She stops following me and even though that should make me feel better, it doesn't.

CHAPTER
TWENTY-EIGHT

Two weeks later – Denver
Isla

I walk into the commercial-sized kitchen, designed to be big enough for three small restaurants to operate comfortably.

Okay, that might be an exaggeration, but not far from the truth. My dad let Liddy go wild with her wish list for the kitchen. Then again, nothing screams money like telling your buddies at the country club that you're rich enough to let your chef design whatever monstrosity of a kitchen she wants.

I'll give it to her, though, she uses every square inch.

The smell of freshly baked bread wafts through the air, and I'm brought back to some of my fondest childhood memories.

The houses might have changed. The stepmothers might have come and gone. But the smells... the smells of garlic and rosemary and freshly baked bread are the one constant. Those and Liddy, of course.

"Tell me about this boy you like," Liddy says, whipping pieces of basil into her world-famous creamy tortellini soup with Italian sausage.

My father requested my favorite dish for dinner tonight and canceled his dinner party. Likely a peace offering after the argument we had yesterday. It's not a complete cease-fire, and I know he'll have to save face in some way to his constituents, but for now, I'm not disowned.

I can't think of a time he's ever done this, but he is tonight.

"It doesn't matter," I tell her, "I screwed it up."

She stops what she's doing and opens the fridge, grabs a flavored sparkling water, and plops it in front of me.

"He's a man. They don't hold grudges that long. Just flutter those long eyelashes of yours at him, and he won't be able to resist you." She grins, her smile lines forming around her eyes.

"Then you don't know Kaenan," I huff under my breath.

Liddy, a few years older than my father, lived an envious life in her youth. before she became a personal chef. She cooked her way through Europe, fell in love with three Frenchmen simultaneously, and skinny-dipped in all four oceans.

Those smile lines have lived life, and I hope someday when I'm sitting in a kitchen recreating her dishes at the same age, I'll have earned my smile lines, too.

"Out with it, Isla. You gave up your company for this man. He must be an animal in the sack." She chuckles.

"Liddy!" I laugh, looking behind me at the kitchen opening to make sure my father didn't just overhear her. "And I didn't give up my company for him. I gave up my company so I can be happy. There's a big difference. This isn't a romance novel where he'll show up out of nowhere, and we'll kiss in the rain," I tell her. "I kept something from him, and now he thinks he can't trust me."

"Can he?" she asks.

"Yes! Of course, he can. I didn't mean to hurt him, and I'd never keep anything from him again. I love him—"

The second the words come out, I know I messed up.

I've been bottling these feelings up, not wanting to utter the words out loud, but there they are. Liddy already knew. I can see the Cheshire cat smile across her lips.

She lets the words I just blurted sink in for a moment.

"So... now... tell me about your guy," she says again, not looking at me but stirring the soup.

"He's... grumpy at times and difficult whenever he feels like it. He can't be reasoned with when he thinks something is a safety issue. He's protective and strong. But not just in that strong muscular way. He's like this big lighthouse..."

The shelter in my storm and my beacon home.

I let out a heavy sigh. "He's completely perfect in every flaw."

She turns halfway towards me, still stirring the soup. "Call him, Isla."

"I can't."

"Why not?"

"Because if he doesn't answer, I might actually die of a broken heart that's being held together by the hope that someday he'll forgive me," I admit in one long breath.

Wow, admitting it all to myself actually felt therapeutic.

I hate how vulnerable I feel when it comes to Kaenan.

But mostly, I hate that I can't do anything about it.

I'm in love with him, and he has every reason not to want to see me, even if Collin and I weren't together anymore.

I understand why he's upset, but I wish he'd let me make it up to him. I wish he'd let me explain.

Liddy dishes up two small bowls and drops a large slice of bread into the creamy soup mixture and then walks them both over to me at the island.

She grabs two spoons out of the metal tin she keeps on the island for quick utensil access and hands one to me.

"It's not ready for dinner yet. It needs to simmer a little longer, but you need some hot soup now," she says, scooting one of the bowls toward me.

"Heart-mending tortellini?" I ask.

"That's what we should rename it. Heart-y-break soup."

"Sounds delicious," I say sarcastically, and we both laugh.

She raises her spoon, and we clink them together before diving in.

Talks with Liddy in the kitchen are better than any therapy session that my mother has ever pushed me to go to.

Thirty minutes later, my belly is full, and my heart is a little bit lighter in some way.

I go back up to my room and start drawing again.

I got an acceptance letter granting me exclusive rights to create a whole line of women's and children's wear for all pro hockey teams in the mail at Vivi's office, and with the money from my buyout, I have more than I need to start my new company. The creative juices are flowing like never before, and I want to get all of my designs down before they exit my brain.

I have an early day tomorrow, with check-in for the race starting at the crack of dawn. I won't be able to draw once I go to bed.

By the time I glance at the time on my phone, it's about an hour past the time I wanted to be in bed, but I came up with three new jersey designs and jackets to go with them.

As I lift my leather design book off my bed to set it on the desk on the other side of the room, a page falls out. It's the page that I used to design Berkeley's jersey.

I hold it between my hands and remember those days before I knew I was falling for Kaenan. Before, Collin showed up and made Kaenan think I was using him when I had a fiancé back at home waiting for me. Back when my days were filled with the sound of sweet giggling and a two-year-old running around the house, instead of clinking wine glasses and high-brow country club members everywhere my father paraded me.

My heart tugs thinking about Berkeley and how much I miss her.

I put away my sketches and change into pajamas. Then I apply makeup remover and brush my teeth before bed, leaving my hummingbird necklace on because I haven't had the heart to take it off since I left Seattle.

I crawl onto the queen-sized bed, and I swear the TV stares back at me from across the room. I've been avoiding turning on the game. I know that the Hawkeyes are playing in Florida and that the game is televised, but I promised myself I wouldn't turn it on just to see him.

I mean, after all, the hockey world is now my world in some ways, right?

I take a deep breath and decide not to be such a big baby.

I turn on the TV and input the channel that I know the game is playing on. It only takes a second for the screen to change, and then I'm face-to-face with a mix of turquoise and white jerseys skating across the ice.

I see Ryker first, slicing between the other team. He sends the puck flying to Briggs. Briggs goes full force speed toward the goalkeeper with the puck kept carefully in against his hockey stick.

I can see he's nearing the goal, about ready to take his shot when a player from Florida comes whipping in. Then out of nowhere, Kaenan slides in and blocks the Florida player, causing two Florida players to collide, and then Briggs makes the shot!

The crowd goes wild, and so do I, jumping up and down on my bed and cheering.

Then, without warning, a Florida player comes up and high-sticks Kaenan to the front of his helmet.

The force knocks Kaenan back on his back, and I watch as his head, protected by his helmet, hits the hard ice.

That had to hurt.

He didn't see it coming, and it was after the play.

Not that it matters. High-sticking is illegal.

Ryker and Brent skate over immediately and pull Kaenan off the ice.

Ryker puts his hand on the back of Kaenan's helmet and leans in, probably asking if he's okay.

Kaenan nods to whatever Ryker asks and then Brent pats Kaenan's shoulder.

The ref skates out instantly, blowing whistles as I scream at the TV from my standing position atop my memory foam that feels a lot like quicksand.

"That's high-sticking, Ref! Two-minute penalty!" I yell as if the ref can hear me and needs a reminder of how to do his job.

The Florida player gets the two minutes he deserves, and there are equal amounts of cheering and booing to the ref's call.

How hockey fans can boo at the ref call, even if it's your team that's getting the penalty, is beyond me. Not only is it illegal, but it could really hurt someone.

I stand there and watch as they pull Kaenan off the ice. The announcer says that they're taking Kaenan off the ice to make sure he doesn't have a concussion.

"It's just a precaution," the announcer says.

I wish I was in Florida at this game.

I wish I could run down to the locker rooms and check on him myself, but we're thousands of miles apart, and he wouldn't want to see me.

I know I shouldn't text him.

It's weak of me, I get it, but I still care, and even if he doesn't respond, I need him to know that I saw the hit and wanted to make sure he's okay.

I rub my hummingbird necklace between my fingers to build up the courage as I pull up his name and look over the twelve text messages that have gone unread by him since I left two weeks ago. He's ignoring me.

Still, I won't be able to sleep if I don't text him.

I pull my thumbs into place and start texting rapidly. I won't do it if I think about this for too long.

> Isla: I saw that hit. I hope you're okay.

I set my phone down, trying desperately not to think about the fact that I won't receive a text from him, and he may not even open it.

It doesn't take long before I'm out like a light, but then by around one in the morning, my phone sounds an alert.

I sit up so fast I just about give myself vertigo.

I yank my phone off the bedside table with enough excitement that I rip the charger cord out of the wall.

> Kaenan: Thanks.

Thanks?

That's all I get?

I have to remind myself that he didn't have to respond at all. It's an improvement, and I'm grateful that he at least read the text.

A few hours later, my alarm goes off, and I wake with excitement.

I fling my comforter off my body and jump out of bed.

The last few months of training have all been for this. Race day.

CHAPTER
TWENTY-NINE

Isla

After Liddy drops me off, I head to the check-in line while she finds a parking spot. It doesn't take long before I'm up next with at least twenty volunteers checking in runners.

"Isla Newport," I tell the woman at the check-in table.

I stare at the large banner that runs along the six pop-up tents of the sign-in tables to make up a back wall. It's a picture of the finish line from four years ago, a race I distinctly remember attending.

It was the last year I ran before I got caught up in what my father expected of me, the new workload of a thriving business, and a new relationship with Collin.

But now I'm finally back, and it's the first time I feel like I'm doing something for me.

The nerves of excitement start to kick in. It's been so long since I've participated in a run this long, but it feels good to be back.

I don't expect to win or even come close. I just want to finish.

She smiles back, her short, spunky ponytail bobbing with enthusiasm.

"Hi, Isla, let's get you checked in."

Within a few minutes, she hands me my packet and gives me a quick rundown of the stops during the run and some safety information.

As I walk away and open the packet, my stomach lodges in my throat when I see my running number.

081

Are you serious?

Is someone messing with me?

I glance around at the crowd forming at the check-in desk, and none of the check-in volunteers stare in my direction.

Could it really be just a coincidence?

I guess when it comes to Kaenan and me, I have to come to terms with the idea that some things are just fated.

Meeting Kaenan, now the greatest heartbreak of my life, the one who got away, taught me invaluable lessons and gave me strength I'll never regret.

And my time with Berkeley will be something I will treasure always.

I will love them forever... no matter what happens from this day on. And no matter what woman gets to call them hers one day.

I head for the starting line and see the large group of other runners already waiting here. Some people are stretching while others are getting help pinning their numbers to their shirts.

I look around and find a good place to go through the packet and wait for Liddy. My legs and muscles are starting to feel antsy. They're craving the feel of adrenaline, the need to be pushed through a long run.

It's not long until I hear Liddy's voice.

"Some turn out, huh?" she says, glancing around at all the contestants.

"Yeah, it's one of the state's biggest events," I say, handing Liddy the number to pin on my shirt.

Seeing the 081 a second time doesn't lessen the burn in my chest.

I wish I knew when the ache of losing him will get easier.

I hand Liddy the number and then unzip my jacket, discarding it down by my backpack. I turn around, giving Liddy my back, and then pull my long ponytail over my shoulder to keep it out of her way.

She pins it to the back of my shirt with ease.

"You're all set, honey. Go knock 'em dead," she says, patting my shoulder.

A pang hits my stomach as Liddy echoes the same encouraging words Kaenan once used for Berkeley at her ballet recital. Will everything be a constant reminder of the life I lost?

One of the event staff members walks out to the front of the starting line, and people start to walk up to the line. The race is about to start, and I need to be in position.

"Thank you for being here with me," I tell her over my shoulder.

She's already bending down to gather my things that she'll keep for me until I finish the race.

She straightens with my backpack, jacket, and paperwork all cradled in her hands.

"You know I'm always in your corner. No matter what," she says. "Now go. I'll be waiting for you on the other side."

I consider reaching out and giving her a hug, but we've never done that before. Liddy has always shown me affection, but it's been in the way of feeding me and showing up for me. Physical touch has never been her thing, and that's okay with me. People show their love in all sorts of ways.

I nod and then turn back and head for the starting line.

A few moments after I'm in position, the horn blows, and the race has begun.

I check my wristwatch, which has my running app on it. I check to make sure everything is on track. My speed, my heart rate, everything is right where it should be, and I'm feeling good.

Runners around me find their speed and rhythm. Some pass me up like it's nothing, while others fall back. Not everyone is trying to win the race; some are here just to see how far they can make it, and some are only competing against their personal best.

Me, on the other hand? I'm here to take back my life. To carve out a world of my own and no longer live as a permanent fixture in the one my father created for me since I was born.

This half marathon is for me.

My new clothing brand is for me.

I keep running, keeping my mind on my pace and my time. I don't need to smash my personal best— I just need to finish. That's the only goal for today.

Kaenan

"Vivi, this is Kaenan," I say the second I hear her pick up her office line.

"Kaenan... this is a surprise. Is Berkeley okay? Is your mother okay?"

"No... I mean, yeah, everyone's fine. I'm calling to see if you know where Isla's race is today."

"Her race?"

"Right."

I don't want to give up too much. I don't want Vivi to give me away by telling Isla anything.

"I thought you were in Florida for a game?" she asks.

"I was, but our last game was last night. I need to know what city in Colorado her race is in."

"Kaenan. I... I'm not sure she would want me to tell you."

I lick my lips— I knew this might happen. I'm sure Isla told Vivi everything that happened at the bottom of the courthouse steps. I don't blame Vivi for being confused as to why I want to know where her sister is. The same sister I banished from my house and ignored her texts for weeks.

"Please, I need your help," I beg.

"You hurt her, and what she's doing today should be about her. If you show up and spark up all these feelings, you run the risk of taking this one thing that she's done for herself, in years, away from her."

Dammit, I know I hurt her. I didn't realize what was going on and what pressure she was under from her own family.

I should have been the man to protect her from it. Instead, I turned my back and let her leave with them.

The wolves came knocking on the door, and I couldn't see the trouble she was in because I was too selfish, desperate for self-preservation, when the first inkling of her leaving me arose.

I knew she was running from something when I met her. Somewhere in my gut, since the moment I saw her when those elevator doors opened, I knew Isla needed protection. She needed someone to speak up for her, and that man should have been me.

I failed her.

But being the selfish asshole I am, I have to see her cross that finish line. I feel like I was a part of the training that got her here.

"I just want to see her cross the finish line. I need to see that she's okay where she is. I need to see that she's happy. Then I'll turn around and leave. I won't approach her. You have my word. Just please... I need to see that she's alright so I can let her go."

I don't usually open up like that to people but I know Vivi is a hard ass and will protect Isla no matter what. I have to give her reason to think I'm not a threat to Isla's happiness.

Vivi stalls on the other line for the second.

"Fine." She sighs dramatically. "I'll text you the information. But so help me, if you ruin this for her—"

"I won't. I swear. I'll leave as soon as it's over."

More like, I'll leave once I see her with Collin.

I need to see that he supports her goals and dreams. I need to see that he loves her with everything he has. I need to know that she's with the better man even though it's near impossible to accept that the better man isn't me.

My phone pings with a notification.

I pull the phone from my ear and see Vivi's text message with the website info for the race. It should have everything I need.

Start times, address, everything.

"I owe you, Vivi. Thank you," I say as I race up to the airport ticket desk to get a flight to Denver.

"Hey, before I let you go..." She hesitates for a second.

"Yeah?"

"I'm not sure if I should tell you this, but Isla won the contract from the NHL."

I smile at the thought that Isla is getting free of her father and making a path for herself.

"She did? Does that mean she's moving back to Seattle?" I say with more hope than I've had in weeks.

"I want her to, but I don't think she will," Vivi sighs.

"Why not? She'd be closer to you and closer to Penelope, Autumn, and Tessa. She'd also be closer to the Hawkeyes."

"Because she doesn't think she can live in the same city as the man she lost."

"Me? Is it me?" I ask, my heart racing a mile a minute at this information.

If this is true, then it changes everything.

She doesn't answer my question.

"Don't forget what I said about not ruining this for her."

"I told you I won't," I assure her.

"She's never picked anyone for herself. She's always taken what's been given to her or expected of her. Let her make the decisions this time. Let her make the call. If she wants to make amends with you and come back to Seattle, then she will."

"And if she doesn't?" I ask, though I don't want to know the answer.

"Then, at least she's finally living a life for herself."

I stop and take a second to think about what she just said.

Let her choose something else.

I don't like it, but she's right. I need to let Isla make the call.

"Thanks, Vivi."

"Good luck."

Three hours later and I'm in a rideshare headed to the race. Based on the time, it's already started. I won't get to see her at the starting line, but I'm determined to get there and see her cross the finish line.

I want to see the look on her face when she makes it across the finish line.

The rideshare drops me the closest he can to the gates, but it's at the end of the parking lot in front of the check-in tables and a quarter of a mile away.

From what I read online, the race takes a long loop and then ends back here.

I can hear the announcer's voice come over the loudspeakers in the parking lot. Runners are within sight, and the first runner will soon pass over the finish line.

I have no idea how close Isla is to the end of the race, but I don't want to miss her.

I pick up the pace and start running through the parking lot and toward the open gates where other observers are streaming in to see the end of the race.

Finally, I make it past the gates, and then I follow the signs for the Finish Line.

I pass person after person, dodging around slower-moving people and almost tripping over a kid stroller.

I make it down to the finish line and stand with a large crowd of people standing on the sidelines, out of the way of runners coming through.

A little farther down, people are embracing, foil blankets are being distributed to a few people, and electrolyte waters are being passed out like candy.

I scour the area but don't see her yet.

If I missed her, and she's already left, I'll always regret not deciding to get on a flight sooner.

Then, through the crowd, I spot her.

She's still down the road but not far. Her blonde ponytail swishes side to side as she runs toward the line.

She hasn't spotted me yet as her eyes are fixed on the "Finish" sign hoisted above the line.

She looks exhausted but determined.

She won't give up until she finishes the race.

That's my girl.

"Keep going, baby. You've got this," I whisper out loud like somehow, all she needs to push a little further is my encouragement.

I glance up at the time listed on the mega light-up board by the announcer towers.

She's going to beat her time.

My chest fills with pride to see her accomplish her goal—not that I thought she wouldn't finish the race. She outran me more days than I care to remember, though, in my defense, I was pushing a heavy stroller with a toddler in it. I'm glad Collin didn't stop her from coming down here.

I watch as she runs across the finish line.

Breathing labored and sweat seeping into her shirt.

She runs out a few more steps and then slows her pace to a jog for a few more steps. Her hands come up and rest on her hips.

Then I see a woman coming toward her—an older woman who hands Isla a water bottle with a Newport Athletics logo sticker on it. This is her world and seeing her in it makes it all seem far more real.

This is where she belongs, no matter how hard that is for me to come to terms with.

Isla takes a long sip while the other woman rifles through a backpack. She pulls out some kind of Ziplock bag with a granola bar or something, and Isla laughs at the gesture.

I've never seen that woman before, but then again, I know so little about Isla's life in Denver.

Could that be Isla's mother?

It's possible, but I thought the woman lived in Italy, and Isla rarely spoke to her.

And where the hell is Collin?

I look around for a minute, thinking I must have missed him. No way he'd miss this.

I don't see him anywhere. My first instinct is relief. Relief that I don't have to witness Isla press her perfect body against the man who took her from me as he takes her in his arms and kisses her to congratulate her. But then I think about how that dickhead isn't here to witness it at all.

Before I rectify that man's shortfallings by walking over to Isla and pressing my mouth to hers to show her how incredibly proud I am of her, I think better of it.

She shouldn't want me here. The last time I saw her, I kicked her out of my house and told her to be gone before I got home.

I fucked up, and now I'm out of the race.

I saw her finish, and now I need to honor what I told Vivi I would do.

Leave Isla to make her own decisions.

I turn and start to walk with the other patrons leaving the premises when I hear my name called.

I'm used to hearing someone call out my name in a crowd, but this voice... I'd know this voice in any crowded room.

It's the voice I hear in my dreams.

"Kaenan?"

I hear Isla call out my name and stop dead in my tracks.

I could pretend I didn't hear her and keep going.

Maybe if I don't stop and turn around, she'll assume she recognized me incorrectly, and then I can still escape and keep my promise to Vivi.

But then I hear the sound of feet running up behind me.

"Kaenan, is that you?"

Now I can't ignore her.

Not when she's running after me.

I turn around, and the moment our eyes meet, her eyes flare in shock, and her mouth drops open.

I guess she wasn't expecting me.

CHAPTER THIRTY

Isla

Liddy brought me my favorite homemade granola bars that she used to make when I ran as a kid.

I love that she remembered; it reminds me of the many races I've brought her to.

But before we can reminisce about the past, my eyes catch on a Hulk-sized man walking in the opposite direction.

It almost looks like...

...but it can't be.

"Kaenan?" I yell out, but the man doesn't turn around.

That dark chocolate hair and the fact that he towers over almost everyone in attendance.

But he should be in Florida. Or at least on his way home. He wouldn't be here. What reason would he have?

"Kaenan!" I yell again, my feet acting on their own.

Exhaustion grips me. Every muscle, every fiber of my body feels spent.

But the dopamine hit from the idea that Kaenan is here in Colorado pushes my muscles one last time to chase him down.

The man turns around this time.

It's him.

Oh my God, it's really him.

My muscles attempt to cramp up on me and I barely make it before I start to crumple to the ground. Kaenan reaches out and pulls me up against him before I fall.

"Whoa, are you okay?" He asks, looking down at me, his eyebrows knitting together with genuine concern.

"You're here..." I say, almost not believing what I'm seeing.

He stares behind us at all the people walking past. The crowds start to exit the area as more people cross the finish line.

"What are you looking for?" I ask.

"Your fiancé," he says, his jaw clenching as he makes one last sweep of the crowd and then peers down at me.

"My fiancé?" I echo, confused.

"I believe the asshole's name is Collin," he says while his gaze scans me, checking for any signs of distress.

Is he avoiding eye contact with me?

He's looking everywhere but into my eyes.

"Why are you looking for him?" I ask, searching his face though his blank expression isn't giving me anything.

Always guarded.

And I'm to blame for part of that, I guess.

"Shouldn't he be here to see you cross the finish line?" he asks, releasing his arm from around me, forcing me to take on my own weight, no longer using him to lean on.

I hate that he's pulling away so soon.

"Given that we're no longer engaged or even in contact, he has no reason to be here. I'm more interested in why you're here. Didn't you have a game in Florida last night?"

His eyes dart up to mine with my confession.

"Yeah." he nods, his arms down by his sides.

My vision glides over the deep vein of his forearm.

I know what it feels like to be wrapped up in them and I'd give anything to feel that now.

"Why are you in Colorado then?"

His vision dips down at the number safety pinned to my shirt.

"081," He says, his eyes almost squinting at the numbers.

"Would you believe me if I said they picked it for me by random?"

"With our luck, yes." He says, his eyes still on the number written across my chest.

"Are you going to answer my question?" I ask again, praying he doesn't say that he met someone else and she ran this half marathon too.

The thought of seeing him with someone else is unbearable, despite my wishes for his happiness.

"Why am I here?" he repeats my question, his eyes lifting up to the finish line banner.

Please don't say, "for someone else".

He swallows, and his eyes drop down to mine.

"I came to see you cross the finish line, and now that I have, I'll let you get back to your life."

Those warm honey-brown irises seem so sad when they connect with mine.

Then he turns and tries to take a step away from me, but I grip his wrist.

"Wait! That's it? You were going to watch me cross the finish line and leave," I ask.

He turns his head back over his shoulder but doesn't twist back towards me.

"Running this race meant a lot to you. I wanted to see the look on your face when you stepped over the line."

My heart thumps wildly against my chest.

He only came to see me cross the finish line.

He wasn't even going to tell me that he was here.

"You're the only man who came here for me."

"He's an idiot."

"That might be true but he convinced my father to let him buy me out of Newport Athletics."

"He bought you out? I thought you loved that company?"

"It cost me too much to keep it."

"What did it cost you?"

"You."

He stares down at me for a moment and when the silence gets too much, I change the subject.

"Besides… those two are better for each other anyway." I chuckle. "And now I have more than enough funding to start my new business. I got the licensing approval," I tell him.

"I heard," his eyes light up for the first time since he showed up here.

"My old seamstresses have my new designs and they're excited for a new project. We begin production in two weeks and our website should be up for pre-orders in a few days."

I try to keep myself from squealing with excitement at how everything is coming together.

He takes a step closer to me.

"I knew you could do it." He smiles down at me, his thumb gliding over my jawline as his fingers wrap around the back of my neck.

My eyelashes flutter softly at his touch.

I reach out up toward the hand he has wrapped around my neck, and I grip his wrist, asking non-verbally for him not to let go.

His eyes dart down to my fingers wrapping around his skin.

"You're going to run the business in Colorado?"

"That depends…"

"Depends on what?"

"Seattle's your city and you wouldn't speak to me when I left. I don't want to step on your— "

"Come home, Isla. I was an idiot. I should have heard you out. I should have never let you leave," he says, taking another step closer, his other hand wrapping over my right hip and around my lower back.

"Home?" I ask, loving the way he refers to Seattle as my home too.

"Knowing how much Newport Athletics is worth, I can't offer you a better financial situation than you already have," he says, searching my eyes. "… but I can offer you the left side of my bed, a little girl who needs you, and a man who doesn't want to live without you."

"Doesn't want to live without me?"

"I love you, Isla Newport."

I step closer to him and wrap my arms around his neck, pushing up on my tiptoes.

"I love you too, Kaenan Altman. Let's go home."

He leans down and presses his lips to mine.

The END

Want to keep reading? Continue the series with Book 4, Rough Score!

To be in the KNOW about all the NEWS, subscribe to Kenna King's newsletter so you don't miss a thing @ www.kennakin gbooks.com.

Thank you for reading and supporting my writing habit ;). If you missed any of the other books in the series, you can find the series by visiting www.kennakingbooks.com or on amazon.co m.

Feel free to reach out via email (kenna@kennaking.com) or Instagram (@kennakingbooks)! I love hearing from you.

Thank you for reading Brutal Score!

To read the next book, Rough Score, you can find it on Amazon or on my website.

Keep up with Kenna by following here:

Made in the USA
Monee, IL
28 October 2024

68769425R00197